Dear Reader,

Here we are again back in the small town of Glory, where things aren't always what they seem, and neither are the people we grew up with. Even with such a close-knit community, the people on the fringes are often the ones who need that community the most.

Just like Reed and Gina.

This story is a little different than the others on the surface, but deep at its core, it's about the same things. Love, hope, and redemption. Finding the courage inside yourself to be the best person you can be, letting love heal the wounds that are soul-deep, and fighting for the happily-ever-after that we all deserve.

Thanks so much for coming back again and checking in on our favorite small town. You know it's not the same here without you.

Happy reading!

Sara Arden

**Also available from
Sara Arden
and HQN Books**

Return to Glory
"A Glorious Christmas" (ebook novella)
Unfaded Glory

SARA ARDEN

FINDING GLORY

HQN™

Recycling programs
for this product may
not exist in your area.

ISBN-13: 978-0-373-77948-2

Finding Glory

Copyright © 2015 by Sara Lunsford

PROLOGUE

"I SAY, DO HUSH, ETHEL." Helga Gunderson rattled the gavel at the podium with all of the authority afforded her station both as the Grand Dame of the Glory Grandmothers and as the chief judge for the first district in Glory County.

Ethel Weinburg, local busybody, knitting genius, and general jill-of-all-trades, squirmed in her seat and made a big show of adjusting the folds of her dress.

Helga warmed. "I want to hear all about your petunias, dear, but we have urgent business on Maudine's behalf."

The woman in question, one Maudine Townsend, sat in the proverbial hot seat up on the small stage. Her blue hair didn't put anyone off—after all, it was perfectly coiffed as it had been every day since she was thirteen. The dye job had been to show school spirit for her old alma mater, but the temporary dye had become more of a fixture.

"As you all know, I haven't been feeling well." Maudine took a deep breath, deciding what she wanted to say next. She didn't want anyone other than Helga to know just what she'd been going through, but she needed them to understand the importance of what she was about to ask.

"Have you tried a cleanse?" Regan Marsh asked, pushing up her glasses. "A good colonic can fix everything. I remember this one time when—"

Heavens save her from people who could only talk about their bodily functions. Maudine held up her hand. "Stop right there. I swore that the day I spoke of such things in public would be my cue to lie down and let them bury me. If that's all I can converse about, it's a sad day indeed." She pursed her lips. "No, what I need is more for my granddaughter, Gina. She has absolutely no life trying to raise Amanda Jane. She's a good parent, but she's too young to have given up on falling in love."

"Maybe her priorities are right where they need to be," Rose Cresswell offered.

Maudine's eyes narrowed. "Amanda Jane needs a father." *And I need to know she'll be loved when I'm gone.*

"I raised my daughters without a man just fine, thank you very much." Ethel crossed her arms.

"No one is saying you didn't. I didn't say Bitsie Weinburg needs a father. I said Amanda Jane Townsend does. And Gina needs the help. Not because she's not capable, but because she deserves to have something in her life she didn't have to fight for. It would just kill me if she missed out on becoming a doctor because I couldn't take Amanda Jane full-time," Maudine confessed.

Gina's story thus far was like a penny dreadful. She'd lost her mother, her sister, and now was trying to take care of her niece and put herself through medical school. She'd found a way to do that with the army, but when she found out Amanda Jane needed her, she'd declined to reenlist. And in doing so, had declined the GI Bill that would've paid for her education. No, Gina wasn't going to end up like everyone else in Maudine's family. She would survive and thrive, no matter what Maudine had to do to make it happen. She couldn't help but feel like she could've done more, done better.

"Honey, no one would expect you to." Helga gave her a sympathetic smile. The kind that you save for kittens, daisies and best friends. Especially when you knew how much pain that best friend was in.

Of course Helga knew what she was thinking. Helga always knew. She was like the FBI.

"Anyway—" She shook her head. Maudine didn't want the conversation centered on her. It was about Gina. Making Gina happy. Seeing her settled.

Maudine knew that Gina could do anything. She believed in her—in her grit, in her spirit, in the fire in her belly that would help her succeed at everything. But her whole life had been a fight. It was time for something good and Maudine was going to make that happen for her.

"As I was saying—" she continued "—I want to see Gina settled."

"Why do they call it settling? I wouldn't think you'd want her to *settle*," Regan interjected.

"Fine. *Happy*. I want to see her happy." Maudine rolled her eyes and wondered how they ever accomplished anything.

"I heard that Reed Hollingsworth is back in town. He bought a big house on Knob Hill," Rose Cresswell added helpfully.

"We all know that, Rose," Helga reminded her kindly. "He's Amanda Jane's father. We've been watching this very closely."

Rose sighed. "I suppose I mean to say what are we going to do about it? I mean, if we're trying to match-make for Gina."

"Exactly!" Maudine pointed a finger at Rose. "That's it exactly. What are we going to do about it?"

Ethel's brow furrowed. "I suppose it depends on what you think we can do about it. What's your endgame?" Ethel had on her game face, the one she reserved for their poker matches after the meeting. Things were getting serious.

"Gina's happiness."

"Duh." Regan Marsh rolled her eyes behind her thick, bejeweled glasses. "But what—" she stuffed a bite of scone from Sweet Thing into her mouth "—do you think her perfect pitch is? What sort of resonance will make her happy?"

"I really wish you wouldn't speak like that, Regan. It shatters your credibility." Helga wrinkled her nose. "And why do you always have to bring everything back to a musical analogy? Wouldn't it annoy you to no end if I did that? If I made everything about the law?"

Several glances cut to Helga sharply and she narrowed her eyes. "Fine. I'll work on that. Anyway, Maudine. What do you think will make Gina happiest?"

"To have a whole family. A man who will love her, and Amanda Jane as his own. To go to medical school without worrying about how we're going to provide

Amanda Jane with the things she needs." Maudine sighed heavily. "I've done my best."

"We know you have, dear. So does she." Marie Hart nodded from her chair.

"We could set her up with my grandson, Greg. He's a firefighter. He's always had an eye for Gina," Helga offered.

"No." Ethel shook her head. "It's too cute. Greg and Gina Gunderson. There are so many *g*'s there, I choked on them."

"Ethel, you cannot expect people to marry or not marry because of their names," Rose admonished.

"The answer is staring us in the face." Maudine's expression melted into a sly smile. "She'll marry Reed," she proclaimed. That was the perfect solution.

"Have you lost your mind?" Rose asked, her expression one of serious concern.

"No, no. I'm serious as Old Man Zorn's heart attack." Maudine nodded emphatically. "She's always had a crush on Reed. Even when the boy had no prospects. Now, he does. He has several billion of them, he's Amanda Jane's father…it solves all of our problems."

"Have you forgotten the part where he was on the drugs?" Ethel faux-whispered.

It was Helga's turn to roll her eyes. "The drugs? As if he did them *all*? That was years ago. He's cleaned up his act. He's CEO of a major international company. If there was the slightest chance he was slipping, his board of directors would oust him so fast it would make your head spin."

"I wouldn't trust him with a child." Ethel crossed her arms. "This is all just so seedy."

"Good thing it's not up to you, isn't it?" Maudine looked pointedly at Helga. She'd be hearing the paternity suit Maudine had convinced Gina to file against Reed.

"You're asking me to break the law. To form an opinion days before I hear a case." Helga shook her head.

"No, I'm asking you, after listening to the evidence for yourself, to consider this option as a relief of circumstances to both parties." Maudine flashed a self-satisfied smile. "Offer them marriage as an option to child support and a custody fight."

"Are you sure you're not the one who should've gone to law school?" Helga eyed her.

"I just know what's best for Gina. That's why we started the Grandmothers, right? To put our life experience to good use." Maudine nodded.

"Do you have any doubts about this? Any at all? A man can change a lot in seven years," Helga asked.

"Yes, I do believe he can." Maudine nodded again, but this time it was weighted with purpose.

"I won't make you any promises. If, based on the evidence presented, this is a good idea, I'll suggest it. But it might not be. I am an officer of the court. So we need a backup plan."

"Your grandson is my backup plan." Maudine grinned.

"That's probably not something you should ever say to his face, dear," Regan added.

"Too true." Helga nodded. "He's a good man. And should be a woman's first choice, not a backup plan."

"You know what I mean. I already love Greg like my own." Maudine tried to smooth over her careless words.

"I know that." Helga sniffed. "So, anyone else have anything to contribute or are we ready to move on to the next item of business?"

Maudine stood. "We can move on to Ethel's prize-winning petunias."

"Actually, I think we should discuss how to get Marie's B and B more exposure," Ethel added. "My petunias are quite special, but they can only do so much, you know."

CHAPTER ONE

A LACY COLLAR lay expertly arranged atop the judge's black robes, like the doily positioned just so underneath the orange carnival glass bowl that held an endless supply of her grandmother's hard, ribbon candy. The kind Gina had chipped her front tooth on when she was eight. Seeing it perched there, so crisp, so proper, caused a heavy knot to turn in on itself in her gut.

"Sit up straight," Maudine Townsend whispered in Gina's ear. "Just because I've played pinochle with Helga Gunderson every Saturday for as long as I can remember doesn't mean she's going to look kindly on you. She'll be fair."

"How is it fair to judge someone by their posture? Especially when I know that you two have *never* played pinochle. You play five-card stud and shoot whiskey," Gina whispered back to her blue-haired grandmother. The woman's hair was literally a light shade of blue. She'd dyed it for the street carnival two weeks back and temporary had turned out to be more permanent. But she'd accessorized nicely, striking an imposing figure in a white vintage Chanel suit circa 1963. Somehow, she'd made it work.

Maudine raised a perfectly drawn eyebrow. "Don't be tart."

"Yes, ma'am." Gina straightened her posture. She was a grown woman, former army, and her grandmother still had the power to make her jump to. She didn't mind it much. Her grandmother was the reason she was a fighter. Her grandmother was the reason she'd made it through high school after her mother died.

And her grandmother was the reason that Gina believed she could be a good mother to her niece, Amanda Jane, after Crystal died a year ago.

There'd been a lot of loss and a lot of sorrow in the past few years. It was a lot for anyone to bear, especially a six-year-old girl.

Suddenly, her grandmother's fingers tightened around hers, the cool metal of her mail-order costume rings digging into Gina's palms.

She looked up and saw him.

Him.

Reed Hollingsworth.

Gina thought she'd prepared herself for this—for seeing him after all these years. For facing him and demanding he do what was right.

No, faced with him, she felt like she'd opened the door to confront the monster in the closet and found out he was real. No, no…Reed wasn't a monster. He was just a guy. A man like any other, even if he didn't think so anymore.

He smelled of money, or she could tell that he would from across the courtroom.

Reed was ushered into the court by some shark masquerading as a man in a suit. They each had haircuts that probably cost more than all the shoes in her closet combined. Of course, that probably wasn't saying much.

His hair gleamed, perfect and golden under the light. Too perfect, she wanted to muss it, push her fingers through it and disturb its perfection. She wanted proof that he was still Reed underneath this shiny veneer. Still the same boy, at heart. Because if he wasn't, how would she survive this?

She'd survive anything, because she had to, she reassured herself.

Gina crossed her ankles and tucked her dollar-store flats underneath her, self-conscious of her hand-me-down dress and the slightly gnawed tips of her unpolished fingernails.

"I'm not worried about the judge, I'm worried about *him*. Don't give him the satisfaction," her best friend and lawyer, Emma Grimes, said from the seat next to her. "I don't doubt he's going to try to pull something here. That attack dog he's got with him looks much too smug."

"Good thing you're better than an attack dog. You're a nuclear weapon." Or so Gina hoped. She'd need it to stand her own.

Gina had never been so angry as the day she found out that Reed had bought a house on Snob Hill. He had money for houses, for fancy cars, for whatever he wanted. Not just what he needed, but wanted. Any little thing—especially coming back to Glory and showing everyone he'd succeeded even when the world had been against him.

Well, that was just lovely for him, but what about his daughter? What about Crystal?

And what about herself?

Gina didn't begrudge him his success and she didn't want a handout. She was more than happy to work for everything she had, but it wasn't fair that she was back to waiting tables, working as an EMT and trying to get through premed, all while raising his daughter with no help from him.

If he didn't want to know the beautiful girl his daughter was, fine. But helping pay for her education, for her food and the clothes on her back was his responsibility, too, not Gina's alone. She'd be damned if she'd let him waltz back into town and lord his money and success over everyone while Gina went without so Amanda Jane could have the things she needed—let alone anything she just wanted.

It was wrong that when they went to the store Amanda Jane never asked for anything. That when she made her Christmas list she put things on it like school supplies for Gina. It was kind, yes. She had a large heart, but Amanda Jane had gotten to know nothing of being a child. Even when she played on the swings, it was done with the grim determination of a chore. Something she was supposed to do.

All because she'd had a mother who loved her high more than her daughter and Reed couldn't be bothered to be a father.

That thought sat cold and false in her mind. Even though she'd seen the proof in his absence, she'd never thought he'd be that way. In fact, when she'd played pretend in her head, she was the sister he'd fallen for, and he was always a wonderful dad.

But in those pretend schemes, he'd never been a junkie, either. Not that he was now; he was clean and sober.

Damn him, anyway.

Why did he have to be so handsome?

Why did he have to come back?

Why did he have to be Amanda Jane's father?

She supposed if she were going to get stuck on that endless loop, she could ask the universe a lot of questions. Why did her mother have to die... It was what it was and the only thing she had control over was the here and now.

Sort of. She had control of her actions. That was it.

Judge Gunderson's voice yanked her out of her thoughts. "Before I officially hear this case—" she peered down at them meaningfully, her presence heavy in the small room "—I want to offer you both a solution that has been suggested to me by concerned parties."

Concerned parties? That would equal one Maudine Townsend. Gina forced herself to keep her eyes forward on the judge and not glaring at her grandmother.

She loved the woman.

She admired her.

Couldn't live without her.

But she liked to meddle where she oughtn't.

"Consider giving the child the stability and permanence marriage will provide."

Maybe the judge was her grandmother's best friend, but damn it.

"I object," Gina said.

"Shh!" Emma and her grandmother said at the same time.

"Of course you do." Judge Gunderson addressed her. "I wouldn't want to marry a man I didn't love, either. But you could do it for Amanda Jane."

Reed's gaze was hot on her, as if she'd just come into the sight of some heat-seeking missile. Well, she wasn't going to look at him and give him the satisfaction.

"So my client is good enough to provide for you, but not good enough to marry? Noted," the shark replied.

"Young man," Helga Gunderson began as she turned her chilly stare on him. "Maybe your theatrics are appreciated in other courts. But you are in *my* courtroom. Being a smart aleck isn't going to win you any favors."

The shark grinned, not at all put off by her words. "Yes, ma'am." He was almost handsome, that predator in a suit, with his boyish grin.

"And, Miss Grimes, please remind your client that she isn't the one who gets to object." Helga looked at them both pointedly.

"Yes, ma'am." Emma nudged her under the table like she had those years ago in study hall.

And her grandmother pinched her on the other side.

"You don't get to object, either. Stop it," she grumbled under her breath at the woman who looked more pleased with herself than she should.

"Miss Grimes, Mr. James, confer with your clients."

Emma leaned over. "It costs us nothing to say you'll consider it. In fact, it could gain us some leverage if we have to appeal. You look agreeable and motivated to do what's best for Amanda Jane."

She snuck a glance at Reed and felt as if she was in high school all over again. She didn't want to be the one to put herself out there. To say yes before he did. It was like admitting she didn't think boys had cooties in the fourth grade. That was so stupid.

"You need every advantage you can get here. He's her father. Crystal may have wanted you to have custody, but legally—" Emma whispered.

"Okay, fine." Oh, God, could Reed really take Amanda Jane away from her? She'd never actually believed that could happen, but sitting here in the courtroom now, it was a sword of Damocles hanging over her head. He had more money, more advantages and no matter what Judge Gunderson's ruling was, Reed could appeal it forever.

Emma straightened and nodded to the judge.

Reed's eyes were on her again; she didn't need to look at him to know that he was the one who watched her. It was almost as if he was trying to see what was under her skin. Or maybe he was just trying to look through her and pretend she wasn't there.

"What about you, Mr. James? Your client's answer?"

"We agree to consider it."

Consider it. Marrying Reed Hollingsworth? That was just insane. The idea crashed into her, bruising her in places she didn't know were still sore.

He was "considering" it. As if he would deign to look down from the castle he'd built for himself and still found her lacking.

She snuck a glance at him and he was still watching her, his blue eyes sharp as blades slicing her to ribbons.

But Gina refused to look away, refused to back down. She'd fight for Amanda Jane with every breath in her body.

"If you decide to go forward, I want a prenup on my desk before next week. If not, we'll be revisiting this case to decide custody, visitation and support."

"This is wonderful news. What are your colors going to be?" Maudine asked. "I'm thinking blush and cream."

"I'm thinking you've lost your mind." She took her grandmother's hand. "If for some reason, this insanity happens, it will be just a signing of papers in Emma's office. No dress, no vows, no—"

"Why would you deny an old woman her last wish?"

Gina snorted. "You're far from dying, Grams." She said it more to reassure herself than anyone else.

"You don't know that. I could get hit by a bus. Or choke on—"

"Then I should never get married so you don't ever leave us." Gina hated how close to the truth that really was and her nose prickled.

"Hush with that." Maudine's thin arm came around her and pulled her close. She smelled like lavender and home. "Come on, now. Everything will be well. I know these things."

After the judge left, Gina wanted to do anything but be in the same room with Reed. She was afraid he'd speak to her; she was afraid he wouldn't. She didn't know how to act.

When she'd been thinking about taking him to court

for child support, this part of it had never figured into the equation. This hadn't been real to her. It had been some fey idea in her head. When Emma asked her if she was sure about taking him to court, she'd been so steadfast. So sure. Now? She was drowning.

She didn't think she'd have to see him, hear him. She certainly hadn't thought she'd have to marry him.

As if that would happen, anyway. Not in a million years. The idea was preposterous.

But then what would she do if he wanted sole custody? Gina needed Amanda Jane as much as her niece needed her. She was her touchstone, her reason for fighting as hard as she had. She might have given up on med school last semester if not for her.

For a moment, Gina wondered if maybe that might be the best thing for Amanda Jane. Reed had all the advantages and she'd never want for anything.

But Reed didn't know how to be a family. His own had been more lacking than hers. She'd at least had her grandmother.

Now wasn't the time for self-doubt. It was the time to be decisive, to charge ahead with confidence, bravery and to never ever look back.

CHAPTER TWO

REED'S FIRST REACTION to the news that he was a father had been anger. Anger that he'd been denied the chance to really be a father. Anger that Crystal and Gina had taken that away from him. Anger that they didn't want anything from him except his money. Because he hadn't known he was a father until he'd been served with suit for child support.

Then under that anger, all the old pain, the old doubt—all the baggage associated with the old Reed—surfaced. He was very much that same kid again who wanted so desperately to be enough.

But something akin to longing vied for top tier when he saw Gina sitting there next to her grandmother.

Beautiful, innocent Gina with her ethereal pale skin, her cloud of dark hair and her soft pink lips that always had a smile for him.

He remembered how smooth and soft her hands were on his forehead, the way she'd tenderly pushed his hair out of his face when he'd been racked with fever and chills the first time he'd tried to get clean. There had been no pity in her eyes, only her kindness to ease his suffering.

One of his darkest secrets was that single time he'd

slept with Crystal. He'd thought it was Gina, and that
made him all kinds of a bastard. Especially when once
he'd realized it wasn't, it had been too good to stop.
Something that finally felt good in a hazy world of pain
and numbness.

He'd allow that he was still a bastard, but he wasn't
that kid anymore. That kid who'd do anything to feel
good, anything to belong, anything to feel like someone gave a damn about him.

He gave a damn about himself and no one, not even
Gina Townsend, was going to take that away from him.

Reed had come a long way since then and Gina obviously knew that. She and Crystal hadn't wanted anything to do with him, hadn't cared about Amanda Jane's
paternity until that article about him had appeared in
Finance Today touting his net worth.

Marriage. What the hell was Gina thinking?

Besides wanting his money?

"I'm on it, Reed. If this is just a money grab on her
part, I'll get you custody of the child, and have her
paying *you* child support before this is over. Parental
alienation. It's a crime." Gray sounded almost cheerful.

That didn't make him feel any better. His ego may
have wanted Gina and Crystal to suffer, but his heart
didn't. No, he didn't want that for Gina and Crystal.
Crystal's suffering was over. She'd died and Gina was
trying to raise his daughter all on her own.

He was still all twisted up. It was like standing there
naked. He'd built this persona around himself, made
himself believe he was this successful billionaire, but
inside, he was still that guy from a trailer park.

There were days he felt as if any minute someone was going to come tell him that it had all been a mistake and he had to give it back.

And sitting in court next to his lawyer in the town that only knew him as poor white trash kept reminding him that it was a possibility.

"I think we should go to the Bullhorn for lunch."

"Isn't that where she works? What are you doing?" Gray shoved his papers in his briefcase.

"I just... I need to see her." Reed wanted to assure himself that despite all of this, everything they'd both been through, that she was still Gina. Gina of the soft eyes, the tender hands, Gina who would be a good mother.

"You just saw her."

"No. I need to *see* her." He hoped that Gray would understand.

He didn't. Gray was made of steel and granite. Everything was very simple for him. "That's what the meeting is for that I'm arranging with her lawyer."

"Are you coming or what?" Well, he'd drag him along, anyway.

"That's what I like about you, Hollingsworth. You live to make my job harder." But Grayson smiled. "How do you know she's going to work, anyway?"

"She'll go to work. That's what she does. A tornado couldn't keep her away." That was, if she was still the Gina he knew. Maybe she wasn't. People were allowed to change. After all, hadn't he?

Half an hour later Reed found himself sitting alone in a corner at Bullhorn BBQ, Gray having opted to have lunch elsewhere to keep plausible deniability. The place hadn't changed at all. It still had that rustic mom-and-pop feel to the place—all the meat was smoked out back in a smoker. You could smell this place for miles.

The tables were covered in plastic red-and-white-checkered cloths, the chairs all a mismatched lottery, some scarred and ancient and others with a little less wear. The food was served in red plastic baskets, the kind you'd see in any diner in Nowhere, USA. There was something about the waxy brown paper that lined those baskets that made the food taste better.

Or maybe that was just a good association. When-ever he saw food served like that, it reminded him of the good times of his childhood. Of Gina sneaking food out the back door to him when his mother hadn't been home in weeks, or she was too stoned to care. The taste had always been like heaven.

It had been years since he'd eaten in a place like this. Now it was all business dinners, charity balls and food prepared by a personal chef.

But as soon as the scent hit him, with a follow-up punch of nostalgia, all that had been wiped away. There was a part of him that wished he was still that screwed-up kid coming to beg food from her. She'd always had a smile for him then. He never had to doubt what she wanted from him.

He'd been worth something to her then.

Some movement caught his eye and he turned to see the object of his thoughts. Having seen her from a distance that morning in court still didn't prepare him for the reality of her. For the hurricane of emotions that swept through him when he saw her. It was like a physical blow that knocked the breath from his lungs.

At first, he didn't think it was her—it couldn't be. She'd been demure this morning, a pale version of herself.

Yet it was her, in all the glorious flesh.

She was wearing a Bullhorn shirt that was stretched snug across her breasts, the horns of the bull curled enticingly over her wares. Gina had never filled out the shirt like that before...

It was tucked into cargo pants that hugged her hips and ass in the most enticing way. And he wasn't the only one looking. Her ponytail swung as she expertly negotiated the floor with trays of ribs and pulled pork, and he wondered if her hair smelled like that flowery shampoo she loved or if she'd smell just a bit like barbecue. Both made his mouth water.

"Gina-bee!" a small voice exclaimed and someone held up a large, red plastic cup. "Root beer, please?"

He froze, his assessment of Gina finished for the moment. That small voice was a cold splash of reality. Suddenly, he was afraid to look. That could only be Amanda Jane. Her blond curls bounced as she wagged the cup around for Gina's attention. She looked so much like him, it was uncanny.

His heart did something in that moment. It froze, it melted, it shattered—it did everything a heart could do. He was overwhelmed by the fact that he was a father. This little person—he'd helped create her. She was part of him.

And he didn't even know her.

His fingers curled into a fist. He didn't know her because they didn't want her to know him. Crystal didn't tell him. He'd have expected Gina to try to get in touch with him, at least.

She had. Now that she knew he had money.

"Certainly not. You've had enough." Gina's voice interrupted his thoughts.

"But I said please." Amanda Jane's lower lip curled into an exaggerated pout.

"Yes, you did." Gina smiled and the expression lit up her face. "Thank you. How about water?"

The pout inflated, but then disappeared. "May I have root beer and ribs tomorrow?"

"I'm surprised you're not sick of ribs." Her voice had an indulgent tone to it.

Amanda Jane shook her head. "Never," she said vehemently.

Gina slid a new glass, presumably filled with water, toward the girl on the way to clear another table.

For a moment, he had a glimpse of a life he'd been afraid to want. Of being a father to a sweet-faced girl who looked much like his own baby photos and being a husband to a woman like Gina.

If he'd had any sharp utensils near, he would have gouged that thought out of his head any way he could. But it was possible. All he had to do was say yes. Gina would do this, if only to keep custody of Amanda Jane.

As if she felt the weight of his gaze, she turned and Gina froze in the midst of wiping her hands on a napkin.

He watched her face change like the ebb and flow of the tide. She was always so easy to read. Reed would've thought the world might have hardened her more, taught her to hide her emotions. But everything she felt bloomed bright on her face with no reservations.

For a second, she was surprised to see him, then there was a happiness in her eyes that startled him. He hadn't expected that—genuine happiness at the sight of him. But it faded quickly into a scowl.

"What do you want?"

"Lunch." Reed didn't mean to sound so cavalier, but it was his only defense against her. What else could he say? *I came here because I wanted to see you?*

He was conflicted about what that thought wrought in him. He didn't want her to be working the same job, stuck in the same cycle, wasting away—all her potential squandered. But if she was chasing his bank account, what else would she be doing?

Still, she didn't seem unhappy.

She was gentle with Amanda Jane, patient. That wasn't the behavior of an addict. That hurt him, pierced his skin and burrowed into his bones. If she hadn't fallen into the same trap that he and Crystal had, what was she doing still in Glory?

"Maybe you should get it somewhere else." Her mouth thinned.

"Maybe I should," he agreed easily. "I wanted to see you."

"Now you've seen me." Her knuckles whitened as she clenched her fists. "Wasn't this morning enough?"

"That I have." He nodded. Reed didn't know what to say to her. He hadn't planned on speaking to her, but he should've known his presence wouldn't have gone unnoticed. "And I'm wondering why you're still working here?"

Her eyes narrowed and for a moment, he thought for sure she was going to do violence.

"Why am I still working here? That's really what you're going to ask me after seven years? The last time I saw you was the night before my sister almost died and all you can think to say to me is why I'm still working at the Bullhorn?" Her voice was almost a growl. "I'm working here to support your daughter. What about you? What are you doing to take care of her?"

He hadn't expected this from her—hell, he didn't know what he expected. Reed supposed that if he didn't believe she'd gotten out of the cycle, why should she believe that he had? The balls on this woman: to sue him for child support and then imply she could somehow mandate the terms of his visitation.

There was a part of him that raged at her for daring to speak of it, for digging underneath his skin and tearing at old scars and still prescient fears. That he'd never be anything more than a junkie kid from Whispering Woods.

But he was. He was so much more than that now. He was a man in control of himself and his destiny. He could buy the Bullhorn and fire her, if he chose.

"Don't push me too hard, Gina. You've already shown you can't take care of her on your own. That's why you're suing me for child support. I'll go for full custody." He kept his tone low and quiet so only Gina could hear him.

"You'd take her away from me, from the only stability she's ever known, because you're afraid of the truth? You're still just like Crys. Maybe you have some nice suits and you got your teeth fixed, but underneath all of that, you're still who you've always been. The high more important than anything else," she hissed back, her voice at the same low pitch to keep Amanda Jane from hearing them.

"You don't know anything about me." For one horrible moment, he was afraid she was right.

Gina paused and pursed her lips. "You're right. I don't. Which is exactly why I don't want you anywhere near my niece."

He saw her hands curl into fists and then splay by her side.

"You want my money." He dared her to deny it.

"I don't know why I thought you'd be different. I guess those rose-colored glasses were just the remnants of my childhood."

"Really?" he snorted. "You thought that you could just throw me away when I wasn't any use to you and now that I've made something of myself, it's convenient to tell me that I might be a father?"

"What I thought was that you might have given a damn. But you didn't. So no, I don't want anything from you but a check." She braced her hands on the table. "That should make you happy. Then you don't have to do anything but put your name on the dotted line or have your shark lawyer do it for you."

"What are you talking about?"

"Maybe you were too blazed out of your mind when Crys told you to remember. But she told you the night she OD'd and she even called your case manager when Amanda Jane was born."

Her words affected him like a physical blow. "Gina, the day I got served with this suit was the first time I'd heard anything about a child."

The fire in her eyes simmered to an ember and she studied him hard.

"There's a part of me that wants to believe you." She looked away. "Part of me that actually does believe you." Her voice dropped an octave; it was almost a whisper.

He felt like the world's biggest asshole. For all her fire, she was still sweet little Gina. And he'd come in here looking for a fight. A place to put all of his pain, his doubt, and a focus for his anger. Anywhere besides himself.

"There's a part of me that wants to believe you, too." He inhaled deeply before making his confession. "And there's this other part of me that thinks you're like everyone else who wants to take everything I've done away from me."

Because he didn't deserve it. He was poor white trash from the wrong side of the tracks and no amount of imported cologne could wipe off the stench, or erase the scars on his arms. He didn't want to believe that, and for a long time, he'd convinced himself that he didn't. Then he found out he was a father. He found out Gina didn't want him. Crystal hadn't wanted him. The people he'd thought were safe weren't.

He shouldn't have confessed that to her, shouldn't have given her anything she could use against him.

Gina sank down in the chair next to him, her shoulders slumped. "I don't want anything that's yours. Just what's hers. If you look at the numbers, I'm not asking for anything extravagant."

That was a glimpse of the person he'd still hoped she was. In truth, she really hadn't asked for that much. She was most likely entitled to ten times that given his income. But he'd wondered if it was just because she didn't know how much to ask for. Except with Amanda Jane's little face looking over at him, he found that thought to be foreign and cruel. If she really was his daughter, she was entitled to his support.

"No, you're not." He didn't know what else to say.

"Reed, I'm doing the best I can."

He wondered what her best was and sure as hell hoped it was better than what they had growing up. Reed was almost afraid to ask, but he had to know. "You're not still living in Whispering Woods, are you?" He mentioned the trailer park community where they'd grown up.

"No. I've got a little house out in the country. Highway 5. You remember the one with the hills that we used to take really fast?"

"Hanging out someone's sunroof? You remember that time you swallowed a moth?"

She turned to look at him. "I thought I was going to die. It was the nastiest thing."

"It's not like you could taste it."

"No, but I had nightmares about what it was doing in there."

He laughed. This…this was what he'd wanted from her—hoped for. Why couldn't he have just spoken to her like this from the beginning? If he was really a better man than he'd once been, he wouldn't need to be so defensive.

Wouldn't need to try to put her down or show her how easily he could defeat her.

Again, he couldn't help but think that he was an asshole. But just like he didn't have to be an addict, he didn't have to be this person, either. He could own his actions and he could choose them.

"I'm sorry, Gina."

It took a long time for her to look up at him and meet his gaze. For a moment, he wasn't sure she would. When she did, he saw something there he couldn't name. All he knew was that it cut him.

"For what?" She cocked her head to the side.

"For being an asshole."

Gina shook her head. "I knew this wouldn't be easy." She laughed, but there was no mirth in the sound. "When I knew you'd been served, I kind of wanted to throw up. I knew you'd be angry with me. I just… Crys said she told you and you didn't want anything to do with us. I never thought she'd lie about that. If I thought for one second that you didn't know about Amanda Jane, I might have gone about it differently."

"You still can."

"What do you mean?"

"I don't want to be a part-time father. I want you to consider what the judge offered." At the sudden look of fear on her face, he held up his hands as if to ward it off. "Not like that. If we're in the same household, I can see her whenever I want and so can you."

She looked as though he'd just punched her. "You've lost your mind."

"Hear me out."

"It would put us at your mercy, right under your thumb." She shook her head. "You just told me that I didn't know you and you're right. I haven't seen you in *seven years*."

"Which is exactly why you should marry me. Don't you think it would be traumatic for her to suddenly be left with a stranger?"

The fear on her face was back and so was the guilty chill slithering down his spine.

"I can't talk about this with you."

He exhaled, sensing that the earlier door to their childhood memories had been slammed in his face.

She stood. "I have to get back to work."

"Gina?"

She turned back to face him. "What?"

He found everything he thought he wanted to say died on the tip of his tongue and it was nothing but charcoal and memory.

"Me, too, Reed." She answered the unspoken questions, regrets, and hopes with all of her own. All the things he couldn't seem to tell her, it was as if she knew them all and had them herself.

Perhaps he'd been wrong. Maybe Gina did know him, after all. She seemed to sense everything he wanted to say but couldn't.

He wondered why it was so easy to say all the wrong things, but the right ones were practically impossible.

As he watched her walk away, he wondered what the

hell he'd been thinking, asking her to marry him. That was pure insanity.

He wasn't ready to be a father. He could barely manage himself. What was he thinking?

Just looking at facts, if he didn't know that it was his own case he was judging, he wouldn't give a child to a man like him. Even with all of his money, all the years between himself and his addiction, all the things he'd accomplished, Reed could only assume he'd blow it and Amanda Jane would be better off anywhere, but with him.

Why he thought he could do a better job than his own absent father—he'd always vowed if he ever had children they'd never know a childhood like his own. It wasn't all horrible; he'd had Gina and Crystal, other friends, but he never had stability or comfort and he was always left with this horrible ache in his chest, this want of things that weren't for him.

A hunger.

And he'd tried to fill it with pleasure—with sex, with drugs, with anything that would make that feeling stop.

He didn't want any child to know that feeling, let alone his own.

He wondered what life had been like for her. If she knew enough now to want what she couldn't have, if it gnawed at her the same way it affected him.

Gina went over to where Amanda Jane was sitting, took the girl's hand and led her back toward the kitchen—away from him. He couldn't blame her.

Maybe she was right to just want a check and his absence.

He closed his eyes as if that could somehow guard him against the sharp blades of that thought. It sliced into him, into every single defense he had.

Part of him wanted to escape, and still another part of him wanted to stay at the Bullhorn just a little bit longer, hoping to catch another glimpse of the woman and child that were the embodiment of a future he'd been afraid to want.

He stayed there in the corner long after he knew she wasn't coming back to his table.

CHAPTER THREE

SEEING REED AGAIN up close and personal had gone better and worse than Gina had hoped. Better because after his initial anger, he seemed willing. Worse, because…

Because he still made her heart flutter like a stupid butterfly and she couldn't stop thinking about him. She wanted to stop. Gina wanted to push him and all of her stupid hopes and resurrected teen desires out of her head. Two days had passed, and she still couldn't stop. Maybe *she* was the addict.

She almost hadn't recognized him at first. His thin features had filled in and it was obvious he was taking much better care of his body. He was bigger, stronger, a hunger inside him striving to get out and obvious in his every action. He looked like the *GQ* model version of Reed Hollingsworth with perfect hair, a perfect suit, but his eyes were the same. In those depths was the familiar hopeful kid she'd known.

Once upon a time, she'd wished it had been her that he wanted and while good sense told her that it was just the leftovers of a high school infatuation, her body didn't know the difference. The hard planes of his powerful body in that suit that had been tailor-made for him, the determined set to his jaw and the ferocity of his expression conveyed that now, there was nothing he wanted that he couldn't have. Gina found that kind of confidence and power titillating, as much as she hated to admit it.

But he wasn't a fairy-tale prince on a valiant steed. He was an addict. That didn't change. He could manage his addiction, but there was no magic cure to free him from the curse. And if there was, it certainly wasn't her. He'd picked Crystal, not Gina. No, he was no hero.

Though she realized he wasn't the villain she'd thought he'd become, either.

She knew that she'd agree to whatever Reed wanted if it meant that she could keep Amanda Jane. And she would never just let her go with a stranger. When it was distilled down to its most basic, Reed was a stranger to them both. Amanda Jane played on the floor with a myriad of secondhand toys. She had a doll in an evening gown riding a fire truck. That was her current obsession. She said she wanted to be a firefighter when she grew up and apparently, she planned on doing it in sparkles.

Which was just fine with Gina. Gina made it a point to tell her that with enough hard work, she could do anything—be anything.

Amanda Jane sang a little song to herself quietly and rather than distract Gina from her studies, it soothed her.

No, what distracted her was seeing Reed Hollingsworth.

Gina had always wondered what happened to Reed. If he'd taken the same path that Crystal had, he'd have been in prison or dead. Then her economics class had been assigned an article about rags-to-riches business-man Reed Hollingsworth.

And the article had pissed her off.

How dare he sit there on his velvet throne looking down on the rest of them while she struggled to feed and clothe his daughter? Crystal may have been fine with no help from Reed, but Gina wasn't. He had a respon-sibility to his daughter. If he didn't want to physically parent, fine. But he could contribute financially. It was the least he could do. The man made millions of dollars a year. Twelve grand a year plus a college education for his daughter wasn't going to beggar him.

Gina was torn between anger, regret, and betrayal. These washed over her all at once and she imagined if the emotions had colors, they'd look like a mess of spilled ink after they'd roiled around inside of her. At the end of the day, there was no discernible difference between them.

She was so tired. She'd just come off a twenty-four-hour shift and she had to study for a test the next day, but she needed to spend some time with Amanda Jane, too. The girl was just getting over the latest bout of bronchitis. Amanda Jane had a weak immune system, but they were lucky that was her only problem consid-ering Crystal's mistreatment of herself while she was pregnant.

Gina sighed and put her head down on the table. She wished she could learn by osmosis, then maybe banging her head against things would actually serve a purpose.

"Are you tired, Gina-bee?" Amanda Jane asked her in a small, scratchy voice.

She smiled. Crystal had called her Gina-bee when she was tiny. It reminded her of the person her sister had been and the hope she had for the person and mother she hoped she could be again. "Yes, darling."

"Maybe it's nap time."

"But you don't like naps."

"No." Amanda shook her head earnestly. "But you like them. So, maybe we should have one."

"I'm fine, honey. I have to study for this test."

"Tests are dumb."

Tests made Gina feel dumb sometimes. She smiled again. "No, they're good. This test means I can go to my next class and then I can be Doctor Gina."

"And Doctor Gina means no more EMT Gina," Amanda Jane recited with her.

"You got it, kiddo." She stared back down at the paper, trying to make sense of the words as they danced over the page, but she didn't see any of them. All she could see was Reed's thin face.

Maybe because Amanda Jane looked so much like him. Or as he had as a boy, before things had gotten so bad.

He'd been so beautiful to her then, so tragic. With a face like an angel and a heart so full of hope, even after it had been crushed again and again. She'd waited for him to notice her as something other than Crystal's sister.

It was ironic, really.

She'd ended up a parent the end of her senior year

and she'd never had sex to prevent exactly that thing. Gina wanted to get an education, a career, before she started a family. And she wanted to do it the right way. She wanted to fall in love, have babies with a man who wanted to be a father and a husband. She wanted the white picket fence and the American dream.

And now, she supposed she had fallen in love, but with Amanda Jane. That girl was her heart and soul, and Gina would do anything she had to do to provide a good life for her. Anything.

Gina had a feeling that the universe was going to test her mettle with that statement, but she didn't care. There was nothing more important to her than giving Amanda Jane the life she deserved.

She knew that meant seeing Reed again and she also knew it meant that she couldn't let her softer feelings for the boy he'd been get in the way. He wasn't that boy anymore. He was a grown man who'd had no problem playing hardball.

But neither would Gina.

She just couldn't reconcile that with the boy he'd been.

Gina looked back down at Amanda Jane's serious blue eyes and found another smile. "Hey, you want to help me study for this test?"

Amanda Jane put down her doll and her small fingers reached for the flash cards. She was probably the only six-year-old who knew the names of all the bones in the human body. She'd been tested as gifted, and Gina wasn't sure if it was because she included Amanda Jane in her studies as a means to double task spending time with her as well as test prep, or if it was because she was wired much like Gina herself.

Either way, it both warmed and broke her heart at the same time. She never wanted Amanda Jane to feel the way that she did growing up. She never wanted her to be the dirty kid who had to eat free lunch, who was the hope in teachers' eyes. That someday, they knew she'd be the story they told to their class about how if Gina Townsend could do it, they could do it, too.

Reed's financial support could change all of that.

She wouldn't care what he thought of her, as long as Amanda Jane was taken care of.

But there was a secret part of her that wanted him to come back to Glory and realize that he'd always been in love with her and they'd get married, raise Amanda Jane together and live happily ever after.

Silly as it was.

Crystal was her mother, not Gina. And if Reed had ever had any feelings for her, he would've told her somehow. Acted on them in some way. She didn't even know him anymore.

She had Amanda Jane. She was going to be a doctor. Nothing could stop her. Not her past, not her sister and definitely not Reed Hollingsworth.

Her cell rang and she saw that it was Emma.

A knot tightened in on itself in her gut. It had to be the meeting to discuss this whole insane idea of marriage.

"Hit me with it," she said by way of greeting.

"What, no hello?"

"Come on, Emma." Gina was sure if she had to wait

another second, the anticipation might kill her. Whatever the answer here was, it would change her life.

"Reed and his lawyer want to meet *today* to talk about the judge's suggestion. He's offering so much more than we asked for and if we can hash this out together, you'll be more likely to get what you want."

"What do you mean?" That was when the knot tightened so hard she thought she was going to be sick. She knew somehow he was going to get his way or she was going to lose custody or something else awful. But she needed Emma to lay it out on the table for her.

"He's agreed to the marriage. Coparenting, cohabitation… Because he's being so generous, the judge will look more favorably on his requests. He's got his lawyer setting up a trust for Amanda Jane and one for you—"

"I didn't want a trust. I don't want his money for myself. I can make my own." She was horrified at the thought. Because she didn't want his money for herself. She just wanted Amanda Jane to get what was hers. She just wanted her to be safe and secure. She didn't need his money.

"You can. But he thinks that time would be better spent with Amanda Jane."

"Excuse me, what?" She blinked.

"He wants you to quit both jobs and focus only on school and being a caregiver."

Her first instinct was to rail against this. How dare he demand that of her? How dare he make the decision for her? He wasn't a king on a golden throne. He didn't get to dictate. But her reasons for fighting it would be simple pride. Deep down, she knew it would be better for her niece. But she couldn't get past how much control that would give him. "And that leaves him holding the purse strings and us his puppets. He wants us totally dependent on him."

That idea terrified her. She didn't want anyone to have control over her. She had worked too long and too hard to pull herself up to suddenly throw herself on his mercy. To be legally and financially bound...

"I think that's part of it, but you can't deny it would be good for Amanda Jane."

"I know that. But it won't be good for me."

"Won't it?" Emma asked gently. "But he doesn't need to know that. Just think about what it will mean to have an address on Knob Hill and his connections. How much faster you'll get to medical school and the internships... Imagine what it will do for Amanda Jane. She'll never be the kid no one wants to sit by, who gets picked last for teams, who has to rely on what she can scrape together for her lunch."

Tears stung her eyes because that's exactly what she feared it would be like for Amanda Jane, but she didn't want to be dependent on Reed, either. What if he slipped back into old behaviors? What if he— She was afraid, not just of the possibility of him, but of herself.

What if she couldn't handle raising Amanda Jane with him without falling for him? She was setting herself up for misery.

"Why don't you think about it for a few hours? But we don't have much time. Judge Gunderson wanted the prenup on her desk by next week."

She thought about Reed again. The clash between

them, but the pain underneath. "Let's get it over with. Putting it off won't make it any easier and frankly, with Crys gone and my lack of income, I'm afraid that he'll take her away from me if we go to court." She sighed. "At least this way, maybe I can get him to agree to some safeguards for my piece of mind."

"I'll tell Gray to come by my office at five. You be here now. Bring Amanda Jane with you and I'll have Missy watch her."

Missy was Emma's secretary/assistant/friend who'd recently come through a horrible divorce from an even worse man and was trying to get back on her feet. She never felt as though she was doing enough to repay Emma for helping her, so she was always looking for extra duties and frequently offered to watch Amanda Jane. They were friends, and Missy never tried to correct Amanda Jane when she wanted her dolls to be firemen rather than beauty queens.

Gina agreed and hung up.

Then it hit her. This was happening. This was real.

That sounded so stupid when she stopped to think about it, but when she'd signed the paperwork to set all of this in motion, it had seemed like some diaphanous thing that wouldn't have any more impact on her life than a changing breeze.

But it would.

It had.

She thought about him at that corner table in the Bullhorn. The restaurant she'd worked at since she was fourteen.

Gina remembered him coming in for scraps, hungry and tired. She'd snuck him the leftovers as best she could. Until the Old Man had caught her. Then she'd washed his car to pay for them. But that hadn't mattered back then.

She smiled, thinking about how horrified Reed had been when he found out she'd had to pay for what he'd eaten and how he'd asked the Old Man for a job himself. And he'd done really well for about two years.

Until the drugs.

Her smile melted into a frown.

Gina wasn't ready for this.

Amanda Jane looked up at her. "Gina-bee?"

She inhaled carefully, filling her lungs slowly, feeling them expand, and when she exhaled she tried to push all of her fear out with her breath. "You want to go visit Miss Emma?"

"Okay." The girl cocked her head to the side. "What's wrong?"

"I'm nervous."

"About what?"

She didn't want to tell her, but Gina didn't really have a choice. Reed would want to see her. "About you meeting your daddy."

Her eyes widened. "He wants to meet me?"

"I'm sure he will."

"What if he doesn't like me?" Her voice was suddenly as small as she was.

"Of course he'll like you. What if you don't like him?" Gina tapped her nose with the tip of her finger and Amanda Jane giggled. "Actually, I'm sure you'll like each other fine."

"What if we don't?"

"What if you do?" She grinned. "Get ready. Bring your travel bag."

Amanda Jane scurried off to do as Gina had told her. Sometimes Gina wished she could bottle that excess energy and borrow a little now and then. She yawned.

Soon, she wouldn't have to work two jobs and go to school. She could just be with Amanda Jane and study.

The idea was so foreign…

And it wouldn't just be with Amanda Jane, either.

It would be with Reed, as well.

She'd be his wife.

They'd been friends once, but she imagined this would be a cold marriage. One of separate rooms, separate lives.

This wasn't at all what she'd imagined for herself. She thought someday, she'd find someone to love. Someone who'd love her.

She supposed she had that, only in a different way. She had Amanda Jane. This was about her, not Gina. She could do this for her.

CHAPTER FOUR

REED PANICKED.

Amanda Jane was his daughter.

What did he know about being a father? Nothing.

Reed had been so sure that when the paternity results came back before the hearing, it would solidify
the foundations of his world, but instead, it had shattered them.

Not because he didn't want Amanda Jane, but because he did. This was his secret hope and desire—
part of it, anyway. Before things had gotten bad, he'd
dreamed of a world where he had a family, a real family.
Not just someone who got a check every month because
she'd managed to bring him squalling into the world.
Someone who loved him, wanted him for who he was.

But Gina wasn't it. Maybe Amanda Jane was. Gina
only wanted his money, and while he couldn't blame
her, it cut him. Because in his pretty fantasy world,
Gina had been by his side.

His fingers curled into fists and he took a deep
breath.

Why had he said he wanted to meet with Gina and
her lawyer tonight?

Probably because he knew that he'd do this to himself. The sooner everything was set in stone, the harder it would be for him to screw it up.

He could do this.

He had to do this.

Reed changed into another suit and tie, the raiment almost like an armor. The expensive clothes shielded him from so many things, kept the boy who still feared he wasn't good enough safe inside that money-green shell.

He met Gray in front of Emma's office. A few kids sat on a park bench outside of the theater waiting for a ride, and the Corner Pharmacy's light had just flickered off. Several couples filed out carrying to-go cups with their signature Green River—a soft drink much like a lime soda.

It was such a pretty veneer, this small town with its quaint bed-and-breakfasts, brick sidewalks and cheery Americana. He remembered how much he used to hate it. It had taken on some goliath proportions in his mind. He'd blamed the town itself for his predicament, as if it had been the town that had pushed him and his mother to the outside.

Not her own actions.

Or his.

Standing there, he realized that Gina had it just as bad as he had, but instead of letting that push her to the margins, she'd dug in her heels and made a place for herself.

A home.

He wanted that for himself and for Amanda Jane.

Reed exhaled heavily. He knew he'd do anything to have that, and to make sure Amanda Jane kept it.

"You look like you've seen a ghost, man." Gray shook his head. "It's like you were standing there lost in it."

"I think maybe I was."

"I can't believe you grew up here."

"Not in this part of town." Reed managed a half smile.

"It must be cathartic to come back here and be able to buy the whole town if you chose."

Reed considered. "I thought it would be, but it's not. There's something about Glory that can't be bought. The people here, the town itself, has to give it to you."

Gray arched a brow. "Yeah, I think I'll stick with the big city, thanks."

"Wait until you have some of the apple pie. You might change your mind," Reed teased.

"Apple pie. That's exactly what this place is like. Everywhere I look, it's all wholesome sweetness. It doesn't seem real."

"It is and it isn't." Reed shrugged. "People here still have their problems. Everyone does. But they choose to insulate themselves with community."

And that was what he'd hated most as a kid, that he was part of what they'd insulated themselves against. He took a deep breath, determined to get his head straight. He wasn't that kid anymore and he wanted everyone to see it. Especially himself.

"You ready to go in or change your mind, Daddy-o?" Reed shot him a dirty look, and Gray flashed him a smirk. He found comfort in that. While everything changed around him, Gray was still Gray. He still had Reed's back. "I'm ready."

He walked into the office and whatever he was expecting from Emma Grimes, this wasn't it. The walls were all a dark, heavy blue, the furniture antique and cherry. The baseboards had been refinished to match. The tin tiles that had once been on the ceiling in this building had been replaced by a painted fresco, in the same dark colors. A night scene by the river and a woman in a ball gown. The ball gown seemed to meld into the river.

"Lovely, isn't it?" Emma asked. "My assistant, Missy, painted it for me. If you'll come this way."

He noticed that while Emma was as pretty as she'd ever been, there was something delicate about her now. Something breakable. Maybe it was the way her short, pixie blond hair framed her face, or maybe it was the clothes she wore. Reed would bet it was all an act to lull her prey into submission.

He knew Emma would be a fierce opponent and from the way Gray watched her, it was obvious he knew it, too.

His gaze was drawn to Gina as soon as the door opened. She sat at a long table, her fingers clasped together, her knuckles white. She was as nervous as he was.

There was part of him that wanted to go to her, to embrace her and tell her that they'd figure this all out. That he didn't want to hurt her and most of all, that she could trust him.

But he didn't know if she could because he didn't know if he could trust himself.

"Hi," she said softly.

"Hi."

Christ, it was as if they were in middle school and he was trying to hold her hand or something. But he guessed neither of them knew what to say.

Gray stepped in. "Thank you for agreeing to meet with us on such short notice. My client and I felt it would be best for everyone involved if we moved quickly."

Reed sat down across from Gina and he was filled with so many questions, waves of different emotions.

"We did, as well." Emma nodded. "We've considered your requests and we have some caveats of our own."

"Being?" Gray raised a brow.

"My client is willing to marry, granted that she and the child each have their own room and—"

He didn't hear the rest of what she said. Only that Gina was willing to marry him. It was a bittersweet feeling, until he heard "separate quarters and separate lives." And then it was all pain. A sharp reminder that he'd never be anything more to her.

"There's no way my client will or should have to agree to that. He's an upstanding member of the business community and has a certain reputation to maintain."

"Reputation? Everyone knows his backstory. It was in *Finance Today*. You can't hide that now."

"Hide it? We're not trying to hide it. But it's where he came from, not who he is now. That's a hard no. We won't negotiate on that."

Emma smiled. "That's fine. We've shown that we

were willing to cooperate and now it's you who won't compromise. I expect a judge would hand down a ruling in our favor on this particular point."

Gina had gone pale and her eyes were heavy and hooded. As if she knew this was going to be the sticking point.

"It's fine," he blurted.

"What?" Gray snapped.

"It's fine. I'll do it."

"There is no way—"

"I said I'd do it, Gray. Move along." He didn't want to quantify his decision in front of everyone; it would be the same as admitting everything to them that he'd just admitted to himself.

"It seems my client is in a giving mood. What else do you want?"

"If you want Gina to quit her jobs, she needs a stipend that will cover her school and living expenses."

"We already—"

"An account in only her name. Reed doesn't get to control the purse strings." Emma lifted her chin, daring him to argue that one.

Argue he did. "Why not? It's his money." Gray squared his jaw.

"And this is my client's life," Emma reminded them all.

"Fine. Whatever she wants," Reed said, even though he hadn't looked away from Gina and she had yet to look at him again.

"Reed!" Gray sounded like a scandalized maiden

aunt. "I really have to advise against—" Gray sighed. "You do know you just wasted my retainer, right?"

"I don't care. Give her whatever she wants." His eyes raked over her as intense as any touch, though his fingers itched for a physical connection.

"Good. I have a revised version of the paperwork right here." Emma rustled some papers.

"But I want you to look at me, Gina." Reed had to see her eyes. She could never hide her feelings. They were always so obvious in her expression.

Gina swallowed hard and raised her head as if all the weight of the world bore down on her.

He could see her fear, her hesitation, the almost cruel hope that lurked there, so he knew she was feeling much the same as he was.

"Yes." He nodded. "Whatever she needs to feel safe, for both her and Amanda Jane." Reed knew it was a weakness, but he'd do anything to get that look off her face. To know that he didn't cause the fear in her heart.

"Me?" A small face peered around the corner of the door. "Is it my turn to come in, Gina-bee?"

Reed almost choked on the strange knot in his throat. "You brought her?"

"What else was I going to do with her?" Gina said quietly. "I thought you'd be anxious to meet her."

It was his turn to look away, to be unable to meet Gina's eyes, or Amanda Jane's. He'd seen his daughter from a distance at the Bullhorn, but the prospect hadn't been expressly real.

Nothing had ever made him feel as unworthy as he did in that very moment—and that was really saying something. Reed was reminded every day with a certain clarity that he didn't deserve all the things he had, and that he didn't belong.

But there was such a purity in a child's eyes... specifically her eyes, that he couldn't stand to be the one to break it.

Gina took pity on him. "No, Amanda Jane. It's not your turn."

"But I'll be good." Her little voice was full of hope.

"Yes, you're always very good. So you can stay up very late tonight and then it will be your turn."

The door clicked shut softly.

"Even if you're not ready to meet her, she's ready to meet you. You can meet us at the house tonight. Seven Sisters Road off Highway 5. Only house on the block."

The part of him that was still a child himself wanted to run. He could just write her a check and he'd never have to face the scorching hope in that child's face again. That was all she wanted from him, anyway.

For one horrible moment, he wondered what it would be like to have one moment of relief from this pain. Numbing this terror. He knew just what would do that for him, but he pushed it out of his head. He was afraid, but he didn't want the numbness, not really. He just didn't want to feel unworthy and he wouldn't give those feelings validation by making them true, by making himself unworthy.

He wasn't a boy. He wasn't a child. He was a man. He'd reached for what he wanted with both hands and he'd gotten it. Now it was his job to protect it.

He nodded. "Thank you, Gina."

She picked up the pen and with a heavy exhale, she scrawled her name and walked out of the room.

When he picked up the pen, it was still warm from her touch. He signed his name next to hers and with every stroke of ink on the page, he felt more confident about his decision.

Gray, however, wasn't as sure.

As they walked out he said, "If you were going to let them ream you, why did you bother to call me?"

"I honestly don't know. But I did the right thing." He was resolute in that knowledge.

"Did you even read it? Did you know you're paying for medical school?"

"I don't care. I have it." Reed shrugged. At the expression on Gray's face, he added, "Things were different for us as kids."

"This is the junkie's sister? How do you know she's not using?"

"Gina? Never. Not in a million years." After setting eyes on her again, he knew that as sure as he knew he was breathing.

"This is going to end badly. I can see the explosions from here. This woman is going to take you for everything you've got." He shook his head. "Do you want me to come with you tonight?" Gray asked, in a low tone, almost like he was telling a secret.

"To meet my daughter?" He shook his head. "No."

"Why didn't you meet her inside?"

"It just wasn't right." He was too afraid, the idea now a reality that scared the shit out of him. And Amanda Jane deserved better than his fear. She didn't ask to come into the world. Didn't ask for him to be her father. Didn't ask for the hand she'd been dealt.

"I get that, man. I really do." Gray clapped him on the back. "If you don't need anything else, brother, I'm going to head back to the city."

"No, I'm good. Thanks." He supposed he was good—this was as good as it ever got for Reed Hollingsworth.

CHAPTER FIVE

"ARE YOU READY to get married yet?" Grams said into the phone when she answered it.

"No." She didn't bother to tell her grandmother about the meeting at Emma's office. She probably already knew.

"That's not what Marie Hart said. She told me that she saw you and Reed and his lawyer at Emma's. Were you playing pinochle or planning your wedding?" Her grandmother seemed to think pinochle figured into everything.

She sighed with only the smallest bit of exasperation. "If you already knew, why did you ask?"

"Because you didn't call me. Why don't you bring Amanda Jane over and we'll watch some movies, have popcorn, and maybe I'll even bake cookies."

"Reed's coming over tonight."

"Oh! Call me later." Her grandmother hung up before she could say anything else.

She shook her head. Maudine had her cell phone attached to her head just like any teenager. Sometimes Gina felt as if she was the old woman and Maudine the grandchild, but only in the vaguest sense.

Gina suddenly had a craving for that ribbon candy. It

reminded her of being a child, when things were good. When they were easy.

It had been strange to be sitting across from Reed in a conference room in Emma Grimes's office.

Strange wasn't the right word. *Utterly insane* might be a better description.

He'd switched faces again so easily it was hard to tell which one was real. The Reed who sat in front of her was the investment genius who got everything he wanted no matter who he had to crush to get it. This suit he wore looked like it cost more than a semester of her tuition. And he wanted her to know it.

She didn't want to look at him like this, but she knew she should be grateful for the reminder. He could never be just Reed again.

Gina thought he'd been there to crush her, to take everything from her, but instead, he'd only given. He'd agreed to everything she wanted. His shark lawyer could've made this so hard, but it seemed like all he wanted was exactly what he said—to be a good parent. Giving her and Amanda Jane safety and security.

That wasn't something she'd ever felt as though she had, so she didn't quite know what to do with it. She wondered if he felt the same way or if he'd taken to his new life without ever looking back? She imagined the latter. She had to say if she was in his shoes, she'd do the same. She knew she was lucky to have had Maudine.

God, why had she invited him out to the house?

He'd be here any minute.

What was she thinking?

Well, besides that this was going to crash and burn?

She sighed. This was the right thing to do. Not just for the financial support, but so that Amanda Jane never doubted she was loved, or that there were people in the world who wanted her. Who would keep her safe.

Gina took a deep breath. This was going to be her life. She might as well start getting used to it.

"Gina, my braids are too tight." Amanda Jane squirmed underneath her hand.

"Sorry." She loosened the length of woven hair. "He's going to be here soon. And I know you won't sit still then. Your hair won't tangle if we do it before you sleep."

"I like his face," she said solemnly.

That was good because she looked just like him. Gina smiled at her. "Go on now."

"I think you like his face, too. You get this funny expression when you look at him."

She'd have to be more careful. "I do like his face." Gina liked a lot more than his face. "We were friends a long time ago before you were born."

"Do you think it's true that he just didn't want to be a daddy?" Amanda Jane cast her eyes down at her bare feet and wiggled her toes.

Gina didn't want to lie to her, but she didn't know the truth. "I don't know, honey. But I can tell you that sometimes people make mistakes and we have to forgive them when they're really sorry."

"Do you think he likes *my* face?" Amanda Jane tilted her head up.

"How could anyone not like your face?"

She smiled. "You're supposed to say that."

"Yes, I am. But do you remember when I promised I'd always tell you the truth?"

"Even if I was ugly like Liza McCaully?"

Gina had to put her hand over her mouth to keep from laughing. "That's not nice."

"It's not nice, but it's true." Amanda Jane nodded, her face serious.

"You can speak the truth without being mean, but yes, I would tell you the truth."

Amanda Jane stuffed her feet into her slippers. "Okay, but now it's time for you to get ready."

"I am ready."

Amanda Jane shook her head. "Your jeans have a hole." She stuck her finger in the hole and tickled Gina's knee.

Gina squealed and grabbed her niece, tickling her in return. Amanda Jane giggled while she struggled to free herself.

"Did you brush your teeth?"

She nodded. "Did you brush yours?"

Gina found the tension draining out of her. "It's not my bedtime yet."

"No, but we should be pretty. You always told me when we meet new people we should smell good."

"I'm brushing everything. Hair. Teeth." She puckered her lips. "Mustache."

Amanda Jane giggled. "Eww. Girls don't have mustaches."

"Some do, but that's what laser hair removal is for."

Amanda Jane nodded sagely as if she were the one handing out the advice.

Gina was brushing her hair when the screen door rattled against the framing under a heavy knock.

Amanda Jane squealed and her blue eyes lit up. "He's here."

Her heart ached for her. This was all so bittersweet.

Reed stood haloed in the yellow light as it cast bright warmth over the hard planes of his features. Her eyes were drawn to the square angles of his wide shoulders and the way the sleeves of his polo shirt stretched over his biceps.

Gina tried not to notice everything about him that turned her on because he wasn't here for her. None of this was about her.

Even though her mouth had gone dry and the words she had died in her throat.

"Hey."

It was such a simple word. He'd said it to her a million times, but this time it was devastating. Both because it was a reminder of times past and while it was spoken in his voice, her attention was once again drawn back to his body.

That and time had made him a stranger.

"Hey, yourself." Also something she'd said a million times. It was strange and awkward.

"Come in? Apparently I need to change clothes. I have a hole in my jeans," she babbled.

Ugh. She hated babbling. Men didn't make her babble. She didn't have time or room in her life to be a silly girl over any guy, especially not Amanda Jane's father. Gina decided polo shirts were the devil. It was the shirt's fault.

He nodded and stepped inside.

Amanda Jane tilted her head back to look up at him. He must seem like a giant to her.

That twisted something deep in her guts. That's what a father should be. Every child should think that their father was some kind of invincible hero. She used to daydream about her own when she was little. Gina imagined him to be tall and strong and that her mother had somehow hidden them from him; that's why he hadn't come to rescue them.

But as she'd grown older, she'd realized it was just a fairy tale like any other and had no place in the realities of her life.

Inside, his presence was even more disconcerting. She hadn't noticed it at the restaurant or in Emma's office because it was filled with other people, but alone together, he dominated the space. He made her feel small and vulnerable without even trying.

Unfortunately, she was both intrigued and uncomfortable. It would all be so much easier to bear if she could get away from the intrigued part.

They eyed each other, both seeming to be wary, but unsure how to proceed.

"Hi." Amanda Jane made her presence known.

Reed smiled at her, a genuine expression that completely changed his face. He wasn't just the cute boy she'd crushed on. She was very aware that he was a man—a handsome, powerful man.

Not that it mattered. She tried to push her brain into EMT mode—where she looked at bodies clinically. Yet, there was still nothing clinical about her reaction to him.

"Gina-bee said you're my daddy."

Gina waited to see what he would say.

He nodded. "I am. Is that okay?"

"I think so. I like your face," Amanda Jane confessed without the slightest bit of hesitation.

He sank down to his haunches, eye level with her. "I like your face, too."

Gina was suddenly hyperaware of the house, the shabby state of things. She looked around the small farmhouse. She'd been happy here, but now that he was coming, Gina found it lacking. She saw every flaw in the molding, the tears in the screen on the front porch, the dilapidated fence posts, the scratches on the wood floors…

But this was also where Amanda Jane learned to crawl, the front yard was where she made mud pies, and those tears in the screens were from the feral cats she always left food and water for.

Even though it was a rental, so much of their lives were entwined in the place and if Reed didn't like it, she didn't care.

He came from worse than this and she wouldn't dare let him judge her.

More important, she wouldn't judge herself.

"Gina-bee said you would."

"She knows me pretty well sometimes."

Amanda Jane nodded solemnly. "She knows most everything."

Gina blushed. "Not everything."

Reed looked up at her. "Probably everything."

Amanda Jane yawned. "You should have come earlier. Then you could read me a story."

"I could read you one now," he offered.

"Oh, no. I'll get too excited and I won't sleep. Story before bath. You could come tomorrow." Amanda Jane looked down at her toes. "If you wanted to."

Gina sighed. "I thought tomorrow was our day."

"Please?"

"Honey, he might be busy. We'll see, okay?" Gina didn't want her to get her hopes up, didn't want her to get too excited about something that might not happen.

Amanda Jane looked up at him and mouthed *Frogfest*.

Frogfest dated back to the first settlers in the area when masses of frogs would converge on the riverbank and low marshy areas around the river to mate and they'd sing a lively tune long into the night. If times had been lean, the frogs provided much needed sustenance during hardship. Although, the modern celebrations didn't include as many frog dishes, but for the occasional vendors selling deep-fried frog legs.

Gina found herself inviting him along. She couldn't resist the absolute joy on the girl's face and they needed to get used to each other—Amanda Jane and Reed. It wouldn't work if they were just suddenly flung into the same household.

"You could come."

"I'd like that."

They'd be playing happy little family. She wondered if there'd ever been a bigger lie.

"Good night," the little girl chirped.

"Where are you going? I thought you wanted to stay

up to meet him?" Gina asked, wondering if there was something wrong.

"The sooner I go to bed, the sooner it's tomorrow. *Frogfest*. Funnel cake."

"Funnel cake with frogs?" Reed teased her.

"That doesn't sound good."

"I don't think so, either." He shook his head.

"You should have tea on the porch. It's my favorite thing to do at night."

"You could come outside with us."

"No. *Frogfest*," she reiterated, as if he and Gina didn't understand the importance of the word. "Can I have your phone to play a game before sleep?"

"Sure, honey."

She ran off, taking Gina's phone with her, presumably to bed.

"She doesn't hesitate to ask for what she wants, does she?" Reed said as he watched after her.

"Emotionally, she doesn't." Having gone without as a child and been afraid to ask for anything, she didn't want Amanda Jane to ever feel that way. She thought about her earlier observations, but she decided she didn't need to drive the financial point home any harder. He got it. He understood. And he'd given her everything she asked for.

"That's good." Reed's voice was brittle.

She swallowed hard. "Do you want a sweet tea? We can drink it on the porch."

"Sure," he agreed.

Gina poured him a glass of tea and they stepped back out into the night. She lit a citronella candle, happy to have something to do with her hands.

He seemed so out of place sitting there in her secondhand rocking chair in his khakis, his polo shirt and
his expensive haircut.

She looked back out into the yard, the symphony
song of frogs down by the pond serenading them and
the flickering dance of fireflies in the dark space.

"You remember when we'd climb up on the roof of
my mom's trailer and hide?" he said, finally.

"Like they couldn't hear us stomping around up
there."

"Or didn't care." Reed shrugged. "Still, those were
the only moments of peace I knew then."

"Do remember that trip to the Lake of the Ozarks?"
Gina blurted.

Reed gave a self-deprecating laugh. "Yeah. That guy
who had that houseboat…he was one guy my mother
hooked up with who wasn't a total scumbag. Too bad
she was so far gone when she met him. Things might
have been different. It's kind of strange to know that
she's that woman for him, you know?"

"Like how all the guys besides him were *that guy*
for you? The ones you thought were trash?"

She watched his face pale.

"I didn't mean—"

He held up his hand. "No, it's okay. I loved my
mother, but that's what we were." He shrugged. "She
managed to hold it together long enough to reel him in,
but then when he saw what was underneath, he didn't
want any part of it. But who in their right mind would?"

"Still, it was a good trip, wasn't it?"

"One of the best times in my life. One of the only good times I can remember."

"I know it was for Crystal, too." She hadn't meant to bring up her sister. Gina wasn't ready to talk about her, even though she knew at some point, they'd have to.

"What about you? Was it a good time for you, too?"

"I thought it was kind of a trick when we were invited along. It was one of the last good times my mother had, too. Even though I know we were just invited to keep you out of her hair, I'll always be grateful for that trip."

"You're talking about everyone else but you, Gina. Is that what it's like for you still? Always thinking of everyone else?"

His question was so pointed that it was sharp. She didn't want to think about that; she didn't want to be any more vulnerable than she already was. But either choice here left her open to his blades. She remembered the last night out on the water.

"It was one of the best for me, too. That's why I brought it up." She exhaled heavily and took a sip of her tea, the sweet tang of it on her tongue making the memory even more vivid.

"The sweet tea," he said as soon as she thought it. Like he knew what she was thinking. "You made a jar of it. That last night, when we were lying on the deck listening to the loons."

"Trying to see the stars but it was too cloudy." She remembered thinking that maybe that night was the one. The one where he'd realize she was alive. That she was a woman.

That he wanted her.

"Talking about how it would be to stay there forever?"

She sighed at the memory. "Yeah. We thought that was some kind of huge dream to have a houseboat there. Or even a little cabin. It was our own nirvana, you and me."

"Crystal always wanted the big city. She wanted lights and people. She wanted the rush, and all we could talk about was sweet tea and fireflies."

"That made her so mad."

"So mad she spent the night with one of the local boys. Your mother was so mad at her that we left an hour late because she wasn't home yet."

"I was okay with it. I wanted to stay as long as was humanly possible." Gina laughed at herself.

"I thought my world was going to change that night. I thought we were finally through the dark," he confessed, looking out into the darkness rather than at her.

She thought that for herself as well, but it hadn't happened. "I'm sorry it didn't."

"I used to be sorry. But if it had, I don't know where I'd be. I like who I am now."

She exhaled. "Can I be honest?"

"That's preferred," he said drily.

Walking down memory lane with him was bittersweet, but it wasn't the past she was worried about. It was their future together. Gina decided to be honest. "I'm glad you like who you are now, but that's someone I don't think I know. I'm not sure what to do here."

"Me, either." The air between them hung heavy and

strange. He took the plunge first. "So today didn't go as I'd imagined it."

"And how did you imagine it?" She wondered if he'd ever had the same thoughts about her as she did about him, but then she dismissed the idea before it could take root. Before it could make this any more awkward than it already was.

"I don't know. But not as it went." A genuine grin curled at the edge of his mouth.

It'd be hard to deny him anything with him flashing that grin around. That was a glimpse of the boy she'd known and it was even more endearing on the man he'd become.

"I wasn't trying to keep you from her." That was as close to a peace offering as she could manage.

"Deep down, I know that." He didn't speak for a long moment and the creaking of the rocking chair against the floorboards echoed with all the force of a gunshot. "But you still have to meet me halfway."

She was torn between being glad he was willing to do that and angry that he could just decide to buy a house because he felt like it and she was working two jobs and going to school trying to raise his daughter.

Worse, if she lived in the same house with him, married to him, how would she hide her attraction to him?

Gina had to remind herself that this wasn't about her. It was about what was best for Amanda Jane. It had never been hard to do things for her. There had never been any question that she'd take her discharge from the army when her two years was up, knowing that Amanda Jane needed her. She knew that would make it harder to go to medical school. Harder to do everything, but it had been no sacrifice.

Living under the same roof with Reed Hollingsworth? Torture.

"I don't know. We may not have the best life, but I like this house. I love that she can run and play here. I like that I can point to a place in the backyard and say that's where she smelled her first flower."

"But this isn't yours. Not really. Wouldn't you rather live somewhere that will one day belong to her? Where she can look at a chair in the corner and say that's where Gina-bee used to read me stories. This is where my dad taught me to ride a bike. God, Gina. If we do this right, we can give her everything that we never had."

All of her protestations died on her tongue. She'd been about to defend herself, the home she'd provided for Amanda Jane, but she realized he wasn't saying it wasn't good enough. He was saying they could do even better together. He didn't say "I can give her..." he'd said *we*.

He had this way of speaking that made her imagine picket fences, family picnics and happily-ever-after. She had to keep herself grounded. There was no relationship between them. He just wanted a chance to raise his daughter.

She hurried to add, "I just don't see how this will work."

"I'm not under any illusion that this will be easy. There will be a lot of compromise for both of us."

"I'll be honest, I'm terrified of moving in with you. I'm terrified that you'll try to control us with the money.

I'm terrified…" She didn't say the rest of what she was feeling. It was too much.

"I'm terrified, too," he confessed.

That was when his warm, strong fingers closed around hers.

"But everything is going to be okay, Gina."

This wasn't exactly what she'd pictured when she imagined one day holding hands with Reed Hollingsworth, but it wasn't bad. Maybe it was better than what she thought she wanted.

The gesture was meant to comfort her, reassure her.

And strangely, it did. She'd felt so alone while going through this, and realizing that he had doubts and fears didn't make her position less secure, but more. To her, it meant that he'd thought about the realities of their situation, but he still wanted to try.

He believed he knew what he was in for.

She held his hand in silence for a long time into the quiet night.

CHAPTER SIX

"AMANDA JANE TEXTED to tell me that Operation Frog-fest is a go." Maudine Townsend put her phone down next to her stack of poker chips.

"Frankly, Maudy, I'm surprised." Helga pushed her chips around. "You know, if this little plot of yours doesn't work, we're going to have to give up our Friday nights. At least until after the case."

"You know, I'm actually surprised that Reed's lawyer didn't ask for another judge."

Helga shrugged. "He probably figures that you know everyone."

"Or he's plotting something." Maudine's eyes narrowed further.

"Not everyone's brain works like yours, Maudy."

"Yes, it does. Don't tell me you're not curious."

"Actually, I think since we're here, we could work on Marie. She's too young to be a Glory Grandmother."

"She's very good at what she does. Her tiramisu is to die for. And that cute little bed-and-breakfast for romantic hideaways? It's perfect. She has a sense about people who belong together."

"She does," Helga agreed. "But her husband has been

dead a long time. Her son, Johnny, is grown and Marie is too young to spend the rest of her life alone."

"Maybe she doesn't want to be with anyone else. After mine died, well…I'm done with that."

"Marie is only forty-five. It's too young to dry up and be the cranky old Italian grandmother. All of her friends are…us."

"There's nothing wrong with us."

"Except that we're sitting in my basement, drinking Herb's beer and playing poker. But we lie and tell everyone we're playing pinochle and sipping tea like the old broads we are."

Maudine sniffed. "I am *not* an old broad."

"You most certainly are. But it's okay. We play cupid rather well." Helga shifted her cards.

Maudine's phone beeped. "Another text. They're on the porch drinking sweet tea and holding hands. Everything is coming together." She sounded like some kind of movie villain.

"Tell that child to get in bed."

"She is."

"You know what I mean." Helga nodded. "And are we matchmaking or playing poker because I'm about ready to beat you."

"I know. Which is why the matchmaking is so much more fun." Maudine sighed.

"You're a sore loser, Maudine."

"I never lose when it counts." Maudine grinned.

"This is like herding cats. I give up."

"You fold? I win." Maudine looked very pleased with herself.

"No, you don't, you old bat. But what are we doing? I don't have that paperwork on my desk yet."

"You will. Tomorrow, we're going to shove them together every chance we get." Maudine started putting the cards away. "Frogfest is magical."

"Not for the frogs," Helga offered helpfully.

Maudine growled.

"Look, I just don't understand why you think they need to get married. Gina has her whole life to decide."

"But I don't have mine."

Helga narrowed her eyes. "Yes, you did. You made your choices and now you've got to let her make hers."

"But they're all *wrong*." Maudine huffed.

"So were yours when you made them. So were mine. And we turned out fine."

Maudine raised a brow. "Maybe so. But I've already lost a granddaughter, the daughter I never had, and my son…who knows. Gina and Amanda Jane have known so much pain and so much loss. So has Reed. I didn't do right by that boy. But I am now and you're going to help me."

Helga harrumphed. "You say that like I haven't been part of every scheme that's hatched in your head like a goose egg since we were babies."

Maudine returned the harrumph, with interest. "You don't seem like you're on board."

"I am on board. With Gina's happiness, not your idea of what it should be. That's for the girl to decide."

"Youth is utterly wasted on the young." Maudine shook her head.

"That's kind of the beauty of it, don't you think?"

"No."

Helga laughed. "She will find her way, Maud."

"Maybe. But we need to help her at least see the path."

"Okay. How do you propose we help her see the path? I mean, we've practically shoved her nose in it."

"Well, I haven't gotten that far. At least not past Frog-fest." She shifted in her seat.

Helga laughed. "Then I suppose we'd better get to plotting, but first, you're going to tell me how you are." She held up her hand. "How you really are. Not what you want everyone else to think."

Maudine shifted in her chair a bit. "Some days are better than others. I've had my last chemo treatment, but I still feel like refried turds. Is that what you wanted to hear?"

"Yes." Helga grinned. "Because I want you to be honest with yourself and me. I don't care about every-one else. But this? You're my best friend and you didn't have to do this alone."

"I did." She nodded. "Because if you were there? I wouldn't have had any courage at all. I'd have leaned on you too much."

"I could handle it."

"But I couldn't, Helga. It was easier to be strong if I knew I had to, if that makes sense."

Helga nodded. "I suppose it does. But I still think you should tell Gina."

"And put more on her shoulders?"

"Wouldn't you want to know if your positions were reversed?"

"Stop playing devil's advocate. This isn't the court-room. It's my granddaughter's and great-granddaughter's lives."

"Exactly my point, Maudy." Helga gave her a dis-approving look.

"Yes, fine. I'd like to know if our situations were re-versed. But that's the luxury of being a grandmother." Then Maudine wilted in her chair. "She's had enough to deal with, and I should've done more when she was younger. I feel like I failed her. I failed Crystal. If I'd—"

"If you'd what, Maudine?" Helga interrupted. "What exactly was there you could've done to save Crystal when she didn't want to be saved? I know this is hard to hear, but you can't help someone who doesn't want it. You did everything you could."

"No. I didn't." She shook her head, guilt weighing down on her shoulders. "If I'd been a better mother, maybe my son wouldn't have left his wife. Maybe then, his wife would've had insurance and maybe she would've had a shot at beating this same cancer."

"Oh, honey." Helga's eyes watered in a rare show of emotion. "I see kids in my courtroom all the time who wouldn't be in the trouble they're in if they had parents who cared. And I see kids who have parents who've done everything humanly possible and their kids are still in trouble. I can tell you, you've done all you could do." Helga straightened. "You know if I thought you'd fallen down on the job at any time, you'd have gotten an earful from me. Friendship does not rose-colored glasses make. At least not for me."

Maudine sniffed, her own eyes watering because she knew it to be true. "Thank you."

"Now are we going to plot or finish up this hand?"

"We're going to plot, of course." Maudine sat up straighter. "Frogfest is going to be the perfect time to push them together. To make them both see what a perfect little family they'll make."

CHAPTER SEVEN

REED FOUND HIMSELF facing the mirror in the bathroom, the harsh lights illuminating all the dark things he'd been trying to hide.

He looked into his own eyes and he reassured himself that he liked what he saw there. Even though there was that part of him that was afraid someone would wake up and realize he wasn't allowed to be this person—that he'd snuck through some invisible barrier to success and they'd kick him back to his rightful side—he knew that wasn't the case.

Reed had worked so hard to get where he was. No matter what that voice in his head told him, he wasn't an imposter. He'd put in the work. He'd earned his place. He'd taught himself the stock market, began with penny stocks until he'd graduated to blue chip stocks, then he'd cashed in some of those and started buying up struggling companies and forming them into something new, something viable, and selling them for a profit.

He also knew that life was full of success and full of failures and he had to choose each day which thing he was going to focus on.

He reiterated all of the things he was thankful for to himself. This was his coping mechanism. Then he tucked it away deep down where no one could see it but him. It was almost a kind of armor that shielded him from the inside out.

Frogfest. He scrubbed his hand over his face. He hadn't thought about that in a long time. Glory was full of small festivals that brought people from the surrounding cities in for little weekend getaways and brought in tourist money. There was something planned every couple of weeks and for the big holidays, the whole town got involved. It was genius marketing, really.

As a kid, Frogfest had been his favorite, as well. Sippin' Cider Days was the least because it meant it was time to go back to school and he'd never had any money for anything. Frogfest was the last time he'd been with his mother when she was sober. She'd bought him a frog plush and promised him that things would be better.

And he'd believed her. He'd clung to that round-eyed, happy-faced stuffed animal every night before he went to sleep like it was some kind of talisman that could force her to keep her word. For a while, it seemed like it had.

Until Walter.

Walter had been the beginning of the end for his mother and for him.

He shoved those thoughts out of his head. They didn't matter. They were in the past and Reed wouldn't live in the past. He lived in the ever better, shinier future where things were still made of unfired clay and could be remolded over and over again until Reed had what he wanted.

Panic clutched at his throat. A sudden fear that everyone would know he was faking it—faking success, faking being a whole person. All the expensive cologne and hand-tailored suits in the world couldn't hide it.

He exhaled, thinking about all the things he could do to quiet that voice in his head.

But none of them were acceptable, none of them were any action he'd ever take again. All he could do was let these feelings run their course.

Reed promised Gina everything would be okay, and it would.

If for no other reason than Amanda Jane.

He didn't think it was possible to feel such an immediate, overwhelming connection to another human being. Reed thought that it would take time to get to know her; that he'd have to sort of fall into feeling like a father. Grow to love her.

The ferocity of emotion that raged in his chest like a lion was instant and eternal. He'd live for her, die for her and everything in between.

But it also made him wonder what was really wrong with him that his own mother hadn't felt that way about him. Why hadn't he inspired such devotion? Was he defective somehow and would that defect burrow into his relationship with his own daughter?

Again, he shoved those thoughts down deep where no one could see them. His life and the life he wanted to give Amanda Jane was going to be about fulfilling her needs, not thinking about his own that went unanswered.

There was no changing the past, only living in the present.

I like your face.

He supposed that was good, because upon close inspection, she did look very much like him.

His brain turned all of these things over again and again, like a cement mixer—combining these thoughts in on themselves, keeping them fluid as he drove back to the small farmhouse on Seven Sisters Road.

He knew Gina wanted to stay there, but even in a small town like Glory, your address mattered.

Amanda Jane waited on the porch, legs swinging and ponytail bouncing in one of the rocking chairs. The door was open and Gina pushed through, handing Amanda Jane a picnic basket and a tote bag while she closed and secured the door. He was glad she'd never fallen into the habit of a lot of residents of the town, especially the ones who lived out in the country, who never locked their doors.

Gina wore another pair of those pants with the pockets and his line of sight was immediately drawn to the flare of her hips and the round curve of her ass.

He was so taken by that dangerous curve that he drove over a garden gnome that stood so brave and welcoming near the gravel drive.

Reed swore and hoped mightily that it wasn't something Amanda Jane had any overwhelming attachment to.

And at the sound coming from his put-upon Audi, he realized they were going to be a little late to Frogfest.

This was the universe reminding him to keep his mind on his daughter, not on Gina. Message received, loud and clear.

Gina ran to the car. "Are you okay? What happened?"

"I think your garden gnome tried to kill me."

The car made an unhappy sound and he switched off the ignition.

"Guess I'm driving." She grinned.

"That wasn't…anything special, was it?"

"No. Just something that was in the yard when we moved in. The previous renters left it. Although, Amanda Jane might make you have a funeral for him. His name was Bostwick. She broke his brother, Fenwick, last week."

A funeral, for a garden gnome? If that's what she wanted, he'd do it.

It must have shown on his face. "Look, um…I hope it's okay, but I don't want you to spend a lot of money on her today."

"Why not?" He'd planned to do just that. He wanted to spoil her rotten.

"She worked for her spending money. Even for her tickets to the rides. She weeded the garden, kept her room clean. I want her to enjoy spending what she earned and I want her to understand how far her money will go. And I want her to know that if she can't have something because she doesn't have the money, that's okay, too."

It made sense to him. He didn't like it, but he understood. "I understand, I do. But you have to understand that there is going to be a bit of spoiling going on in the near future and yours isn't the final say."

"And yours is?" Her tone wasn't confrontational. Or at least he didn't think it was. The T-shirt she wore clung much too tightly to her breasts for him to think clearly. "No, we'll have to compromise."

"So neither one of us will get our way is what you're saying."

"Basically."

She laughed. "I guess I can live with that. So, do you mind riding to Frogfest in Bill?" She pointed to her tiny, aged Kia.

"Are we taking the KiaPet? I wanted to ride with Daddy," Amanda Jane said without any hint of a pout in her voice.

"Daddy is riding in the KiaPet, too."

Daddy.

They meant him. *He* was Daddy.

That was still quite something for him to wrap his head around. There was so much hope and expectation wrapped up in that one word. Not just Amanda Jane's, but his own. He'd never expected to wear that title and now that it was his, he didn't want to screw it up. He didn't want to be anything like his father. Or Gina's father. He had this fey vision of himself that he knew wasn't real. Couldn't be. No one could be all the things he wanted to be.

"Aren't you?" Gina prompted.

"Yeah." He nodded and followed her to the car. He'd worry about fixing his later. It'd give him an excuse to spend more time with them—if he needed one.

Bless you, Bostwick, he thought to himself. He'd given his life for a good cause.

With Amanda Jane buckled in her car seat in the

back, and all of Gina's bags loaded into the trunk, they headed toward Riverfront Park and Frogfest.

The whole town had come out for the festivities as they always did with every fair or festival. At the first strains of the carousel music, Amanda Jane's energy was practically frenetic. Or maybe that was Reed himself? He suddenly found that being here with Amanda Jane brought back all of his childhood joy at the prospect of Frogfest. The park had been closed off and the entry gate had been made up to look like a giant bullfrog head.

Activities had been divided up into things for older kids, like the octopus ride, and the ball pit and inflatables were for younger kids.

"She'll bounce in the inflatable for a good hour and a half." Gina smiled.

Then, he saw the kissing booth.

That brought back a lot of memories.

Crystal, Amanda Jane's mother and Gina's sister, had worked the booth one Frogfest and it had been the first time he'd kissed her. So many memories in this place.

Gina followed his gaze and said, "Oh, lord. Look who's behind the booth."

It was Gina's lawyer, Emma. She headed over to the booth, laughing as she went. "What are you doing?"

"Isn't it obvious? I lost a bet." She scowled, obviously unhappy to be there.

"That's not a very kissable expression on your face." Reed threw in his two cents. It wasn't just unkissable, she looked downright hostile.

"It's not supposed to be. If I don't look kissable, no one will kiss me, right?"

"Isn't this to raise money for the hospital auxiliary?" he asked.

"Yes, and they can damn well get someone else if they want to make any money."

The jar was abysmally empty. Reed dug a five out of his wallet and stuffed it in the jar.

"Buddy, I hope you're paying me not to kiss you." Then her eyes narrowed. "Gina can handle my light work."

He looked at Gina and her eyes had widened so far that she looked like a small animal in the glare of an oncoming truck.

If she'd been any other girl but Gina Townsend, he would've taken her up on Emma's offer and kissed her senseless. Because he didn't care about kissing any other girl but Gina. But he wanted to kiss Gina more than he was comfortable admitting.

"I paid *you*, Frog Lady."

"I hope you don't think I'll turn into a princess."

He smirked, but instead of kissing her grudgingly proffered cheek, he took her hand and kissed it like a gentleman from days of yore.

Emma blushed, all of her prickly demeanor gone. "You, sir, are dangerous."

"No, no, no. That's all wrong," Amanda Jane said. She pointed at Reed and then at Gina. "You are supposed to kiss *her*. And she *will* turn into a princess. I know these things. Grammie told me."

Gina was the first to respond. "Nope. I've got both my shoes."

"You're confusing fairy tales again, Gina-bee." Amanda Jane didn't seem amused. "Do it correctly, please."

He loved that she was like a mini-adult. She was so polite, but knew exactly what she wanted and how things were to be done. She would find that frustrating as she grew up, but it would also serve her well. She reminded Reed a lot of what Gina had been like as a child. She'd had this amazing intellect that had been completely wasted on those around her. Even him.

"Correctly? I'm too old to be a princess. You, on the other hand, are just right."

"She can be queen and me the princess?" She seemed to consider the scenario for a minute. "I suppose that could work." Amanda Jane still sounded doubtful.

Reed knelt down and embraced her carefully, giving the child the opportunity to squirm away if she didn't want him to hug her. Instead, she flung her thin arms around his neck and he dutifully placed a kiss on her cheek.

"I like this game." She planted one on his cheek in return and then ran to the ball pit.

Her affection and expectation of such came so easily. He thought of all the ways people could use that against her, could hurt her. He found he couldn't breathe.

"I know, right?" Gina said quietly. She understood.

"You're all doing it wrong." Gray's voice surprised him.

"What are you doing here? I thought you were going back to the city?" Reed asked as he got to his feet.

"I had to try out this infamous Frogfest. I heard there

were going to be carnival games and maybe an exhibition match of some local talent." He shrugged. "I see everyone takes these things seriously around here." He eyed Emma.

"If we did it wrong, maybe you should show us how it's done?" Gina cast a sly grin at Emma.

Emma's gaze cut to Gray so fast, Reed was sure he actually saw it slice the air. "You wouldn't dare."

"Oh, I more than dare. Especially since you think I wouldn't." He pulled out a hundred-dollar bill and stuffed it in the jar. "That's the best reason to dare."

"Damn," Emma whimpered.

"You got that right." Gray grabbed her and bent her over the back of his arm and kissed her.

Gina lifted her chin and nodded at Reed. "That's what she gets for calling you light work."

Reed laughed. "Oh, really? Well, compared to that, I guess I am light work. He's got a lot more game than I ever did."

"It's for a good cause, anyway." Gina shrugged. "Sorry Amanda Jane put you on the spot like that. I'll talk to her if you want."

"No, it's okay. I think it's probably pretty normal. We're her caregivers. Wanting to see us that way is searching for a kind of stability, I imagine." Reed remembered having those same wants as a child with every new man his mother brought home. After a while, he'd gotten numb to those wants and eventually, started dreading each new encounter because it was always the beginning of the end.

Gina's expression changed from light and open to

concerned as she spread out the blanket and arranged the bags and basket just so. "Do you think she feels like her life is unstable?"

If he were more of a bastard, he could use this moment to pounce, to give himself the upper hand for further negotiations. But he didn't want Gina to feel unsure of her choices. He knew that she'd done the best she could. Once he got past his own issues, he could see that.

"No. An unstable child wouldn't ask for what they want like she does. She expects all of her needs to be met because they have been. You've done a great job, Gina."

He didn't expect her to melt into him the way she did, for her arms to lock around his waist and for her to bury her face in his neck. Reed embraced her carefully and tried not to think about how good she felt wrapped in his arms.

How good this whole day was turning out to be, despite having murdered Bostwick the garden gnome.

"I'm sorry, I just...I've tried so hard. I wanted her to have better than we did."

"And she does. You're a good mother."

She broke away from him and everything in him wanted to reach out and pull her back against him. "But I'm not her mother."

"You are in all ways that matter. You've been a good father, too. You've been everything. But you're not alone now."

Gina's eyes fluttered closed. "You know, when I took her after Crystal died, I told them they couldn't just give me a child. What was wrong with child services that they could just hand this child over to me?"

"I would've felt the same way, but I would've been right in my case. She's happy, healthy, smart and kind. What more can you do?"

"I guess keep doing what I've been doing." She looked away from him to scan the ball pit and then back at him. "So this is really happening, right? We're getting married?"

"Yeah. If you say yes."

"I think there are some things we need to talk about that weren't addressed in the agreement." She took a deep breath. "Are you dating?"

That was the last question he expected from her. "What?"

"Dating. Seeing someone. Hittin' and quittin'..." She used their old high school slang for one-night stands.

"Uh, no, Gina. None of that."

"Me, either. I don't want a string of people in and out of her life."

Her answer unknotted something tight in his chest. "I don't really date at all. So that's not a problem."

"Why not?" She cocked her head to the side and looked up at him.

Her eyes were so clear, like the cloudless sky, and her bow mouth was pursed waiting for his answer. The distance between them began to disappear slowly but surely as he leaned in, perhaps to tell her a secret.

He hadn't intended to kiss her, but he found himself leaning forward, anyway.

"Daddy! Come play with me," Amanda Jane yelled.

Her voice startled Reed out of whatever spell had drifted over him and he launched himself to his feet and went to go play with his daughter.

CHAPTER EIGHT

HAD REED BEEN about to kiss her? Gina wondered.

The more important question was, would she have let him?

This kind of complication was the very last thing she needed.

She pressed her fingers to her lips, imagining just what she would do if he did kiss her. After kissing him back, of course. The part of her that wanted to know what it was like to kiss Reed Hollingsworth hadn't grown out of it, perhaps never would.

She'd spent much of her teen years wondering what it would be like if he ever turned to her, if he ever leaned over ever so slowly, what it would be like. Would her world explode or dry up until it was nothing but dust?

Would his kiss be like a man's or a boy's?

She'd been infatuated with him as a girl, but now that she was a woman, all of those thoughts and feelings came rushing back tenfold.

But for him, she wondered if it was part and parcel to playing house with her. He suddenly had this ready-made family and maybe he figured she was just part of the deal. Take her, keep her happy, or maybe it wasn't even that blatant.

Gina flopped back onto the blanket and stared up at the bright, endless ocean of sky. A gentle breeze played over her hair.

She'd spent so long trying to make sure any prospective boyfriends understood that Amanda Jane was part of the package, she forgot that she wanted someone else to want her for herself, too. She'd always kind of assumed that was a given.

Nothing could ever be so easy with Reed. He made her doubt herself on all fronts without even trying. In fact, he'd been nothing but encouraging and she found that she desperately wanted his approval.

She'd never worried about anyone's approval but her own.

Until now.

Now her stupid brain wouldn't do anything but think about why he'd almost kissed her, and what would've happened if he had, and if it was a sign from the universe that Amanda Jane had called out to him when she did.

Didn't she have enough on her plate?

Apparently not.

She watched father and daughter play in the ball pit. The easy affection that had blossomed so quickly between them. Gina decided that maybe he'd be a great father, if he'd let himself.

Then Gina decided that she might be the most horrible person on the planet.

It was always in the back of her mind, sometimes the front, that Amanda Jane was her niece. Crystal had been her mother. Gina's poor, tragic sister. It hadn't had to end like it had, if only she'd fought more, done more…

But thinking about Crystal having this with Reed… days like today. Moments like the last one where he'd almost kissed her, it made her jealous. As jealous as she'd been when they were in high school and she kept waiting for Reed to notice that she was pretty, too. That she was smart. That she was the one who really wanted to be with him.

For the first time, Gina thought that Crystal hadn't deserved these moments.

Who was she to judge? She knew Crystal'd had her own demons to exorcise and she knew there were things that lived in the shadows of memory that had always had a tight fist around her sister's throat. She wouldn't trade places with her for anything in the world.

And she couldn't build her dreams on the hopes of her sister's pain and suffering.

She'd just have to make herself right with things the way they were. And that definitely meant no kissing. This would be a marriage of convenience. A business partnership so everyone got what they needed, most especially Amanda Jane.

Except if she was being honest with herself, she didn't want that. She wanted this version of white picket fences.

She shook her head and realized it was only the leftovers of a childhood dream. Not of Reed, but of how she always thought life was supposed to be. It was like a family sitcom where there was a mom and dad and everyone lived together in an average split-level with a yard that needed mowing and cars that needed washing.

She wanted Amanda Jane to have that.

Hell, since she was so stuck on honesty right now, it wasn't just for Amanda Jane. It was for her, too.

Only life wouldn't be like that. It wouldn't be an average middle-class split-level. His house, their new house, was practically a mansion.

But maybe that was okay.

Maybe, regardless of what she and Reed felt or didn't feel, they could give her that together.

She pulled out a book to study for her finals, but just as she did, Amanda Jane dragged Reed back from the ball pit and wanted a funnel cake.

Gina pulled out the small coin purse where Amanda Jane had saved her money and handed her the five dollars for the funnel cake.

"Are you sure you want to spend it on that?"

"Very sure." She nodded emphatically.

"Okay." Gina let go of the bill and Amanda Jane ran toward the nearest vendor.

"Do *you* want a funnel cake?" Reed asked Gina.

"No, thanks. I can barely fit into my work pants as it is. Too many nights eating at the Bullhorn." Why had she said that? She sounded like some girl who was fishing for compliments.

"It's funnel cake. Buy bigger pants."

She laughed. She liked that he didn't care. Liked that he didn't rush to reassure her. It was refreshing. "Not so much. I'll be pushing maximum density if I'm not careful. I ballooned freshman year because my diet consisted of ramen. I watch my carbs."

"That sounds kind of miserable." He wrinkled his nose. "I will never eat another cup of noodles. I think even if I was starving, I couldn't bring myself to put them in my mouth."

"Yeah, you ate a lot of them, didn't you? We all did." She nodded. "It was miserable. But so is being too big to do my job. So I'm going to just have to *smell* the deliciousness of the funnel cake."

"I'll make you a deal. Have the funnel cake, and go protein all week. I'll do it with you. You can't go wrong with steak and bacon."

She decided it wasn't the polo shirt that was the devil; it was him. That grin on his face made her want to agree to anything he suggested. "Fine, but the funnel cake and steak are your treat."

"Of course." He cocked his head to the side as if he couldn't fathom why she'd even bother to say that, as if it were just something to be understood.

"And the new pants, if I need them," she teased.

He frowned. "You do need them. Gray should have those accounts set up for both of you this coming week."

She shouldn't have said that. Gina had only been teasing him about getting fat after eating the funnel cake. "I wasn't actually asking for money. I was teasing."

"I want you to have the things that you need. And you were right, you shouldn't have to ask for them."

Gina felt like pond scum. She knew he was sensitive about being wanted for more than his money and she talked about it like she was entitled to it. She'd only been kidding, but she was the first to admit that sometimes those careless words could cut deeper and more precisely than the most strategically aimed barbs. "Money is a hard thing for people like us."

"It doesn't have to be."

"But it is. I wanted to say that maybe I should have tried to get in touch with you and ask if you knew about Amanda Jane. I just—" She sighed. "I'm sorry. If I'd been thinking, I'd have thought about how that made you feel. Instead, I was so angry that you had so much and I was working so hard for so little."

His expression was unreadable. "Maybe if I'd seen things from your perspective, as well. I was an ass when I showed up at the Bullhorn."

She found herself smiling at him and wishing maybe he'd try to kiss her again. "I guess we need to work on our communication skills."

"And our needs pyramid."

She snorted. "Don't go using all your therapy weapons on me. I have no defenses."

He laughed and was silent for a long moment. "Who would've thought all those years ago this was where we'd end up?"

"Not me, that's for sure. I enlisted in the army and I thought that I'd stay in until I earned my MD. Then Crystal died." She shook her head. "This isn't anywhere near where I thought I'd be."

"At turns, I can't imagine you in the army, and yet, it seems like the easiest option to escape Glory. Do you still want to be a doctor, or is it just what you've trained yourself to want?"

The question startled her. She could admit that it had taken on some epic proportions in her brain. Becoming a doctor had morphed into a place she was going rather than a thing she was doing. It was wild how he seemed to know that. But that change didn't make her want it any less. She knew logically that when she received her MD, that paper wasn't going to be any kind of magic wand.

But it was a key.

It was a key to a world beyond the one she knew, not just financially, but in her heart, too. She'd have the means to help people and not just people who could pay. All people who were sick or hurting, she'd have the skills and the tools to help them.

Her own mother had died from a cancer that had a high survivability rate, if only it'd been detected sooner. But because she didn't have the means or insurance, she let it go way too long before finally trying to get in at the clinic.

She studied Reed for a long moment. "I do. I'll make a difference. Be someone."

"You are someone." His eyes studied her, as if he was trying to figure out exactly who that someone was.

"You know what I mean. I'll be someone who matters. Someone people will listen to, and I'll be able to help people."

"How could you ever think you don't matter, Gina? You matter a lot. Everywhere you go, you bring light with you."

Her face flamed at the compliment and she hated both that his words affected her so and that he said them. "That's some poetry right there." She didn't know what else to say.

"It's true. It always has been." Again, his eyes on her were almost like a physical caress.

She was thankful for the interruption when Amanda Jane bounded back over to them. "Missy is here. Can I go see her, please?" She pointed over by the strongman games where Sheriff Judd Wilson was currently trying to win a giant frog.

Missy waved for Amanda Jane to come over.

"Sure, but don't wander too far." She looked back over at Reed. "I thought you were bringing funnel cake?" She needed to put some distance between them. She had to remember her role.

"Done." He got up and went off to procure the sweet.

Whatever this was happening between them had to stop.

Why, the voice in her head argued. Why did it have to stop? They were going to be a family. Maybe not in the traditional sense of the word.

What if things didn't work out? What if this arrangement lasted much longer than she anticipated?

She desperately needed to stop thinking about all of this and study. She could angst later.

He returned all too quickly bearing the fruits of his efforts: four funnel cakes.

"What is this? Are you trying to kill me?" She laughed and noticed the plates were purple. They were from Sweet Thing, a still relatively new bakery in town opened by

Betsy McConnell. Of course, relatively new in Glory meant it had been opened in the past ten years.

"I couldn't decide. She had plain." He pointed to one. "She had maple bacon, which I had to try. Modeled after her Better Than Sex donuts. Had to try that one, too." He pointed at another one. "I thought Mrs. Beasley from the Bell Ringers Church Choir was going to have a stroke and then she ordered three."

Gina grinned, imagining the stern-faced, bekerchiefed little old lady in her orthopedic shoes ordering Better Than Sex anything. "What else did you get?"

"Cocoa and hazelnut, and there's a peanut butter and banana."

"Which one do you want?"

"All of them." He arched a brow. "What about you?"

The Better Than Sex was just too appealing. "I've tried those donuts. So I think that funnel cake has to happen."

She crammed a bite into her mouth. The flavors seemed to just melt into her tongue and when she inhaled, she could smell the maple, the bacon and something else that she couldn't quite put her finger on, but she rather imagined smelled like happiness.

"What's the verdict?"

"What?" she asked behind her hand, trying not to talk with her mouth full.

"Is it actually better than sex?" He took a bite of the peanut-butter-banana one.

Gina swallowed. "I wouldn't know. I've never tried the other."

He choked around his bite and for a moment, Gina

thought she was going to have to give him the Heim-lich. "Don't make me give you mouth-to-mouth while you've got food in there. That's so gross."

He made another choking noise and grabbed a can of cola and guzzled it. "Me, trying to kill *you*?" Reed managed, eyes watering with the effort of not dying.

"So you find my lack of experience as startling as I find four funnel cakes?"

"I find your lack of empathy for your friend chok-ing to death startling."

"If you can make noises, you're still getting oxygen. You're fine." She smiled. Gina hadn't meant to confess her current state of virginity. That wasn't something he needed to know. But it had just come out, much like that bite of funnel cake that a bold pigeon snatched up and flew away carrying.

She hoped he'd just let it die, but his reaction told her he'd probably beat it to death. He'd teased her about it when they were in high school, but she'd been deter-mined that she wasn't going to let anything get in the way of her dreams.

The silence between them was suddenly heavy and she wondered if they were both remembering that same night when he'd offered to be her first, just to get it over with, if that's what she wanted.

She remembered what it had been like wanting so badly to say yes, but the fear that kept her back. The fear of what it could mean not just for her future, but for her heart. She'd known then that he wasn't in love with her. They were friends. He thought he was helping her, when all he'd done was break her heart.

Amanda Jane came back with Missy in tow and they spent the rest of the afternoon enjoying the games, the food and the people of Frogfest. She noticed that her grandmother was suspiciously absent. Gina just knew she was somewhere getting up to the dickens.

She was finally able to stop thinking about Reed and what all this meant for her and simply enjoy the time she got to spend with Amanda Jane.

It wasn't until they got back to the house and Amanda Jane asked, "Gina-bee, can we have a sleepover?"

"Tonight?" she asked as they unloaded the car.

"Yes, with Daddy."

She closed her eyes. How did she answer this one?

Reed stepped up and took it out of her hands. "If it's okay with Gina-bee, how about I stay until you fall asleep? Then it's like a sleepover, but not as messy."

"Can we watch a movie until I fall asleep?" She eyed him carefully.

"Sure." Reed looked at her. "If that's okay?"

Gina wanted to say no. She needed a breather, space from him and all the feelings that he wrought in her. But when she looked down into her niece's eyes and saw the excited hope there, she couldn't say no.

There was no reason not to let him stay.

"He did promise you a story tonight. Story, then bath, then bed?" Gina offered as a consolation prize to denying the actual sleepover.

"Story, then bath, then movie until bed?" she countered.

"Okay."

Amanda Jane darted into the house.

"Where does she get all that energy?" Reed asked.

"I've wondered the same thing. Specifically, if I could bottle it." She was always tired these days, but maybe that would change when she wasn't working a million hours, trying to study and taking care of Amanda Jane.

"Thank you for today, Gina."

He scrubbed his hand over his jaw, the motion making her think he had more that he wanted to say.

She just couldn't do it. She couldn't process any more. "You're welcome. Her favorite books are *Goosebumps*. She can read them herself because they've been read to her so many times, but she still likes to be read to. There's a stack of them on her dresser. First door off the kitchen is hers."

Gina took the time to sit down and get settled with a hot cup of tea to soothe the tension of the day. She found that since she was always on nitro speed, she needed something to signify to her brain that it was time to wind down—it was okay to be silent and still. She had little luck with anything but a steaming cup of chamomile. Even the ritual of preparing it immediately soothed her nerves and caused much of the tension in the back of her neck to slide away.

Hearing the sounds coming from her bedroom, Amanda Jane's and Reed's voice as he read her the book, it wasn't something she thought Amanda Jane would ever have.

Agreeing to what Reed wanted was absolutely the right thing. If he stayed this version of himself.

She must've drifted off to sleep in her chair because the next thing she knew, the television had flipped to a blue screen and the DVD logo bounced across the space. Gina saw they'd watched something about a baby dinosaur.

Reed was sprawled out on the secondhand couch, his left arm dangling down to the floor, his left leg doing the same and his head tilted back on the edge of the couch. He completely dominated the tiny bit of furniture.

It hadn't seemed so tiny when she'd hauled it from Goodwill by herself.

What got her, though, was the sight of Amanda Jane curled up on his chest like the most contented of kitty cats that could ever be found wearing superhero pajamas.

One of her small hands was up by her ear, and she tugged every so often in her sleep, almost as if she were making sure it was still there. Her tiny bow mouth was parted and her narrow back rose and fell with even breaths in time with Reed's.

It was a lovely moment and she snapped a picture on her phone to commemorate the moment both for Amanda Jane and for herself.

Tears pricked the backs of her eyes like tiny little thorns. She'd never had this. Reed had never had this. Was it possible that wanting to get it right would be enough? They had no idea how to be a functional family unit.

She clutched the phone, looking at the picture rather than the actual tableau because she needed a barrier between her and this thing. Seeing this made real, a father and his daughter, all the things that she'd been taught a father was supposed to be, it ignited her fears.

Fears about permanence. If he'd get tired of playing house with them and leave. She knew what that was like. Knew how it felt because her father had done the same to her mother. She didn't want him to get close to her if that's how it was going to end, but she was no fortune-teller. She couldn't predict the future.

Or maybe she could. All things considered, the way they both grew up, how could it end any other way?

She thought about her grandmother and the absolute surety with which she'd declared Gina should marry him. Her grandmother was old-fashioned to be sure, but she was also her role model. The guiding hand that had helped her come this far. She wouldn't put Gina and Amanda Jane's happiness after some outdated idea.

No, she and Amanda Jane were her grandmother's number one.

She'd had faith in the woman thus far, she could trust her a little more. She could try to trust Reed.

Gina could try to trust herself.

CHAPTER NINE

REED AWOKE TO a singular sensation: discomfort. He'd spent the whole night on Gina Townsend's couch. He felt like an old man, his joints twisted like the root system of some ancient tree.

Not exactly what he'd had in mind when he imagined spending the night with her, but he hadn't ever believed in a world where Amanda Jane Townsend was possible, either.

He'd have to fix that, as well. He wanted her to have his last name. Gray was probably working on that already, but he dug around for his phone and sent him a quick text.

Reed realized the child was no longer on his chest and looked around for her and Gina. Gina, who wouldn't be Gina Townsend anymore, either, but Gina Hollingsworth. *His wife*. The thought floored him. He hadn't really expected things to go this way.

They were at the kitchen table and Gina was studying flash cards, and Amanda Jane was helping.

Gina seemed to sense his presence and looked up at him. "Coffee's on the counter."

"You get going early out here, don't you?" His voice was scratchy with disuse.

"There's a farm down the way that has roosters. They always wake me up."

"Did you know, Daddy, that roosters don't crow at dawn?"

"They don't? When do they crow?" he asked as he poured a cup of the steaming black brew into the other cup that was on the worn Formica counter.

"Whenever they want to. They crow for food, they crow to warn of predators, they crow to—other stuff I don't want to talk about."

He laughed. "Okay. Fair enough." Reed sat down at the table with them, his eyes still heavy and gritty with sleep. "What are you two doing today?"

"I called Johnny at Hart's Automotive. He came out and got your Audi," Gina supplied.

"On a Sunday?"

"Yeah. One of the perks of small-town living." She shrugged. "And I promised him a plate of Bullhorn's three-alarm special on the house."

"Thanks." He sipped the dark gold and sighed as it clicked the wheels and cogs in his brain to life. "I was thinking that today maybe I could take Amanda Jane to the house and let her pick out her room."

Gina pressed her lips together tightly before speaking. "I don't know."

Amanda Jane's eyes widened. "I have to move?"

He wondered if this was when she was going to get upset. "With me."

"Is Gina-bee coming?" It seemed as if she wasn't too sure about these new developments.

"Yes," he answered.

"As long as Gina is coming, I'll go."

"I think you'll like it." He looked at Gina. "This is the spoiling part."

"I figured as much." Gina eyed him.

"And you can study in peace and quiet."

"Bribes aren't going to work every time." Gina smiled softly, indicating that she was only teasing him. "I guess so. But don't buy her anything crazy. Like a pony."

Amanda Jane's eyes widened farther. "I can have a pony?"

"You can have anything you want," he promised her easily.

"I knew I was going to regret this." Gina shook her head, but there was a smile on her face.

Amanda Jane launched herself from the chair to go put on her shoes and socks.

"You know, I was only half kidding. Really, no pony," she reiterated, raising her eyebrow in abject disapproval.

"Why not? She can have lessons. I handled some investments for a guy whose daughter rides at a barn on the other side of town." Reed held up his hand. "Before you object, his daughter takes care of the animal herself. She has to groom him, feed him, and exercise him herself. It's not all a walk in the park."

"I can't believe we're actually having this discussion." She shook her head.

"We're not, not really. She hasn't asked for a pony."

"Reed, I'm serious."

"I am, too. Spoiling. It's happening. You taught her

a lesson yesterday about money, and today, I get to be Dad. Remember, I haven't gotten to do this."

Gina made a helpless gesture.

"Study. Don't worry, we'll be fine." He waved her off.

"Reed, I have to say this and it's going to make you angry. And if it hurts, that's not my intention. But it has to be said."

He steeled himself for whatever it was she was going to say.

"For a man who wants to be more than his bank account, you're not doing too great a job showing us what else you have to offer."

She was right, it did make him angry, but more than that, it stung like a bitch.

"Just spend time with her."

"I will. But she also has a room that needs to be decorated so it feels like it's hers. I'm trying to make this move easy on you both. Every time you tell me no, you're making it clear that you're the parent and I'm just a contributor to her genetic makeup."

She flinched. "I just… Fine. Do whatever you want with her room." Gina took a few deep breaths before looking up at him. "Are you going to decorate my room, too?"

He knew she was trying to soothe the barbs she'd flung, but he didn't have the heart to spar with her at the moment. "Whatever you want."

"What I want is for this to be easy." Out of all the things that she had to deal with, it would be nice if something could just…work. If all the pieces would fit where they were supposed to when they were supposed to.

"Then let me make it easy. You don't have to control everything." He knew her better than she thought.

"But I do, Reed. Don't you understand? The things in my life that I can control, I have to. There's been so much that's beyond my control, so many things thrown at me. My mother's cancer, her death. My father leaving. My sister. Amanda Jane." She motioned in the air. "These things that I can control, they help keep me sane. Otherwise, my brain goes all sorts of wild places. What if, what if, what if. It plays on a loop all the time and if I listen to it, all I can think about is pain and loss. Can you understand that?"

"I understand that control is your drug of choice. It numbs all the pain, all the fear the same as those other things did for me."

How dare he compare the two? They weren't the same. Not by a long shot. "It's not the same," she snarled. "Controlling the things I have power over doesn't hurt anyone."

"One could argue that me putting a needle in my vein didn't hurt anyone but me."

"How can you even say that so casually?" She couldn't even think about it casually.

"Because you're so buttoned-down that you're not living and you're teaching Amanda Jane that same habit."

"Do you really want to talk about teaching habits?" she threatened.

"You're really angry, Gina. Maybe you should think about why."

"Why? You show up here and start making demands and—"

A small sniff made them both stop and look at Amanda Jane.

"I don't need anything new. I'm sorry," the little girl said.

"Oh, honey." Gina's upset seemed to diffuse instantly. "Come here."

Amanda Jane got up obediently and went to Gina and she hugged her.

"This is just new territory for both of us. I'm sorry we were disagreeing loudly."

"You were fighting."

"No, we weren't fighting. We were just discussing and we disagreed. Loudly," Reed added. "It happens sometimes."

"I don't want you to leave. Promise you won't leave." She flung herself against him and he hugged her.

"I won't leave." Whispering those words made him feel like the biggest heel. Not because he planned on leaving, but because he hadn't been there to start with.

Gina looked lost and afraid, too, as if she believed that he'd suddenly disappear like a petal blown by some unreliable breeze. And he couldn't blame her. All they knew was impressions of each other and who they used to be.

"How about we shop for your room all together? Today we'll just go to the zoo."

"It's okay. It's just a room, right?" *No pony*, she mouthed.

"Really, it's okay?" Amanda Jane blinked, eyes wide.

If Reed didn't know better, he'd say that the girl had Gina wrapped around her little finger. But the expression was guileless.

"Yes, it's fine. I'm grumpy because I'm stressed trying to study. Go. Have fun," Gina reassured her.

"Okay, but only if you kiss and make up."

"I… That's not what we do," Gina stuttered.

"Yes, it is. When we get mad at each other, we always kiss on the cheek and make up. Gina-bees and daddies should do it, too." Amanda Jane seemed determined that this was simply the way of things and they had no choice but to comply.

Reed wasn't sure what possessed him. Maybe it was what she'd said about not showing them what else he had to offer. He could give her this. If she wanted it. He leaned over and pressed his lips to her cheek, just barely missing the corner of her mouth.

"There. All better? Are we friends again?" His voice was low, almost guttural. He'd meant to be light, teasing, but he was too affected.

Gina flushed and nodded.

"See? All better." Amanda Jane looked satisfied.

"Let's go outside while I call the rental company so Gina can study." He held the door open for her.

"You can call her Gina-bee, too. She won't mind."

"Oh, I think she might." Reed was sure that to him she was most definitely not a Gina-bee.

"We can ask her when we get back. Can I really have a pony?"

"Yes."

"Can I have a castle in my room?" She skipped over to the tire swing.

"Yes."

"Can I have a fire truck in my room?"

"Yes."

"When are you going to say no?"

"When you ask something worth saying no to." He found all of those requests to be reasonable. They were things he could do, easy things. It was just money.

"I like this game."

"Me, too."

And while he pushed Amanda Jane on the tire swing in the yard, he thought about what it felt like to press his lips against the smooth softness of Gina's cheek and how easy it would've been to lean over just a bit more and taste her lips.

He might've, if he'd been able to brush his teeth instead of just guzzle coffee.

This was dangerous territory, thinking about kissing Gina.

What if she didn't like it?

What if she did?

He'd never really be sure if she was with him for Amanda Jane's sake, or because that was where she wanted to be.

He pushed it out of his head and decided to focus on Amanda Jane. That was why he was here. To get to know her. To be her father. Not to try out his moves on the girl's aunt.

Reed took her first to the house on Knob Hill where he showed her where her room would be. Where Gina's would be.

Then he took her shopping in the city and didn't feel the least bit bad about buying her everything she pointed to.

All in all, it turned out to be another great day. He'd just started to wonder when she'd hit him with the hard questions. The ones about Crystal, about himself. Reed knew he'd have to have answers for her, and while he didn't want to lie to her, he didn't think he could bear to admit all his failings to her either.

There had to be some kind of middle ground. Somewhere when she was old enough to understand, she wouldn't think less of him.

He wondered what Gina had told her.

He didn't have to wonder long.

They were on their way back to the farmhouse when she asked, "Gina said that once you were sick like Mama."

"Yes." That was the truth.

"But you got better."

"I did. And it was hard, and took a long time."

There was a long silence in the car and she'd been chattering almost all day. So it was strange now to sit in the weight of her silence.

"Why didn't Mama want to get better?"

"Who told you that?" When he found out he'd—

"She did. She told Gina-bee the last time we visited her before she went to heaven. She took us off her visiting list and told her not to bring me anymore."

"Does Gina know you heard this?"

"No, I was supposed to be playing. But I wanted to see my mama, not play."

"You should tell her that you heard it. Then you can talk about it with her."

"But I want to talk about it with you," she said pointedly.

"Why?" He didn't understand her at all.

"Because you were sick, too. Gina never gets sick."

"The kind of sick we were…" He wasn't sure how to explain it.

"Makes it so you don't want to get better."

"Sort of, yeah."

"I think Gina would be upset if I told her, but I want her to be my mother. And I don't want her to have her own room separate from you. Mommies and daddies share rooms and fight over potty seats."

He swallowed hard. "Honey, things are the way they are." God, that was a stupid answer. "I can't change who your mother is."

"Emma did. She said that according to the law, Gina is my mom."

"I really think you should talk to Gina about this." They hadn't discussed what they were going to tell her or when they were going to tell her. This was all new territory.

"But I want to talk to you. Gina would get upset."

"Why do you think I won't get upset?"

"You just won't." She sat back in the seat. "I had a good time today. Did you?"

"I did."

"Are you ready for me to be quiet? When I talk this much, Gina says she needs quiet time to hear herself think. I don't know how you couldn't hear yourself think because you think in your own head."

"I think it's been a long day. But if you have something to say, you can tell me."

"No, I don't have anything to say. Not really."

He laughed. He liked Amanda Jane. Reed supposed he was expected to think that, but he knew in reality that you didn't have to like someone to love them. And he liked her. He liked her personality and the shadows he saw of the person she was going to be. He knew that part of that was Gina's influence.

"Can we watch a movie again like last night?"

"If it's okay with Gina. But I can't stay all night like last night. I have to work in the morning."

"When are we going to move in to the pretty house?"

"When Gina says." That was the easiest and truest answer he could give her.

"She's in charge of a lot of stuff." Her eyes narrowed. "I want to be in charge of stuff."

"She is."

"Is she the boss of you?" Amanda Jane cocked her head to the side.

"In some things."

"And in some things you're the boss?" She nodded. "I think that will work."

They pulled into the driveway and Amanda Jane bounded into the house. He was hesitant to follow her. He didn't live in the farmhouse with them; this wasn't his space.

"Gina?" he said at the door.

"Come in."

He stepped inside and realized he smelled an apple pie. "Did you bake?"

"Maybe." She grinned.

His brain started to short-circuit. There was nothing sexier than a woman baking. Unless that woman was Gina Townsend. "Weren't you going to study?"

"I was, but I had some apples about to go bad and sometimes baking helps me think."

"Sometimes eating helps me think." He grinned.

"I cut a piece for you already. We can have ours at the table while she takes her bath. You were gone for such a long time, I was worried."

"I was trying to give you some peace and quiet."

Amanda Jane mouthed *peace and quiet* along with him while wearing a serious expression.

"After so much noise, all this quiet is kind of foreign to me now." Gina smoothed her hands down her jeans.

"Pie?" Amanda Jane perked.

"Breakfast. Not before bed," Gina said. "Bath."

"You let her have pie for breakfast?"

"It's fruit." She shrugged. "We try to do some fun things, you know. I'm not all doom and gloom."

"I know that." When they sat down at the table he said, "She asked me to stay and watch another movie. Is that okay?"

"Sure. I'm glad you guys are spending some time together and getting to know each other."

"That's had me thinking, Gina. Maybe you and I should spend some time together. We don't know each other anymore. And I'd like to." That little voice in his head said that he wanted to know her for himself, too, not just for Amanda Jane.

She paused, pie midway to her mouth. "I'd like that, too. It makes me feel better about everything." Gina rushed to add, "I think it's because I don't know you anymore that I'm afraid."

"I hope you don't think that I'm not afraid. I am. Amanda Jane is this amazing little person and every time that it occurs to me that she's my daughter, I don't know how it can be real. Or who thought it was a good idea." He gave a self-deprecating laugh.

"When did you want us to move in?" She took a bite of pie.

"As soon as possible. Amanda Jane is going to start first grade in the fall. It would be good if her legal residence was the new address."

"Okay."

"Okay? You don't want to argue?" he teased. Actually, Reed had expected this to be more of a battle.

"No, I don't want to argue. That's fine. I agreed to be your wife." She blushed. "I mean, to cohabitate."

"You can say getting married. That's what you're doing."

"It just sounds so intimate. It sounds like our relationship is something it's not." She looked away from him.

"We're raising a child together, Gina. It doesn't get much more intimate than that, does it? The ins and outs of everyday life are more meaningful than bodies slapping together."

She blushed.

"Why did that make you blush?" Using his forefinger, he tilted her chin up so she had to look at him. He loved that she blushed, but he didn't want to embarrass her. He wanted to know what she was thinking and if it was the same thing he was.

"It's stupid, right? I'm an EMT. I'm going to be a doctor. I see bodies all the time. I see them in various states of dress, undress, and activity. Like the last call I got before I was off shift? A guy got his tongue ring stuck on his girlfriend's piercing. Didn't bother me at all. But when you say things like that, I—" She pinched her lips together, as if she just realized she was going to say something that she didn't want him to know.

In this, he was more experienced than she was and he knew where her mind had gone. "Did that make you think about us? What I said? If it was our bodies?"

"Reed!" She looked away from him again.

"Did it? You can tell me, Gina. I'm not an animal. I'm not going to assume that you want to screw me just because you might have wondered what it would be like. People have thoughts about other people all the time. And there aren't orgies in the streets. Really." He was determined to keep his brain and his dick on the straight and narrow. He'd told her he wasn't a beast and he was determined to live up to that promise.

She bit her lip. "Fine, okay? Yes, it made me think about it."

Then he knew he was a damn liar. Because he wanted nothing more than to grab her and really kiss her. Not that peck from earlier, but taste her lips and devour everything she had to offer until she was a writhing, pleading mess in his arms begging for all the pleasure he wanted to give her.

"Look, the world didn't stop spinning." No, if anything, it spun faster, out of control.

"No, it didn't." She pursed her lips. "But I'm still vulnerable."

"No, you're not. You're safe with me, Gina. I swear." He was determined not to screw this up.

"Safe?" She looked back up at him. "I'm not that, either."

"Do you think I'd hurt you?" That kept his libido in check. The idea that she'd be afraid of him was better than a bucket of ice down his back.

"Not on purpose. God, Reed. Are you that thick in the head? Didn't you see the way I looked at you when we were kids?"

He knew then that he would never be able to do all those things to her that he wanted. Somehow hearing that she wanted him made him think about what it would have been like if he had known.

"No, and it's probably lucky for you that I didn't."

He would've ruined her, taken all she had to give and drained her dry. He wouldn't have done it on purpose, but the person he was then, that's all he could do. He didn't know how to be a person, how to love, because he'd never had it.

CHAPTER TEN

LUCKY FOR HER that he didn't notice her making mewling calf eyes at him? Why? What did that mean? Would he have taken her up on it? She shivered, little frissons of delight spreading through her at the thought.

"I thought about it then, too, you know?" Gina confessed.

"What?" He looked at her.

For a moment she wondered if he just wanted to make her say it—speak the words aloud that she wanted him to be her first. But he really didn't know what she was going to say.

"When you offered to take care of that 'pesky cherry' for me." She licked her lips. Her mouth had suddenly gone dry.

"Oh, Jesus, I was an asshole." He shook his head. "You should've kicked me in the face for talking to you like that. I was so high, if you'd said yes, it would've been on your list of regrets, I'm sure."

"I don't know. Maybe not." No, she imagined not. No matter what happened between them then, what she would've regretted was what she regretted now. That she hadn't been bold enough or strong enough to reach for what she wanted.

He shook his head again and stuffed another bite of pie in his mouth and she thought about that kiss from earlier. It was a little bit of nothing, that kiss. It was just his lips on her cheek, and it hadn't been anything special.

Or maybe it wasn't *supposed* to be special, but it was. Sparks ignited through her body at the contact and it had taken everything in her not to turn into him and demand he kiss her for real.

But then where would they be?

A one-night stand with a man who couldn't go home because he was home? They had Amanda Jane to think about.

There was that part of her that kept thinking about fairy tales and white picket fences that thought this was the best course of action for both her and her niece. If she and Reed were involved, they would be almost the perfect little model family.

But the realist in her reminded her that he'd just said they didn't know each other anymore. He wanted to spend time getting to know her, not getting into her panties.

And he was right.

She only knew the idea of him.

What was more, she couldn't ever let herself forget that he had the same problem Crystal did. Maybe he'd gotten help, maybe he was clean, and that was what he had to do to be in Amanda Jane's life. But what if he relapsed? What if he left?

On an emotional level, Gina simply couldn't go through it again. She'd been through as much as she could stand with Crystal. Amanda Jane couldn't go through that again.

"Was this maybe a bit more personal than what you meant when you talked about getting to know me again?" She laughed off what had almost become an irreparably awkward moment.

"Maybe, but I'm not sorry for it."

"Since I just told you something so personal, maybe you'll tell me something." She was hungry for some new morsel, anything about him.

"Whatever you want to know, Gina."

"You said you don't date. Why not?" Why had that been the first thing she asked? Some things never changed.

He seemed startled by her question and blinked. "You don't hesitate to go for the throat, do you?"

"If you don't want to answer—" She was ready to backpedal at full speed.

"No, I'll tell you. That's fine. The question was un-expected, though."

"Why? Most playboy types are...well...playboy types." She'd imagined him running around with this jet-set life-style with more money than cares.

"Having money doesn't automatically make me a 'playboy type.' So far, my many residences include a condo in the city and the house on Knob Hill. It's not like I bought a yacht and went to Monaco."

"Why not?" She wouldn't go to Monaco, but she'd go to Paris, Venice, Rome, London...she'd see the world.

"That's three questions," he teased. "But they all have the same answer. It's not practical. I could lose this money easier than I made it. And I remember what it's like living in Whispering Woods. I never want to go back there. Not just the place itself, but the mindset. The fear of being hungry." Reed shrugged. "I'm not going to let some gold digger take it from me, either."

"You think the only women who want to date you are gold diggers? That's pretty cynical." That would be a rather lonely existence, she imagined, thinking that everyone she met would want something from her.

"I think we live in a culture where we're taught to value money over connection."

That wasn't the answer she expected. He was different, but there were things about him that were the same. She couldn't argue with his logic. "Dating doesn't have to be serious."

He arched a brow. "No? Is that why you're still a virgin?"

Gina blushed. "Point taken."

"It's not just the money, Gina. I won't lie and say it doesn't matter because it does. But it's about me, too. If I invite someone into my life, they have to accept every part of me. Not just who I am now, but who I was. And who I have the potential to be, both good and bad. Now I have Amanda Jane."

Gina looked down at her hands. "And me. I'll be your wife. I can't imagine what woman would tolerate this arrangement."

"That's just it, Gina. She doesn't exist. Because I would never put her before Amanda Jane." He was quiet for a moment. "Or you."

She looked up at him again, the possibilities of fairy

tales glittering like stars in her eyes. She blinked, trying to wash away all the sparkle she saw there. It was easy to speak of these things, much harder to do them, and Reed had always had a certain way of describing things that made the impossible seem likely.

"That's not my place, Reed." As pretty as it sounded, that wasn't fair to him.

"It is. We will be married. You're vital to Amanda Jane's happiness."

Part of her wished so desperately that he'd say she was vital to *his* happiness. As childish and silly as it would sound.

"Do you really think that we can do this?"

"We're already doing it."

She sat up very straight, realizing that she hadn't heard Amanda Jane in a while. "I need to go check on her. I'll be right back."

Amanda Jane was in her room, hair braided, nightgown and slippers on, dressing up one of her dolls.

"Hey, what are you doing in here? I thought you wanted another movie?"

Her blue eyes were wide. "You were talking."

She nodded. "We were. But only because we were waiting for you."

"Do you like him?" Amanda Jane asked as she carefully brushed the doll's hair.

Gina suddenly couldn't face the purity in her eyes because it burned through to her gut and splayed everything wide for anyone to see. "Of course I like him. He's your daddy."

"No, Gina-bee. *Like* him, like him." When Gina

didn't answer, she continued. "I think I'd like it if you liked him–liked him."

"That's not possible, little one." What was she supposed to say to that? How did she explain to Amanda Jane that things couldn't be that way? How did she explain it to herself, because obviously, her body wasn't getting the message.

Her brain was receiving it loud and clear, but that didn't stop her from thinking about him 24/7.

"You don't get to pick who you like-like, Gina-bee. It just happens." She put the doll down on the bed and hopped up beside it.

Gina sighed. "Sometimes, there are people that we may like-like, but for whatever reason, it's just not the right time for it to happen."

"How can things happen at the wrong time?" She cocked her head to the side. "If they happen, they're supposed to. That's what you always told me about Mama."

She'd talked herself into a corner. "That's enough questions out of you. Time for bed."

"That's what you say when you don't want to answer me." The girl climbed into her bed with no fuss.

"Yep." Gina grinned at her and Amanda Jane returned the smile.

She tucked her in and when she left the room, she found Reed standing in the hallway. His presence made it hard to breathe in the small space and she was so very aware of his size, his strength and the fact that while he wore his familiar face, he was very much a stranger.

"Is she okay?" Concern marked his features.

"Yeah." She found the space between them shrinking, her eyes somehow too heavy to lift to meet his gaze. Gina swallowed hard, her whole body heating at his proximity.

Was she blushing? Her cheeks felt as if they were on fire.

"So I guess she doesn't want a movie." He chuckled, the sound low in his throat.

There was a different timbre to his voice now. Gina didn't know what had changed—maybe nothing. Maybe it was just standing alone with him in the dark.

She ached to touch him, to reach out and fall into his arms, their lips colliding. She could take him up to her room and—hell. What was she thinking? It had been so long since she'd been held. Kissed. And this want in her had been silent for these long years. She'd given up on wanting anyone—or anyone wanting her.

Gina knew this was situational. Logically, it was being thrown into this position with him, not just in the immediate moment, but the idea of raising Amanda Jane together. It made him safe.

But Reed Hollingsworth was anything but safe. He could wreck her from the inside out.

"What about you? Do you want a movie?"

"I should probably go to bed. Back to work tomorrow." Bed. Yeah, with him. She shook her head at the direction of her thoughts.

"Gina."

"What?" She still wouldn't look up at him.

"Why won't you look at me?" His voice rumbled low and caused a heat to wash over her.

"I can't," she squeaked. She hated that she squeaked.

His fingers were warm and strong on her chin, tilting her head up to the confession she didn't want to give him. She knew he'd see her want in her eyes and then what? It couldn't go anywhere even if he did want her.

How pathetic was that? How awkward would it be if he didn't?

She wanted to turn away, to hide, but there was something reckless in her blood that suddenly flared to life. Let him look, let him see, and let the things fall as they would like leaves from the giant oak in the front yard.

And he did. He saw it all. His blue eyes were suddenly shadowed in the half light, darker—deeper.

"Hell," he mumbled and the space between them was gone.

Her arms tangled around his neck and the contact felt so good, after so long, just to be held by someone. He didn't stop there, though.

Crushed against him in a dark hallway, she finally got her kiss.

It was everything she dreamed it would be. He was masterful, powerful, but tender, as well. He tasted of all the things she wanted, but never thought she could have.

She wanted his hands everywhere; she couldn't get close enough.

Reed Hollingsworth was kissing her.

It was as surreal as the rest of the things that had happened to her in these past weeks.

He was the one who broke away first and she felt the loss of him, his heat, his strength so acutely she shivered.

Gina had never once thought of herself as small and alone, and she'd never felt that way until this moment.

Standing there, heart pounding like a drum and her senses fogged with desire, it was as if she were a lone bit of flotsam on a river whose current was too strong to fight.

"I'm…" He scrubbed his hand over his jaw.

"Sorry?" she supplied, breathless.

"That's just it, I'm not sorry. But I shouldn't have done it."

Her lips were bee-stung and warm and she was having trouble thinking of anything but that kiss.

But he was right. "No, you shouldn't have. Now things can never be the same."

His expression was pained. "Could they have ever been?"

She shook her head. "No. I guess not." Gina swallowed hard and moved toward the living room. What would she have done if Amanda Jane had chosen that moment to open her door? It would give her ideas that were best left untouched and unknown.

He followed her, and she was hyperaware of his presence at her back. "Do you want me to go?"

"No." She pursed her lips. "But maybe you should?" Gina didn't mean for it to be a question, but deep down, she wanted him to stay. Only, this couldn't only be about what she wanted. "Maybe we should put some distance between us. And what just happened."

"I'd say that we should pretend it never happened, but I can't do that. Can you?"

She was both relieved and terrified by his response.

Relieved that she wasn't the only one, but terrified for the same reason.

"No, but I don't want to play house," she blurted. "I don't want you to have feelings for me just because the arrangement makes it easy."

Reed looked away from her. "Nothing about this is easy, Gina." He exhaled heavily. "Is that what you think being married will be like? Playing house?"

"Maybe. I don't know." She shrugged and bit her lip. Her mouth still tasted of him, of his kiss.

Of playing house.

"I won't do it again." His eyes were dark and hooded.

Gina thought for a moment she saw a flash of pain. "It's not that I didn't like it." It was her turn to look away. "I think I liked it too much."

He laughed and it was a cold, bitter sound. "Never heard that before."

"You don't understand at all, do you? I wanted you. I wanted this with you." She hadn't meant to confess this, but she couldn't let him think that she didn't want him. It had seemed like the worst thing in the world if he ever found out how she'd felt, but now it was if he didn't. She couldn't stand that look on his face.

His eyes widened. "What are you saying?" As if the words didn't make sense in the way she'd strung them together.

"Our current circumstances aren't the incarnation I dreamed about, but I kept waiting for you to notice me and I really believed one day we'd be together. When Crystal had moved on, you'd realize it was me you wanted. And we'd have a real family. Now here we are." Her throat constricted. She couldn't believe she'd just confessed this. It was her deepest secret, although not her darkest. Her darkest was that she was jealous of Crystal for having him. She'd have traded her brains to be the hot sister. At least back then.

"Yeah, here we are." He gave another mirthless laugh. "And it's nothing like what you dreamed of." Reed shook his head. "You know, there was a part of me that wanted to be the white knight on the horse for you. For Amanda Jane. But that's not real. And those kind of expectations—"

The sadness scrawled on his face was too much. "I don't have any expectations," she rushed to reassure him. "Nothing outside of what was agreed upon in Emma's offices."

He nodded slowly. "Good. Because that I can do. Anything else..." He shrugged as if the motion could sum up everything else that his voice couldn't.

"Jesus, Reed, do you think I still have all of those little-girl dreams and expect you to fulfill them?" Although, speaking the words aloud, she knew that there was a part of her that did.

"Don't you?"

She blushed. "That's just the little-girl part of me I haven't managed to outgrow yet. I know it for what it is."

"That's the damnable part of it, I guess. Because the kid I used to be, he wanted to be with you more than anything. But he knew that you were going places bigger than me."

Something stung behind her eyes, in her nose. She

couldn't breathe. "But we're not those kids anymore. We know how the world works. And we have Amanda Jane to think about."

His eyes were guarded again. "Yes, we do. Emma should've received the account information by now, and if not, she will shortly. So I expect as per our agreement that you'll be giving your notice at the Bullhorn and to the city."

He was all business now—closed off, his vulnerability hidden from her. As soon as he tucked it away, it was as if it had never been. Gina wanted to see it, touch it, know it was real and that she wasn't alone.

Otherwise, it was as if he was some kind of stone statue, moving like an automaton warrior—slicing through anything that stood in his way.

"Yes. I'll do that." She hadn't wanted to give up the EMT job. She liked working as an EMT. But she knew that the hours weren't conducive to Amanda Jane's needs or studying. She could catch up on some courses during the summer, too.

"Let me know when you want to come see the house. I'll have packers and movers here this coming weekend. Just let them know what you want to take."

The reality of her situation slammed into her again and her stomach twisted into knots. "I'll be on shift. I just don't know when."

"I'd like to take Amanda Jane instead of sending her to day care for those days."

"What about work?"

"Benefits of working for myself. She can come to the office with me."

She nodded slowly. "Okay, but if you need anything, call me or Missy, or even Grams, okay?"

"Actually, I was going to see if Missy wanted to pick up some extra hours, if it was okay with Emma."

Gina exhaled a heavy sigh of relief. "That's great."

But the look on his face said he knew the exact direction of her thoughts.

"I'll pick her up tomorrow morning."

"I have to be there at eight."

"I'll be here at seven."

He headed toward the door, but there was something unfinished. Something that hung in the air between them, heavy and awkward.

She called out to him, and when he paused, she flung her arms around his neck and hugged him.

Gina's instincts had been to reassure them both, not to feel how strong his arms were around her, how hard his chest was, or to inhale the delicious scent of his expensive cologne.

Fey, misty of visions of what it would be like to surrender to this thing between them washed over her. The memory of that scalding kiss made it all the more real. As did the press of her arousal against her belly.

Her breath caught and she wondered if it would always be like this. If every encounter with him would ignite her into this thing of burning need.

And how she was supposed to live without the possibility of surrender.

"It's all going to be okay, Gina."

When he broke the embrace and she stood in the doorway watching his taillights disappear down the drive, she struggled against the pinpricks that signaled a wave of tears.

No one who had the power to make it so had ever told her it was going to be okay. That was Gina's job. It was what she was good at. And until Reed had spoken the words to her, she hadn't realized how badly she needed someone to say them to her.

And most important, mean it.

CHAPTER ELEVEN

"DADDY, YOU WORK in a castle," Amanda Jane said as he led her inside the metro towers where his offices were located in the city.

Reed looked up at the glass-and-metal construction and supposed that she was right. It was a beautiful building, but imposing as well—like a castle should be. "I guess I do."

"Are there dragons to slay?"

"Not so much to slay, but pay." Yeah, he'd go with that comparison.

"You pay the dragons?" She wrinkled her nose. "I don't like this."

"No one does." They were preparing for the end of quarter, and that always meant more hours and more labor and more checks to be written.

"You're funny." Amanda Jane barreled through the door ahead of him.

There was part of him that was afraid of being here, of doing this—of being a father—but another part recognized that this was what had brought him to this point in his life.

"My grammie says you're going to marry Gina-bee. I keep waiting for you to tell me, but you haven't. So I wanted you to know it's okay. If you want to."

"If I want to?" He raised a brow and offered his hand.

She tucked her small hand into his. "I don't think you should marry someone just for someone else. Even though Grammie wants you to."

"Grammie wants us to?" He kept parroting her. Each new thing she said was more of a surprise than the last.

She nodded. "We were trying to get you to spend more time together at Frogfest, but it felt like tricking you. I don't want to trick you. I want you and Gina-bee to be happy."

Her words, innocent and honest, tugged at his heart strings. "We will be. As long as you're with us."

"I don't know about that. Gina-bee and Grammie tell me I'm full of the dickens."

"As all children should be, I think." Yes, she was definitely full of the dickens.

The elevator stopped and he walked in to his offices with Amanda Jane in tow. They'd had a lovely morning shopping, spoiling her just a little bit rotten before work.

His assistant, Rae, was looking her usual cheerful self. "Gray is in your office," she said and handed him a sheaf of papers. "And who is this young lady?"

"I'm Amanda Jane."

"Rae, this is my daughter."

"Are you helping your daddy today?" Rae grinned.

Amanda Jane shook her head. "Yes, but I can help you if you want."

"And how would you help me?" Rae knelt down to be on Amanda Jane's level.

"I'd tell Mr. James to take you to lunch."

Rae grinned and looked up at Reed. "I approve."

"We'll see what Mr. James has on the docket today." Reed grinned. "Actually, Rae, would you mind taking Amanda Jane for a hot chocolate to start her day?"

"Not at all. Come on. You like whipped cream in your cocoa?"

"Definitely."

Reed went into his office and turned to watch his assistant walking away with his daughter, then turned his attention to his lawyer. Because he was sure that's the hat he was wearing at the moment.

"So, get it out before she gets back."

Gray smirked. "Look, I just want to make sure this is what you want to do."

"I signed the paperwork, didn't I?"

"This means you're going to marry her. As in join for life."

"I believe the paperwork says until Amanda Jane is eighteen."

"Whatever." Gray's eyes were intense. "For all of this wanting to protect yourself, all the safeguards you have in place, you're just willing to give this woman everything."

He'd been about to protest, but realized Gray was right. "I know you had it hard coming up, too, Gray. Neither one of us had a silver spoon. But it doesn't have to be hard for my daughter. You've seen Amanda Jane; you've seen how Gina takes care of her."

"You know you're paying for medical school?"

"For my daughter's caregiver, her aunt, to have an education? Yes, yes I am. It's nothing to me. What her education will cost, I make that in a week."

"It just doesn't make any sense."

"It does to me. That's all that matters." He realized why it made sense to him. For all of his insistence on being wanted for himself, he was afraid that wasn't good enough, but he desperately wanted to be. So he was content to fill the holes that were lacking in himself with money. It was something he had. Something he could give them both that they'd not have anywhere else.

He knew how wrong that thinking was. His initial fears of being wanted only for his money were always present and he worked hard to keep them secret, keep them hidden, and now it seemed as if they were splayed wide for all to see.

He couldn't have that.

"I guess tonight you'll be putting your money where your mouth is, Reed."

"What?"

"The governor's dinner?"

"Shit. Who has a dinner on a Monday night?" Reed groused.

Gray raised a brow. "Spoken like a true snob."

"I can't show up alone, but taking Gina puts her in the spotlight. I don't know if she's ready for that. Hell, I don't know if *I'm* ready for that."

"We can't beg off. We need those connections if you want the stockyard deal to go through."

"They're not going to sour the deal just because I don't go to their little party." He rolled his eyes.

"No, but neither will it make them amenable to your terms, which obviously we can get around, but why do it the hard way when all you have to do is show up and tell Gina to look pretty?"

"We're not…" The sheer magnitude of what he was proposing was impossible. Wasn't it? They'd discussed the idea of marriage. They'd agreed to it. They'd hammered out the financials, but not the rest of it. Not the little things that made up living.

Like this.

There was no real reason for her to attend. Except what about when she was his wife? It would look strange to this group of people if his wife wasn't on his arm. If he ever wanted to take his company public, the opinions of others mattered a great deal.

This wasn't something Gina had signed up for, and to his own chagrin, not something that he'd thought about.

Taking his company public, they'd need to believe this was a love story.

"The implications of all this finally starting to hit home?" Gray asked gently.

"Nothing can ever be a simple proposition, can it?"

"Here's what's going to happen. You're going to call that judge. She's going to marry you in her chambers and we'll issue a press release saying that you were married quietly…"

"Hold on. I need to talk to Gina." He wouldn't do any of this until he'd cleared it with her. He knew she was already dealing with so much and he wanted to make things easier on both of them, not harder.

"Then I'm going to assume that what I overheard from Rae and Amanda Jane is an offer. Your dime, of course." Gray plucked a seemingly invisible bit of lint from his suit.

He shook his head. "Yes, by all means take my assistant out to lunch and allow me to pay for it."

"Don't mind if I do." Gray grinned. "She's not going to bite, right?"

"That's between the two of you."

"I think I need Amanda Jane to protect me." Gray's grin widened.

Reed shook his head and laughed. "If she doesn't want to go, she can stay here. I just have to call—" He looked up to see her standing in the doorway; Gina with her face flushed and her eyes pools of concern.

"What's wrong?" Why was she standing here in the middle of the day? She should've been on her shift.

"I…"

"And that's my cue." Gray nodded to Gina and left them alone.

"I just needed to see her. She's never been so far away from me before." Gina wrung her hands.

A cold sensation washed down his spine. "You didn't trust me with her?"

"It's not that. I just… This is new." She glanced around at everything in the room, but at him. That spoke volumes.

She looked so small, so breakable, that all of the indignation he felt, the burning sparks of anger, they were washed away and he could only think about wiping that expression from her face.

"As you can see, we're fine. She's fine. Rae made her some cocoa. They were going to an early lunch, actually, because I needed to call you."

"A conversation that she can't overhear? What's happened?" Obviously, Gina had assumed the worst.

"Nothing's happened. Sit down, Gina."

"I'm sorry." She didn't move; she still seemed lost and adrift somehow.

"For what?" He wanted her to feel as though she could talk to him, and he tried to turn off his own feelings, and push down his own needs. He wanted to stop thinking about how much it stung that she didn't trust him.

Logically, he understood. He really did. He couldn't imagine leaving Amanda Jane with a stranger and that was still what he was, at least to her. He reminded himself that she'd been doing this alone for a while and her distress was probably natural.

But that didn't soothe the burn inside. It only made it burn hotter, only added fuel to the fire and gave that voice that told him he wasn't good enough, that he was going to fall, that he was going to fail, a pulpit.

"I shouldn't have come." She seemed so distraught.

He pushed a hand through his hair. "Gina, if you can't come to my office when you need something, how are we ever going to be married? It's okay that you're here." He took a deep breath. "It's even okay that you didn't trust me."

"It's not that I don't trust you. It's that I can't control you." Her face flushed. "Not like that. It's that so many bad things have happened."

"You're having a mild panic attack." He put his arms around her and he hated that she felt so right there. No, maybe it wasn't that he hated it, he hated that he noticed it. That her world was seemingly falling to pieces around her and all he could think about was being able to touch her.

"This has never happened to me before." She clung to him, burying her face in his neck.

Suddenly, it was more than comfort. It changed, their embrace. It was hot and…completely inappropriate.

"It's okay that it did. I'm sure there's going to be a lot of growing pains as we adjust to this."

She pulled away from him, seemingly bound herself together with some invisible glue. "You said you were going to call me?"

"This isn't the right time."

"It must've been important if you were going to call me." She looked so hopeful, as though she just wanted to forget the past fifteen minutes had happened.

"I, uh, have a thing tonight."

"So you won't be able to keep Amanda Jane, after all?" Her brow furrowed.

"I need you to go, too. It's just a dinner, a fund-raising thing."

"I have a shift."

"That's handled."

"What will we do with Amanda Jane?"

"Missy. We don't have to stay late."

"Why do you need me to go? It's not *my* money they want." She shoved her hands into her pockets.

"Because you're going to be my wife. Because I want to take my company public. Because I need to make a good impression. Because…" He took a deep breath. "Because I want to take you to dinner."

She hadn't had much of a reaction to anything he'd said until he got to that part. The scary part. He rushed to add, "We talked about spending time together. Getting to know each other again. I don't want to spend the next eighteen years married to a girl I used to know."

"I don't have anything to wear." She laughed dismissively, blushed and then looked down at her feet. "That sounded so…will-you-buy-me-something-gold-digger. I didn't mean it like that."

"I'll take care of it. I'd be a dick if I didn't. It's not like either of us can show up in jeans."

"You're a billionaire. You can do whatever you want." She looked back up at him and he saw all of her vulnerability in those depths.

That was the crux of it right there. She felt powerless. She thought he was some kind of playboy. As though he hadn't worked hard for every penny he had. As though the rules had changed for him.

He guessed to a certain point, the rules had changed for him. Money could do a lot of things. But there were chains that came with that money, too. Not that he was complaining. He'd rather be chained in gold than barbed wire.

"Everything has its pros and cons, Gina. Like this. You're going to be part of this world. I know that's not what you signed up for, but your education will be paid for. You'll be a doctor. The best part? Amanda Jane can be anything. Anything at all. There won't be any doors closed to her if we do this right."

"And here I thought it was just dinner and now you're saving the world." Her expression was shy somehow.

"It was different for you. You had your grandmother to show you another way to live. All I had was me. So to me, yeah. Having these connections, this life? Giving those to my daughter? It's better than saving the world."

"Why didn't you feel this way when Crys told you she was pregnant?" Gina asked in a small voice, seemingly searching for the answer to be written on his face.

He dared to touch her, braved the contact of flesh to make her look at him. He wanted her to be looking into his eyes when he answered her.

"I swear that she never said anything to me, Gina. Never. The last time I saw her was when she OD'd that first time and I went to juvie. I never saw her again. I never heard from her."

"So you really didn't know until you got the papers?"

"No." He searched her eyes. "I didn't even know Crys had passed until I got the papers."

"I'm sorry."

"You keep saying that. Let's not do sorry. It doesn't help anything. Let me take you to lunch and buy you a pretty dress. Marry me and let's just look forward."

"I guess we can try that."

"Yeah, I know it wasn't your dream proposal and I'm not your dream guy, but it doesn't have to be bad. We can be friends again."

"Do friends buy each other expensive party dresses?" She looked unsure.

"Sometimes."

"Is Amanda Jane okay with Rae?"

"She'll be fine, but we can take her if you can pry her away from her hot cocoa." Reed checked his phone and saw a text from Rae. They'd just left. "Or that new dinosaur restaurant on the Plaza."

"I guess that's okay." Gina bit her lip. "I need to let go a little bit, I know."

"You can let go with me, I won't drop you."

"Do you swear?"

"Always." God, what the hell was he saying? Why was he making her promises he didn't know if he could keep? He didn't even know what they were talking about now. What was between them, or…

The dress. He'd think about the dress instead. "Let's go pick out a dress, yeah?"

She seemed relieved. "Okay."

"If I'd remembered about this thing, we could've had one made."

"Funny, that." She shook her head.

"How so?"

"I used to get made fun of because my mother made some of my clothes when I was little. That was poor white trash." She laughed. "Now, having something tailor-made just for me is what the people with money do."

"How about tonight, we don't worry about the past? Let's think about the future."

"Sometimes I think the past is our only common ground."

"Then we need to change that."

"You make it sound so easy."

"I'm under no illusions this will be easy, Gina. But maybe tonight we can approach this like we just met."

"And what, ignore all the baggage that we have together?"

"Yeah." He nodded. "Who dumps all their baggage on a first date, anyway?"

"Is that what this is? A date?"

He couldn't read her expression. "We're going to be married. I think it's okay if we date."

"You know what I mean."

He never should've phrased it that way. Reed motioned, at a loss for what to say.

"Maybe we don't have to put a label on it. I'm sorry I'm such a spaz," she said.

"You're not."

"You were trying to make this easier and I just..." She sighed. "Let's go shopping."

CHAPTER TWELVE

THIS WAS LIKE some kind of Cinderella fantasy, Gina thought.

Reed was standing there, his black card at the ready, and anything that the salesgirl had to show her was hers for the taking.

The very idea made her itchy. As if it was all a joke and any minute someone would pop out and tell her she was on some hidden-camera prank show. She felt very out of place. She never imagined that she'd be playing dress-up at some fancy shop in the city where a stocking probably cost more than what she made in a week.

The salesgirl was nice; she did nothing to make Gina feel unwelcome or like she didn't belong. All of that was in Gina's own head. She'd never had a problem with who she was or where she came from when she was growing up.

Even when she got picked on for her handmade clothes and secondhand shoes.

But somehow, this made her feel like she was lacking. Maybe because that was what her fears were—underneath all of her bravado, she was afraid that she wasn't good enough and that she couldn't do this. Couldn't be a wife and a mother because she didn't know how.

The glass slipper wouldn't fit because it was never hers to begin with.

"What sort of event are you attending?" the girl asked with a smile.

Gina looked to Reed to answer for her because she had no idea. She could quote philosophy, speak about current events and politics, even discuss the newest advances in medical research, but she had no idea which fork to use or what to wear to an event like what he was talking about.

"Evening gown. Charity dinner."

"Of course, Mr. Hollingsworth. I should've known." She smiled and guided them toward a fitting area.

Have fun, Reed mouthed.

Fun? How could she possibly have fun? Half the dresses she spotted had price tags that were ridiculous.

"Red, I think."

"What?"

"Your dress? I think red would complement your coloring."

"You're the expert." Gina shrugged. She couldn't imagine herself in a red dress. It seemed too decadent. Too…everything. Which was silly. It was just a color. It wasn't like one dress was going to change her life.

"Yes, I am." She nodded. "I've opened a store charge for you upon Mr. Hollingsworth's request. I'm Amy, by the way. I do work on commission, so if you decide you need a new wardrobe, I hope you come see me again."

"New wardrobe?" She supposed that she'd be expected to do this sort of thing more than once. She'd need to look the part. "That's terrifying. I wear jeans, T-shirts and work pants. That's about it."

Amy laughed. "We'll fix you right up."

Part of this felt as if he was trying to make her over into something she wasn't, but she knew that wasn't how Reed thought. Or it wasn't how he used to think. And since when had she become so stuck in her ways that she wasn't willing to try something new? That she'd refuse to fit in on principle? That was not who she was.

This was just a dress.

Just outer wrappings.

When Amy presented her with the dress to try on, she immediately noticed how soft and diaphanous the fabric was against her skin.

"Doesn't that feel marvelous? The most important part of dressing up is feeling wonderful. So many women stuff themselves into clothes that aren't comfortable and say beauty is suffering. I think that's garbage. A woman never looks more beautiful than when she's comfortable and confident in herself."

She went into the dressing room and stared at the dress for a few long moments before she committed to putting it on. It was just a dress.

Only it wasn't.

When it slid down over her body, it was like sliding into a dream. The red chiffon had a high halter neckline, wrapping around her throat like a choker, and bloused slightly at the waist. It was sleeveless and managed to both disguise and accentuate her ample cleavage at the same time.

Gina turned to the side and then saw the back was

open all the way down to where her spine began to curve down toward her bottom. It was risqué, but not. Elegant, but comfortable. The dress itself was a lot like Gina in so many ways. It was at odds with itself, but it was still beautiful. That idea, thinking of herself in those terms, made her feel like maybe everything really would be okay.

And maybe a dress really could change her life and perhaps that wasn't a bad thing.

"Let me see," Amy demanded.

Gina opened the door and stepped out onto the mini platform in front of the tri-fold mirrors.

"I was right. Stunning." Amy held up a pair of simple red kitten heels. "Try these."

Gina lifted the floor-length skirt and Amy knelt down to slide the shoes onto her feet.

"That one," a deep voice said from the doorway.

She looked up to see Reed, but it wasn't a version of Reed that she knew. Not this one. His eyes were dark and hungry—not just hungry, but ravenous. At first, she thought maybe she felt like a mouse and he was a giant predator. But she knew in this dress, she was no mouse.

Gina liked the way his regard felt, almost as if she could physically feel his hands on her. The sensation was better than any daydream she'd had about him because it was real.

She couldn't resist smiling. "You like it?"

"I like it very much." He didn't bother trying to hide his assessment of her or mask it for anything but what it was, raw desire.

Or maybe that's just what she wanted it to be?

"You haven't seen the back yet." Amy directed her to spin.

She turned, looking back at him over her shoulder. "Is it appropriate?"

"Very."

"There is a lovely set of matching undergarments, designed especially for the cut of the dress."

Gina's face flushed when she saw the scraps of lace, because she wasn't imagining what she'd look like in them. She imagined what it would be like with Reed taking her out of them.

"We'll take those, too." His regard was still heavy on her skin, touching her in places it had no business touching.

"Oh, will we?" she teased. Gina couldn't believe how flirty and breathy she sounded; it was as if it wasn't even her voice.

"Unless you'd rather go without?"

Was he actually suggesting she go commando under that dress? "I…no. We'll take those, as well." She hoped she didn't sound as flustered as she felt.

Gina felt as if she was all over the map. Sex kitten one minute and blushing virgin the next. Although the blushing virgin part was the truth.

"Very good." Amy grinned. "I have a few other things for you to try on. Just in case you need them before you do this shopping thing up right."

When they were alone, he said, "You know the biggest question here is whether you like the dress."

"I love it." She did. She'd never been one to play

dress-up, not like Crystal. Gina was more the mud-pies-and-catching-frogs sort of child.

"Good."

The tension in the room was suddenly thick, gravid with expectation—but of what, she didn't know.

"So are you going to pick me up in a pumpkin carriage?" She tried to break the tension.

"I could, if that's what you wanted."

It didn't dissipate. If anything it became more intense. His voice was still low, so much deeper than the boy she remembered. It reminded her that Reed Hollingsworth wasn't a boy. He wasn't a "safe" daydream. He was a man. He was real. And their actions had very real consequences.

"No. That would be silly. And extravagant."

"How about a limo?"

She tittered, high-pitched and nervous. "That would still be extravagant."

He was suddenly close enough to touch and his hand reached out to do just that. Maybe he was going to push her hair out of her face, maybe he was going to touch her just for the sake of touching her, but he dropped his hand. And her skin was bereft at the loss. She wanted his hands on her more than she could say. Even if it was just his fingertips grazing the surface of her cheek.

"What's the point in having this money if I don't spend a little of it?" Except it seemed as though he was asking her more than that, there were more layers to the question. She just couldn't see what else was there, what he wanted her to say.

"You're already spending a little of it."

"You know how you said you don't know how to be?"

She'd said that the night they were out on the porch drinking sweet tea. Gina nodded.

"I still feel like that sometimes."

Then the moment was gone as suddenly as it had come, dissipated like a cloud.

"I'll leave you to your privacy."

Gina was torn between relief at his exit and wishing he'd come back. She couldn't wait for these feelings to pass. She was sure they would, after they got used to each other. After they were friends again.

When Amy returned, she handed her several more things to try on. "You two are such a lovely couple."

A denial was on the tip of her tongue, but they were a couple, weren't they?

After she'd made her selections, Amy said, "Thank you so much, Mrs. Hollingsworth."

She wasn't Mrs. Hollingsworth. But she was going to be. Gina Hollingsworth. How many times had she written that in the back of her notebooks?

Fear knotted in her gut all over again.

Maybe if she just kept thinking about the dress. The dress that fit her so well. The dress that she never would've dreamed would be her perfect fit was.

She could only hope this new part of her life would be like that.

But even if it wasn't—at the very worst, she got to go to medical school. Amanda Jane got to have a father. No matter how scared she was, this was the right thing. If only she could keep from freaking out and screwing it up.

She'd been so worried about Reed, and she still was. Trust took time to build, but it wasn't him she needed to focus on. It was herself.

Just like today. Not trusting him to handle his own daughter for a day by himself. He'd shown himself to be nothing but patient and kind with Amanda Jane.

But it was hard, and seemingly naive at best, and irresponsible at worst not to take his past into consideration.

Gina exhaled and decided that for tonight, she wasn't going to worry about these things. She was going to give that voice in her head the night off. It could use a break, and so could she.

"Can you pick me up tonight at my grandmother's?" she said once they were in the car.

"As you like. Where are you parked?"

"In the south garage. C-17. By the elevator."

"Well, that was precise." He laughed.

"I don't like to lose my car. Especially in the city."

He pulled up behind the KiaPet, as she called it, and when he brought the car to a stop, she leaned over before she could think better of it and brushed a quick kiss on the hard plane of his cheek.

"Thank you for the dress."

She hopped in her own car before he could say anything and drove home to Glory, determined not to think about him or kissing his cheek the whole way home. Instead, she rolled down the windows and turned the music up.

COMING DOWN THE STAIRS from her old room, she found Amanda Jane and Grams waiting for her.

Maudine looked ridiculously pleased with herself, but there was something else in her expression, too.

"What are you looking at?"

"Just you, my pretty grandbaby." Maudine smiled at her.

"Don't go counting your chickens, Grams. I know you must've said something to Helga. I know you were that 'concerned party.'"

"We already had this discussion. And so what if I was?" Maudine suddenly found something on her dress that was intensely interesting.

"I don't want you getting your hopes up and thinking this is more than it is."

"Me? Child, you're the one going to marry him."

"There's nothing set in stone."

"You signed a prenup."

"And neither of us put a date on the wedding."

Maudine narrowed her eyes. "I'm feeling another song coming on."

"That you're not going to chirp in the judge's ear. We'll get to things in our time in our own way."

"I don't like your way."

"I don't like yours." Gina fought the urge to stick out her tongue at the older woman.

"I was just telling Helga that youth is definitely wasted on the young."

"You had yours to waste. Now let me waste mine."

"But I don't want you to waste it, dear. That's the point."

"Maybe I need to waste it."

"Have you been talking to Helga?"

"Not since I saw her in court." Gina winked at her, which was better than sticking out her tongue because in her way, Gina was much like Maudine. Always up to something and she always seemed to enjoy it way more than she should.

"You look elegant." Maudine gave her a genuine smile. "This dress is perfect for you."

"It's so red."

"Yes, it is. And every eye will be on you. Especially Reed's."

"It's just a dinner."

"Where you'll be introduced to people as his fiancée."

"Stop it, Grams. I already feel like I'm going to throw up."

"What's a fian-cy?" Amanda Jane asked.

"You didn't tell her?"

"Not exactly."

"Tell me what?" Amanda Jane ran her fingers down the skirt of the dress with a giggle. "It's so soft."

"Would it be okay with you if I married your daddy?"

"Oh, I knew that part."

"You did? How did you know that?" Gina asked.

"I told Daddy it was okay, but only if you want to. I don't think you should get married just because of me. You should be best friends and want to do all the things together and have slumber parties."

Gina really liked Amanda Jane's idea of marriage. It sounded kind of perfect.

"You leave that part to us and you do your part." Gina ruffled her hair.

"What is my part?"

"Being good for your grammie while I'm gone."

"Of course. I know that. I have to have a job besides that."

"I don't know. That's a pretty hard job for someone as full of trouble and fairies as you are."

Amanda Jane nodded solemnly. "I know. It's hard work. But I'll do it."

Maudine grinned.

"Two peas in a pod, that's what you two are." The bell rang and Gina's guts twisted. "Do I look okay?"

"Okay enough that I think you should have a slumber party." Maudine smiled.

"You're terrible, Grams." Gina shook her head.

"I know." She grinned and answered the door.

Reed was wearing a tuxedo and if she'd thought the polo was devastating? The man wore a tux as though he'd been born for it. As though his sole reason for existing was to walk around wearing that and giving hapless virgins heart attacks.

"You look lovely," he said, his appraisal softer than it had been in the store.

Maybe *softer* wasn't the right word. Having his eyes on her still stirred things that they had no business stirring, but it wasn't that scalding lust. No, it was more terrifying because it seemed as if maybe there was something more.

Or worse, maybe the something more was only on her part. Reed looked every inch a fairy-tale prince and he was here to pick her up in his carriage, to take her to the ball and...

"You look pretty, Daddy," Amanda Jane said.

He didn't hesitate to pick the girl up, unmindful of wrinkling his tux or worried about a little girl's sticky hands. It didn't matter to him.

She found that ridiculously attractive.

"Daddy is handsome, not pretty."

"No, pretty. He's very shiny. That's pretty," Amanda Jane insisted.

Reed laughed. "I'm glad my girls think I'm shiny and pretty."

His girls. Part of her wanted to correct him, but the instinct that won was to ferry that bit of ownership to a small part in her heart and wrap it tenderly, only to bring it out when she needed it.

"Stay out late, do something you shouldn't, but be safe," Maudine advised.

Reed leaned over and kissed Grams's cheek. "Thank you for taking her on such short notice since Missy was…"

"Pish." Maudine waved him off. "Go on with you."

"The car is waiting," he said to Gina as he put Amanda Jane down.

"Are you sure you want me to go? Maybe I should just—"

"Maybe you should go." Maudine literally moved her toward the door with a gentle push.

"I think your grams has definite ideas about where you're going."

"I think so, too." Gina meant her words to imply that her grandmother had ideas for her in more ways than just tonight, but more like her life path in general.

It was so strange to be with him like this, to feel his hand on the small of her back burning her skin. Imagining what it would be like if he touched her everywhere. She had to stop this.

Once inside the car, complete with a driver, he leaned over and spoke low in her ear.

"You have no reason to be nervous. Everyone will love you or they'll hate you because you'll be the most beautiful woman in the room."

"You don't have to say those things." She looked away from him.

"They're true. I've never lied to you before, Gina. I wouldn't start now."

"No one has ever told me I'm beautiful. Not like this."

"If it makes you uncomfortable, I won't say it. But I can't stop thinking it." His breath on the shell of her ear, his nearness, it all spiked her desire.

"I'm still just Gina, but you're not just Reed."

"Yes, I am."

No, he wasn't. The Reed she knew didn't smell like expensive aftershave, his presence didn't suck all the air out of a space, her face didn't burn with shame over this want of him. She'd thought she had a crush on him when they were kids, and she'd yearned for him with all of her young heart. But this want now was a strange kind of fire. It consumed her in some twisted backdraft.

Gina felt very small, awkward and out of place on his arm. His gentility was something he pulled on like a mask, a costume. He became that other Reed. The finely polished gentleman with the perfect hair. Someone who wasn't real.

Or maybe she was the one who wasn't real. Maybe she'd disappeared like so much flotsam. Walking around on his arm, it was a stark reminder of how much things had changed.

And how she'd stayed very much the same.

The ballroom at the Kansas City Convention Center had been decorated to the nines and anyone who was anyone on the KC scene was present and accounted for.

She hadn't thought that so much business or so much money had its roots in KC, but it did. It shouldn't have surprised her. The mob had used the city as a gateway to the west when Vegas was young and brought in businesses and did some great and not so great things for the local economy.

So many people, so many fake smiles, so many questions. She wanted to run and hide, but at the same time, she wanted to study these people like bugs under glass. She wanted to see what made them so different from herself and Crys, if there was something genetic that was somehow better.

Gina realized that she was making herself feel like she wasn't enough. Reed thought she was enough. He thought she mattered.

Just because these people had more than she did didn't make them any better. They were all painted up and pretty to give money to the university and to medical research. They were doing good things. This was a good thing.

She shuddered to think how much her ticket had cost to come to this event. She recognized a few people from her research on KU Medical Center. People who were on the board. People who could do great things for her career, if she managed to open her mouth and speak. Or maybe it was better that she didn't. She'd just be quiet.

Gina spotted Reed's lawyer, Grayson James, moving through the groups of people. He spoke with everyone and she noticed that he turned some people toward them and others he maneuvered away.

He was very smooth.

"Gray is earning his keep tonight, I see."

"He's very good at what he does."

"He'd have destroyed us in court if we hadn't agreed to this marriage of convenience."

"I never wanted to destroy you, Gina. I just wanted to protect myself."

"And I see you're good at it."

"Why does that sound like a sin?"

She exhaled heavily. "It's not. But you have all the power here."

"Can we talk about this after the event? Any number of people here could use this against me and the company. That means against you, too."

"Okay." They made it through more conversation, drinks, dinner and finally dancing. She thought the night would never end. Being a princess, well…the glass slipper didn't fit at all.

"There's someone I want you to meet." He led her over to where a beautiful couple stood.

The woman was tiny, but there was something regal about her. Something inescapably powerful. The man she was with—then she realized where she knew them from. It was the princess and the ranger. Last year, hometown hero Byron Hawkins had rescued a real-life princess and stolen her away from the bad guys trying to ruin her country. He'd brought her home to Glory. She'd never actually gotten to meet the princess, but she knew who Byron was.

He'd been one of the bad boys, the bad crowd. He'd gotten into all kinds of trouble that boys from his side of the tracks tended to keep on the down low. Now he was a national hero.

Maybe he was proof that a person could leave their past behind. They could become someone not only better, but... She looked at Reed.

"Do you remember Byron? And this is his wife, Princess Damara."

The petite woman smiled. "Just Damara, please. My home country is a democracy now."

"And this is my fiancée, Gina Townsend."

"You're Crystal Townsend's little sister, right?" Byron said. "I remember her from high school. How is she?"

Gina pinched her lips together, the words locking in her throat. She'd told plenty of people about Crystal's passing. Accepted their condolences, all without crying or being upset. It was automatic, a social response. But talking to Byron somehow hit deep.

Luckily, she didn't have to say anything else.

"Oh, I'm so sorry. I didn't know. I've been out of the country for some time."

"You've been a little busy saving princesses, freedom, and all that," she teased, moving the focus of the conversation back to him.

Damara seemed to understand exactly what she

wanted and hopped on the train to move the discussion. "Since we're stateside, we were going to visit Glory. Byron said I'd really have enjoyed Frogfest. But honestly? All I want are French fries and donuts. You know they taste better when I get them at the source." The woman offered her a kind and radiant smile.

"Betsy's? She's the best." Gina was glad to have something else to think about.

"So have you set a date?"

Something else except that. "Um, no. We're not really making a big affair out of it. Private. Very private." She nodded.

"You're in the public eye now, or you will be. Private might be a thing of the past."

"That's part of why I bought the house in Glory," Reed said.

Just the sound of his voice calmed and reassured her. It shouldn't have, but it did.

"I know what you mean. It's why I took Damara to Glory. The whole hide-in-plain-sight thing. There's something about that place. It's kind of mythical in that for all that it changes, it never really does. There will always be a closer-knit, insular sort of unit. Sure, they'll fawn over you a little bit when you do well for yourself, but you'll always be one of theirs. There's something comforting in that. A kind of protection," Byron said.

"Exactly that. I thought maybe part of it was because I'd made all this money and I wanted everyone to see I was more than a kid who scrounged in the dirt in Whispering Woods. But it's because I know if there is any unwanted paparazzi sneaking through my yard, they're going to get the wrong end of someone's rolling pin or escorted to the county line by the sheriff with a cordial invitation to take a long walk off a short dock."

Gina liked his reasons, but the look on his face didn't exactly match up with what he said. Even though he smiled, there was a tinge of bitterness beneath. She couldn't blame him. She'd at least had her grandmother to insulate her from feeling so ostracized. Reed had had nothing but her and Crystal.

She found herself linking her hand with his, as though maybe she could anchor him there somehow.

His fingers were strong and his grip solid. And maybe he was the one anchoring her there instead of the other way around.

"How long are you stateside?" Reed asked. "My daughter would love meeting a princess. Especially one like you."

"One like me?" Damara raised a brow and then grinned.

"She's the kind of girl who likes to dress her dolls up in evening couture and then they go fishing or drive race cars."

Gina shot him a look. She'd just made a similar comparison herself the other day. She must've really gotten into princess pretend the day that Reed had taken her shopping.

She tried to imagine him dressing up and having a tea party with her and found she had no trouble with that image at all.

He would've had to have played with her to know how she played.

"She sounds amazing." Damara smiled. "I'd love to meet her. We'd love to have you and your family visit us in Castallegna. She'd like the castle."

Gina noticed there were some groups of people waiting to speak with the princess. Their eyes met. "Ah, duty calls, eh? The business of building a democracy requires a lot of networking and politicking."

"Of course." Gina gave her a genuine smile.

"I'll have our secretary get in touch with Reed's and we'll set something up."

"You're a natural, sweetheart."

His praise slid over her, warm and smooth like a good whiskey. "Because she was nice."

"That's why I wanted you to meet her."

"I guess Glory is moving up in the world. A princess. A hero. A billionaire."

"A doctor..."

"There are plenty of doctors in Glory," she deflected.

"Not like you."

"Hush with that." For some reason, this embarrassed her. She didn't know why.

"No. I won't. It's okay to reach for what you want and to actually expect to get it, Gina."

"I expect to get it."

"But you expect it to be hard."

"Because most things are." If she expected to work hard, then it was no surprise when she had to.

"Not everything has to be a struggle."

"I'm feeling like you're trying to say something about my current situation, not just life." She raised a brow and accepted a flute of champagne.

"It could be applied to our present situation, yeah."
He nodded.

A few guests had gathered around them and conversation veered away from intimate matters immediately.
Talk of current events, Reed's plans for his company, the delicious shrimp cocktail and everything else merged into the flow of conversation.

After some moments, music began to play and couples began to dance.

Reed excused them from their companions and pulled her against him. "You're doing great," he said, whispering against the shell of her ear when the music started.

"Dinner, huh? This is more like a ball." This was so much different than what she'd expected.

"He called it a dinner."

"Did you get what you needed?" she asked.

"Why, are you already trying to run away?"

"Most definitely. I hadn't expected…all of this. It's so bright. There's so much glitter and gold. I don't know how it doesn't blind you."

"Because I remember my life without it. I always remember."

She was pressed against him, her palm in his. And maybe a too-tight glass slipper wasn't so bad, after all. If it meant she got to be in his arms like this.

Gina couldn't stop inhaling his scent—the mix of aftershave and cologne, and that underlying note that was uniquely him. She wanted her clothes to smell like him, she wanted to be able to hang this dress in her closet and when she put it on, she wanted to be lost in the memory of what it was like to glide around on a cloud under the stars wrapped in him.

But it wasn't a cloud, it was just his practiced steps. And the lights weren't stars.

And this life? It wasn't hers. It was pretend, a game.

Then he pulled her closer, impossibly close, yet somehow not close enough.

His hand on the small of her back, she decided, was a seemingly innocuous gesture but really more like a tool in the hands of the devil.

All of her focus had centered on that one, single sensation. She wanted his hand to be everywhere. She wanted that burn all over her skin. She wanted to tilt her face up and look into his eyes and see that same hunger she'd seen when he first saw her in the dress.

She wanted it to be there for her. Not because she was convenient, but because she was what he wanted more than anything.

The way she wanted him.

This was a passing fancy, it had to be. Only because he was familiar and unfamiliar at the same time. There was a built-in kind of intimacy, but with all the excitement of a new chase, a new person. It would pass.

It would fade to dust long before Amanda Jane was eighteen and she'd be married to a man who wasn't married to her, not in his heart.

But there was a voice in her head that told her that if she wanted him, she should reach out and take it, the experience of him. She knew better than anyone that tomorrow wasn't guaranteed. Later wasn't always an option. Time should be spent with the same reserve or abandon as money, depending on how one looked at it.

Or maybe she was just trying to rationalize doing something wild.

"You dance well."

"Me? I'm just following your lead."

"I took lessons."

She tried to imagine Reed taking dancing lessons, comportment like some kind of Pygmalion. And it wasn't that hard to see.

Gina was instantly jealous of any of those women who'd thought they'd make him a project, change him, then claim him for their own.

Although, obviously, it hadn't worked. Because he was here with her. She wished sometimes her brain could just stop spinning, stop analyzing every breath or every sigh. She wanted to just live in the moment. For once.

Gina allowed herself to lean into him, to seek just a bit more closeness, to think about the way the lapels of the tux felt under her cheek, her fingers, the warmth of his embrace.

"Ah, the happy couple. May I cut in?" Gray asked.

She wanted to say no, but Reed handed her off. She felt the loss of his arms acutely.

"I suppose I have to go dance with Natasha Wallingford."

"You did promise and I've been amusing her all evening. Your turn," Gray said.

"Do you mind?" Reed asked her.

Yes, she minded very much. But she'd never say so. "No, go make nice. Secure your investors."

In a surprise move, Reed kissed her cheek. "That's my girl."

He'd called her his again. She wondered if he knew he was doing it, knew what it meant to her. He couldn't possibly, nor should he. That was something she should keep to herself.

Too bad Gray was as perceptive as he was.

"This really isn't about his money for you, is it?" he said, guiding her in a smooth motion across the floor.

She'd rather have his shark lawyer think she was a shark, too. Not some sad little cuttlefish looking for… whatever this was. "Of course it is. It's about my niece's future."

Gray laughed. "You can lie to everyone else. Even yourself. But I know people, Miss Townsend."

"No, you're a predator that knows prey." She didn't doubt for one minute that Gray was still sizing her up. But she couldn't be angry at him for it. He was just protecting his client and his friend. Nothing that Emma wouldn't do for her.

He laughed again. "I won't deny that. But I can see it in the way you look at him. He's always been the one for you. But your sister got him."

"Don't talk about my sister." This was territory she wasn't ready to explore. None of it was, really. But her want of Reed and her own motivations, she couldn't do this here. Her grip on her emotions was already tenuous at best.

"My apologies."

She arched a brow. "That was unexpected."

"What, that I'm not a total asshole?"

He was a great dancer, as good as Reed. His movements were precise and elegant. It was no chore to dance with him and she was suddenly grateful for all the Sundays spent in her grandmother's living room gliding around with her while she whispered the steps one-two-three-four...

"Yes," she said honestly.

"When you marry Reed, I'll be your lawyer, too. I'm not trying to hurt you. I don't want you to hurt him, if you can understand that."

"As if I could hurt him." She didn't want to think she had that power. If she did, it meant that maybe there was more beneath the surface between them. She couldn't risk it.

"You could destroy him. You could break everything he's built for himself."

"I'll do my part." His words burrowed deeper, stirring things they had no business stirring. Giving breath to ideas that were better off dormant and light to hopes better left in the dark.

"It's more than that. More than the investors. More than doing your part. You're a piece of his past. A past that he's tried to make peace with, but a reminder of who he used to be and all the bad things that went with that."

"There were good things, too." She hadn't forgotten those and she knew that he hadn't, either.

"You should tell him that."

"Why? As a member of the top of the food chain,

why would you ever suggest anyone show their weakness?"

"Is it really a weakness to tell a man that you can see how far he's come and that the past doesn't have to overshadow the future?"

When he phrased it like that, no. But when she factored in all of her feelings, her wants, it was terrifying and left her terribly vulnerable. She'd worked too hard to pull herself out of the gutter too. She just couldn't.

"Think about it."

"I'm thinking I don't like Natasha Wallingford." She watched as Reed glided with her around the floor and laughed at the things she said, the way the woman tilted herself into him.

Gray laughed. "No one does. But she owns the last piece of property that we need for this deal. Then we're taking the company public. It'll be a good thing. Both for the health and longevity of the company, and for Amanda Jane's trust."

Reed and Natasha wound their way over and up close, Gina couldn't help but notice that the woman was actually quite lovely.

"Darling," she said, addressing her directly. "I'd like to trade you, if you don't mind. This one can't stop looking at you and he's playing hell with my ego." She gave her a genuine smile.

This was at odds with the impression she'd first had of the woman and what Gray said about no one liking her didn't make sense. She was actually rather charming.

"Thank you. This one," she said, using Natasha's

phrasing, "is playing hell with my ego, too. A switch is in order."

"Delighted." Natasha grinned.

Gray shrugged and took the sharp woman in his arms.

"Really, we should do lunch. I mean, trading men warrants a cucumber sandwich or two, don't you think?"

She didn't know what to say, so she agreed. "Come to Glory. Best bakery in Kansas."

"Oh, honey, I don't eat carbs."

"You don't eat these. You experience them."

Natasha seemed intrigued. "You've got my attention. I'll have my secretary get in touch."

Reed led her away. "So you have plans with a princess and a shark. Thanks for saving me."

"Why don't you like her?"

"She's terrifying."

"Gray seems like he should be able to handle her."

"They have a history."

"I think Gray has a history with every woman. Except me.

"And Emma," she added helpfully. "I think they're going to have history."

"Glad I'm not the only one. I think it would be good for them."

"You sound like my grandmother."

"That's really not what a man wants to hear from the woman on his arm."

She laughed easily. "No, but you do know that my grandmother fancies herself some kind of matchmaker, right? She and her friends."

"Oh, obviously." He nodded with a grin. "But I understand where she's coming from. She wants the people she loves to be taken care of. And she doesn't want them to be alone."

"Alone isn't the worst thing in the world."

"That's true. But would you want that for Amanda Jane? I mean, if positions were reversed. If you were the grandmother and Amanda Jane was you?"

"I suppose I would be a bit eager." She shrugged. "But still, I think it would be interesting to see what would happen if we sic Grams on them. I bet she'd have them married, too."

"Actually, I think Emma would be really good for Gray."

"So now you want to play matchmaker?"

"Sure. Why not? It'd be a cute story to tell their kids. They met on opposite sides of the aisle in the courtroom."

"I think you're a romantic at heart," she teased.

"You didn't know that?" He didn't bother to try and hide it.

"I didn't." She found herself staring into his eyes way too long and much too earnestly.

"You haven't asked to see the house," he said, finally.

"I haven't had time. This is all happening so fast." Gina smiled at her own words. "I sound like some silly girl, don't I? Oh, Mr. Hollingsworth," she mocked herself.

"Not at all." He smiled down at her. "Would you like to?"

She thought about what it meant. This was going home with him. What would happen?

What did she want to happen?

Or maybe this was all much more innocent than she'd made it out to be. Maybe he just wanted to show her the place where she and Amanda Jane would be living.

"Yes. If we can be done here, I'll go anywhere you want me to."

He laughed. "I think Gray can handle the rest of it. No one would begrudge me leaving early to spend time with my lovely fiancée." He eyed her. "Speaking of, have you talked with Amanda Jane about this?"

"It seems my grams took care of it."

"Good. I was worried. She said something to me and I wanted to make sure we were on the same page."

"Me, too. She said you'd talked."

"I didn't believe in love at first sight until I saw her, you know. She looked up at me and that was it. I thought I'd have to get to know her, but I'd do anything for her. Do you know that?"

"I do know how that feels." She nodded and teared up. Gina hoped her makeup wasn't running down her face. "And I wanted that for her. From you."

He seemed as though he wanted to say something else, but he didn't. Instead, he pulled out his phone and called for the car.

CHAPTER THIRTEEN

REED WASN'T SURE how he was going to keep his hands off her. He liked touching her, loved having her in his arms. More men would take dancing lessons if they knew what it was like to have a woman in their arms like that.

He wanted to touch her again. Wanted to hold her. Wanted to have her pressed against him, soft and sweet.

No, if he was being totally honest, he wanted her pressed beneath him, hair splayed out behind her and her cheeks pink from— He had to stop thinking of her that way. This whole idea of marriage wasn't about their relationship. They didn't have a relationship, at least outside Amanda Jane. This wasn't fair to either of them—and especially not to his daughter. There was more at stake here than some heated attraction.

But with her close to him in the dark, the partition up between their space and the driver, it was like a little alcove. A world secret and outside their own. Especially with the way she leaned into him.

He slipped his arm around her. "Thank you for tonight."

"I didn't do anything."

"You did. You showed up. You interacted. You were

your charming self. Everyone adored you and everyone is sure this is a love match. It's just what we needed."

She patted his arm. "I'm glad."

The death knell. Patting his arm. As if he was a kid who'd done something cute. He had to stop thinking of her this way. Had to stop imagining something was there that wasn't. Or even if it was, it couldn't go anywhere. Not unless they could guarantee forever.

Not unless they could guarantee Amanda Jane forever. Sure, they were getting married, but it was a piece of paper, a business venture. If things progressed between him and Gina, there were emotional repercussions for all of them.

He took her hand anyway, liking the feel of her skin against his. "I need to buy you a ring."

"No, you don't."

"I do. Part and parcel." He wanted to see it on her finger.

"A plain gold band is fine. The best really. I'll have practicals and be washing my hands, wearing gloves…"

"When will you let me spoil you?"

"When will you believe that while this is about money, it's about money for Amanda Jane. Not me."

"I know that. I do."

"I want to begin as I intend to carry on."

"That's probably for the best." He released her hand.

"I wish I could do that."

"What?"

"Fit so easily into that world. Be so comfortable."

"You charmed Natasha."

"She said you kept looking at me. Were you worried Gray was going to make me angry?"

"Not really. I just liked looking at you," he confessed.

"I liked looking at you, too. You should wear a tux all the time."

He laughed and might have preened just a little. "If it pleases you."

"Can we really do this? Can we join our lives like this? We don't have to, you know? The judge can't demand we get married. If we work out custody and…"

"That's what Gray said. But this is really the best thing for the company and for Amanda Jane. She'll have a secure, stable household. And so will you. She'll have access to both of us anytime she wants it." He took a deep breath and asked the real question. "Would it really be so bad being married to me?"

"I'm afraid."

"The prenup is there to protect you, too."

"Not of that. Of having feelings that I shouldn't. Of being easy and convenient, not real."

He was so glad that it was about that for her, too. "You are the furthest thing from convenient, Gina." He pulled her just a little closer, and he didn't encounter any resistance. "I'm afraid of the same things. If we cross a line because we're playing house, there's more at stake than just our feelings. Marriage will keep us in the same house, but we both know what it's like when both people aren't invested."

"I would never want that for her."

"Me, either. But right now? We're both invested in her. I guess I didn't ask, but was there someone you wanted to date? Someone you have feelings for? You can tell me, Gina. I'm not going to be a dick."

No, he wouldn't be a dick, but he still anxiously waited for her answer.

"No. There's no one."

Relief swept over him. "Then we'll have our family. It'll be a different kind of family, but it will be ours." He rested his chin on the top of her head and inhaled the scent of her shampoo. "Hers."

"You said I could be honest. Right now, this feels more than platonic."

He knew he should release her. Should let go, but he couldn't. He didn't want to. And she wasn't pulling away.

"Two beautiful people alone in the dark after champagne and glittering lights? Of course it does."

Neither of them moved away and they rode together in silence until the car pulled up to the house on Knob Hill.

"We talked about this house when we were kids."

"I told you someday I'd live here." Reed had always dreamed big, even when he was lower than the gutter.

"And now you do."

"So do you," he added.

"That's going to take a while to sink in."

He held the door for her and helped her out of the car and dismissed the driver. Reed led her inside.

She looked up at the arches, eyes wide. "I never thought I'd see the inside of this house. Let alone live here."

"Do you want to see your rooms? Amanda Jane's is here," he said when he led her up the stairs.

What he really wanted was to show her his room.
His bed. The pleasure he could give her with his fingers, his mouth…his tongue. He wanted to taste her.
He wanted to watch her face as she savored the pleasure he'd give her.

He opened the door on the opposite side of the hall.
"This is yours. The furniture that's there came with the
house. You can do it up any way you like."

It wasn't just one room, it was a suite of rooms. Almost like her own apartment. There was a sitting room
area, a bedroom, a walk-in closet that was as big as their
whole trailer had been as a kid.

It even had a wet room—complete with a waterfall
wall of showers and a Roman-style bath that could hold
four people. She could practically swim in it.

There was even a small alcove off the sitting area
that had been closed off with glass doors and there was
a desk and bookshelves inside. A little office.

It was lush, extravagant.

But it had been toned down, too. She knew with his
money, he could've done so much more. He did more
where it mattered. Like the high-end computer, the latest medical references on the bookshelves… Those are
the things that mattered to her. Those were the things
that touched her.

She ran her fingers carefully over the back of the
couch in the sitting room area, but suddenly, there was
a tension in the room, a weight. They both felt it.

Gina turned to face him and almost as if they were
moving through water, they were drawn together slowly.

He liked how easily she came into his arms, the way she fit against him.

That electricity sizzled between them again and he could feel the undeniable pull of her lips.

"Do you feel it?" she asked and searched his eyes. "We're poised at the edge of something and I think I'm going to fall off the ledge."

"I've got you. I won't let you fall."

"I don't think either one of us has power over that." Her lips were parted as she took a deep, slow breath.

"Maybe not." He spoke to keep his mouth busy, instead of kissing her.

"We're trusting each other right now, aren't we?" She wet her lips.

"Yes, I think so." God, he wanted her so bad. He wanted her more than he'd ever wanted anything.

"Remember when you told me that we could tell each other things and you weren't going to 'pounce on me' just because I'd thought about something?"

"I remember." Oh, did he remember. He was so hard right now, there was no way that she didn't know it.

"I'm thinking about it now. About you kissing me. I can't stop thinking about it. I think about how good it could be."

"Are you asking me to kiss you?" He needed her to say it, had to know it was really what she wanted.

"Yes. No." She lifted her chin higher, bringing her face closer to his. "I don't know. If I wanted you to kiss me, would you?"

She was killing him ever so slowly. They were moving into dangerous territory because she was offering him everything he wanted with both hands. He wasn't naive enough to take it at face value, though. Her needs weren't to be kissed, they were to feel safe. At least at the moment. He knew that.

"That's not what you want, Gina."

"It's not? How do you know?" She lifted her chin in rebellion, but it brought her lips ever closer to his own.

"Because I've done the work on myself." He brushed his lips against her forehead. "And I know that right now, you want to feel anything else than the fear."

She leaned back to give him the perfect angle. "And we can trust each other now, right? That we can have a moment of something that just feels good with no other bullshit attached?"

"I like how you're calling relationships and expectations bullshit. But I don't think that's how you really feel."

"You know what I mean, Reed."

"I do."

And he knew better, but that didn't stop the slow arc of descent as he pressed his lips against hers. There was an undeniable magnetic polarity between them, this collision inevitable.

She tasted of sweet mint, of memory and possibility.

Gina shifted and drew him to that plain, beige couch and she straddled him. Her breath hitched in a gasp when the hard length of his erection was pressed so intimately against her.

"Still want to kiss me?" he asked, offering her a way out and half hoping she'd take it.

Reed was under no illusions that this would lead to

sex, or was anything more than momentary comfort or distraction on her part. He wouldn't let it. He didn't want there to be regrets between them. After all the times she'd cared for him, this time, he could take care of her.

"Yes. But I'm scared of this, too. When did I turn into such a coward?" Her words came in a breathy whisper.

"You're one of the bravest and strongest women I know, Gina."

She leaned down, her dark hair brushing against his cheek like silk, and pressed her lips to his. "Your kisses are as pretty as your words."

"You're killing me." He twisted his fingers in her hair. "Especially since I know that when you tell me to stop, when you're done being scared, you'll wish this hadn't happened."

She cupped his cheek. "It can't go any further than this, but this is just a kiss. A kiss never hurt anyone, right?"

It could hurt him. Because it was Gina. It was taking out the things he dreamed of in the quiet and the dark and playing with them, dressing them up and leaving them like discarded toys when they were done.

But he wouldn't tell her no.

This was what she needed and if he was being honest with himself, it was what he needed, too.

He needed a connection with someone, and he definitely had that with Gina. It was more than touch, more than desire, it was something on a deeper level. And it felt too damn good.

A creak on the stairs jerked them both back to reality and Gina retreated to the far side of the couch, breath coming in short gasps. Her lips were swollen and bee-stung, eyes heavy-lidded with desire.

For him.

They both looked for the source of the sound, and it was just the giant Maine coon cat that he'd allowed Amanda Jane to bring inside.

"That thing's a beast. I didn't know you were a cat person."

"I...not so much. Amanda Jane found him. This is supposed to be temporary until we see if anyone claims him, but I think we're his forever home."

The cat had to be twenty pounds. He stomped down the stairs, swishing his tail. And before Gina could say anything about it, he reminded her, "You didn't say no cats. You said no ponies."

She laughed. "That is what I said. What's his name?"

He shrugged. "Boris."

"He kind of looks like a Boris. He's very stern, isn't he?"

"I tried to talk her into a kitten, but she was set on him."

"It'd be easier to tell her no about things if she made more of a fuss, wouldn't it?" Gina said, straightening her skirt.

"She's so...easy to be with." He didn't know if that was actually the descriptor he wanted, but it was close.

"Yeah."

"She's a lot like you were when we were kids."

Gina cocked her head. "What do you mean?"

"You always kept your head down. You never asked for things unless you really needed them. You tried not to be a drain on anyone. Helped where you could, never got in trouble. And really, you never got to have a childhood."

Gina flushed. "I didn't want that for her."

"I'm not saying you've done a bad job with her. I think maybe little girls with big brains see things much too clearly before they should have to, regardless of their circumstances."

"Maybe you're right." Gina bit her lip.

All he could think about now was kissing her again, but the moment had passed and it would be easier on everyone if they didn't speak of it.

His dick wouldn't be forgetting it any time soon, though.

"So, what happened…"

"We don't have to talk about it. I assumed you didn't want to." He didn't think he could stand another round of telling him he wasn't what she wanted.

"I shouldn't have put that on you."

"Put what on me?"

"My…peace of mind." She nodded slowly as if she'd just realized that was what it was. "That's on me to find for myself. I shouldn't have to crawl in your lap and beg you to kiss me just to get my head straight."

"I'll kiss you anytime you want me to, Gina." Damn it, why had he said that? If she took him at his word, he'd just be opening himself up for more feelings he didn't want. He'd be her go-to, her crutch, and when she found herself and fell in love with someone else, he'd be left with a lot of lonely nights, fantasy and memories of kisses that were never his.

She blushed. "You like kissing me?"

"That's a stupid question."

"I like kissing you, too. So we probably shouldn't do it, right?" The earlier heat between them had faded and all they were left with <u>was</u> the consequences of their actions.

But Reed was sure the scorch marks would never fade. "Probably not. Are you still good with the movers coming this weekend?" Talk about banality, everyday little things that were nothing compared to that kiss.

Or he was going to take her to bed, the consequences be damned.

"Yeah." She bit her lip. "So, when do you want to do this wedding thing?"

This wedding thing. That was exactly why this could go no further. "This week, if it suits you."

"My grams wants to do a big thing, but I'd rather just…I'd rather save that, if you know what I mean."

He did. He knew exactly what she meant. She wanted to save the pomp and circumstance for when it mattered. Not that he thought he didn't matter or this didn't matter, but this marriage was a business arrangement. A familial arrangement. It wasn't about what weddings were supposed to be about.

It cut him, even though he knew it really shouldn't. This wasn't about them, not really.

"I understand."

"I care about you," she whispered, seemingly trying to dull the blow she'd dealt him.

"I care about you, too." He knew she wasn't trying to hurt him, but just as he'd predicted, even only kissing her had demanded its price.

"I should go."

"I think that's probably best." Because he couldn't stop thinking about her, thinking about that kiss and wanting so much more than they'd been given. "I'll call you a cab."

"I'll walk to Grams's. The night air will do me good."

"I feel like I should protest, but this is Glory."

"Yeah, I'll probably have Caleb or Judd on me in a second stuffing me in the back of a car or insisting on walking me, anyway."

"That's not what I'm supposed to do here, right? Insist on walking you home? It'd be the gentlemanly thing to do, but I'm pretty sure you're a grown woman who can decide when and where she wants to go."

"No." She laughed. "It's not a trick or a test. I do know exactly where I want to go."

"At least text me when you get home so I know you got there safely? If you don't text me in an hour, I'm coming looking for you with guns blazing, sweetheart."

She laughed again, the sound musical. "Okay. If you insist." Gina paused at the door. "You should know, my grandmother would love that."

"Wait a sec." He grabbed his keys and took the extra key to the house off the ring. He pressed it into her palm and closed her fingers around it. "This is yours."

She bit her lip, as if chewing over something she wanted to say, but wasn't sure if she should. Then she blurted, "You should know...this key? It means more to me than any conglomeration of metal and jewels you could put on my finger."

"I know." He still had a hold of her hand. "So let me buy you the ring, anyway."

"When you put it that way, I guess it's okay."

"You might be the only woman who has ever said no to diamonds."

"Just a band, remember? Practicals."

"Right. Just a band, then." He didn't want to let go of her hand, but he did and he watched her walk through the door without looking back.

CHAPTER FOURTEEN

THAT WAS A DAMN LIE, to be sure.

Gina had no idea where she wanted to go. No, that was a lie, too. She knew where she wanted to go, but she also knew that it was wrong. Some big fancy wedding to Reed, all to feed her fantasy? No. She'd buy the dress, she'd do the whole thing when she was getting forever.

Gina definitely shouldn't have kissed him again.

She blushed just remembering making out with him on that sofa, straddling his lap. The hard evidence of his desire so obvious.

Her face, and all sorts of other places, flamed when she thought about it. She couldn't believe how...wanton she'd been. That was an old word, outdated and applied to hellions with flaming red hair on the back of frothy horses. Not plain old Gina Townsend. Yet, it was the only thing that came to mind. She'd demanded he kiss her, clung to him, rubbed herself all over him.

And it had been so good.

His touch made her wheels stop turning so furiously, it centered her. Being near Reed grounded her, until she started thinking of him as a man—a handsome, virile man, and then it launched her off into the stratosphere, but in a good way. She couldn't explain it and sounded like a lunatic, even to herself, when she tried.

The night air wasn't exactly cool, but it was enough to push the heat from her face.

She took her shoes off and walked barefooted toward Grams's. Gina needed the time to think. To process. Or maybe she needed the space between her and everyone else. Walking at this time of night, there was a certain freedom there. She didn't have to go back to the real world yet. She could remember what it was like to be in his arms. To spin around on a cloud… It was okay here to think about that kiss, to think about what things might have been like.

Only it wasn't.

Without the bad times, he wouldn't be the man he'd become. So she couldn't have any regrets.

Her steps slowed as she approached the warm light spilling from Grams's windows. Inside that house was still a haven, but it was in the real world nonetheless. With Amanda Jane. Inside, she had to think about what that kiss would mean not just for Gina, but for Amanda Jane, too.

She wanted this moment to herself just a little bit longer. Then she'd go inside and snuggle up to her niece where she slept in Gina's father's old bedroom.

But Helga Gunderson opened the door. "Well, are you going to stand out there mooning all night or are you going to come in? My old bones need to go to bed."

Gina laughed. "I'm coming in, ma'am."

Once she was inside, she put her shoes down on the chair.

"I see you didn't lose a shoe," her grandmother said. "I haven't decided if that's a good thing or a bad thing."

"I say let the girl decide."

"I suppose." Maudine sniffed.

"Well, are you going to tell us or what?" Helga was impatient.

"It was just a charity thing. He asked and I went because we're, you know, getting married."

"Yes. About that." Helga nodded. "This is agreeable to you? I know you signed the prenup, but I want to know if this is really what you want to do."

A way out. She should've known that Helga wouldn't push her to do something that she didn't want to do even if she thought it was best for her. A tension she didn't know she'd been carrying was leached out of her.

"Helga," Maudine began.

"Hush, you meddlesome woman. I'm talking to Grandbaby now."

Maudine crossed her arms over her chest and harrumphed.

Helga, when she wasn't being official, always called her Grandbaby. As if that was her name. She found it strangely endearing.

"Yes. I'll say Grams was right about this and so were you." She eyed her grandmother. "Don't let that go to your head." She sighed. "But it is the best way to give Amanda Jane stability and security. Reed isn't… He's…" She looked for the word to best describe him.

"He wasn't a bad kid, even though he got involved with a bad crowd," Helga said helpfully.

"He really is a good man. I think it's obvious by

the way he's willing to do anything for Amanda Jane. Anything for me to feel safe about this, even though I think it hurts him."

"So if I said to be in my chambers tomorrow at four, we could proceed." Helga eyed her carefully.

The question hit her like a brick—hard. It numbed her for a moment, but she knew she'd feel something else when that numbness faded.

"We'd talked about proceeding, so I don't see why not. Yes."

"Good. Let the groom know. Now I can go to bed."

She picked up her phone and texted him.

Wanna get married tomorrow?

Her phone buzzed with his reply. I'll be there.

Judge's chambers. Four.

See you soon. Glad you got to Grams's okay.

This time tomorrow, Reed Hollingsworth would be her husband.

"You don't even have a dress. Come up to the attic with me."

She followed Grams up to the attic while Helga showed herself out. There, draped over a dress form, was a simple, flowing white dress. The only decoration was the pearls sewn like a crown into the empire waist.

"Grams, I…"

"Yes, you can. And you will. This is your dress and

it will be Amanda Jane's. Just as it was mine, and your mother's. Maybe you're not marrying Reed because you're in love with him, but this is a big thing. You should have your family with you. This way, we can all be with you. Even your mother."

Her nose prickled and her eyes watered and she found herself at a loss for words.

"You'll at least let me do your hair?"

She nodded. "Whatever you want."

"Good. Because we bought a dress for Amanda Jane, too."

Gina laughed. "Of course you did."

"I also gave your notice for you when Reed asked me to call in for you." She said this as if she was simply adding something to the grocery list.

"Grams!"

"Shannie at Bullhorn said it was about time you quit and wishes you the best. And the city, well, they weren't as thrilled. But in a few years, those guys will be bringing patients to you."

If she was honest with herself, she was glad her grandmother had done it for her. She didn't want to leave the family she'd found at the Bullhorn or her job as an EMT. But something had to give and those two things were it. She'd be more available to her niece, and again being honest, she'd be more available to herself. She'd be able to study, to do all the things she needed to do without burning the candle at both ends.

Well, most days, anyway.

"Since Amanda Jane is already asleep, why don't you stay here tonight?"

"Okay, Grams. But only if you make us waffles for breakfast."

"Always with the bribing," she teased. "Of course I'll make you waffles, silly girl." Grams hugged her.

"I love you, Grams."

"I love you, too, sweetface."

"Want to watch some old movies and eat popcorn?"

"I certainly do."

Gina changed into the pair of jammies she had in her old room, careful not to wake Amanda Jane. Then she crawled into her grams's big bed and accepted the giant melamine bowl of popcorn.

"This is a rather tame bachelorette party, but I think it's good." Grams crawled in next to her, complete with bunny slippers and hair in rollers.

"Just like when I was little." When things got too tough at home, when she was too tired to deal with it all, she would come to Grams's. Here was where she got to be a child. Here was where it was safe. Here was where she'd gotten her sense of self and the steel in her spine, but only because this was where she didn't need it.

"Everything is going to change tomorrow, honey. And it's okay. It's supposed to."

"I don't want to think about that." Because it was all she had been thinking about.

"No one will ever be able to take Amanda Jane away from you. Or Reed. Or your future."

She leaned over. "I'm still scared."

"There's nothing to be afraid of. You've been a grown-up for a long time. Longer than you should've had to have been."

"Maybe not. I've always leaned on you and now it's like…I don't know. The buck could still stop with you. But now it stops with me."

"I'm always here for you if you need me."

"Why did you pick Reed?" She wondered what had sparked her grams's absolute faith in the man she hadn't seen in years. Why had she picked him for Gina?

"I didn't. You did."

"When I was twelve," she snorted.

"Sometimes, the heart knows what it knows."

"You've got some interesting ideas, Gram."

"Helga thinks so, too. Now that we've got you settled, Helga and I think we should start on Marie. You know that boy Johnny Hart?"

"Yes, Grams. I know him." He was the one who'd fixed Reed's car on a weekend for a plate of Bullhorn.

"His mother. Who do you think would be a good match for her? You're going to be a married woman and that entitles you to some input into The Grandmothers."

She laughed. "No rest for the wicked?"

"Never," Maudine declared.

"I don't know. Marie is very sweet, but very traditional."

"I think she needs something to shake her up. What about that lawyer?"

"Oh, lord, Grams. Gray? No. Plus, I'd kind of like to see him with Emma."

"You're a natural," Maudine cackled, sounding a bit like a wicked witch. "Think about Marie. I need to get in some more trouble. It keeps me young."

"I think maybe it does. I was just threatening to sic you on him."

"Oh, really? And what does your future husband think of that?" Maudine cocked her head to the side. "Not that he gets a say, but…"

"He thought it was a good idea."

"I knew I liked him. Now let's watch this movie and pretend we're sniffling for the characters and not ourselves."

WHEN IT WAS TIME for Gina to get ready to go to the courthouse the next day, she seriously considered climbing down the portcullis and running away.

What if she'd made the wrong decision?

What if by doing this, she was letting Amanda Jane in for more heartache? It was all fun and good times right now, but what about later? What about if Reed changed his mind about being a parent?

She didn't have control over that.

The only things she could control were her own actions, and the only way to protect Amanda Jane from that was to have never allowed him back in her life to begin with.

And it was too late for that.

Her mother used to say sometimes you've wandered so far into the forest that you couldn't turn around. The only way was through.

She guessed that this situation was like that. She just had to push through, see it through. And with Amanda Jane's hand in hers, she'd walk through any forest, any mountain, any fire.

The little girl was dressed in pink, with matching shoes that clicked on the hardwood floor when she walked. Which was one of her favorite things to do.

She clicked and clacked merrily up and down the hallway while Grams and Emma fussed over Gina, painted her face and curled her hair.

She wondered if it was much the same for Reed, minus the makeup and hair curling. Gina tried to imagine Gray fussing over him and it just didn't present a very believable picture.

Knots twisted in her belly.

"Don't be nervous, Gina-bee. It's just Daddy."

Just Daddy. Yeah. Sometimes that little girl was so spot-on with her observations. "I'm not nervous," she fibbed.

Emma cocked a brow. "Then why are you pacing? You've been ready for ten minutes."

"I don't want to be early."

"You don't want to be late, either. It's not too late. I can still drive you to the movies instead." Emma grinned.

"No, I want to do this."

"Then let's get to doing it."

The ride over was quick; she could've walked. But no one would hear of it.

When they arrived, she was surprised to see a small crush of news vans and when they saw her, they darted for her, but Glory's finest was on point, keeping them from access.

She hadn't expected that.

"He is a billionaire, Gina. Did you forget?"

"Maybe." She sucked in a deep breath.

"Everyone wants to know who captured him. The sweet girl from his misspent youth and that's how they'll play it. That's how you should, too."

"Like he's some kind of exotic animal? He's a person."

"Yeah, good thing you see that. A lot of those people don't. Remember that."

When the small chamber doors closed behind her, she saw Reed. He was wearing a tux again, this time with a rose pinned to his lapel, and he was holding a single bloom, which he offered to her.

For some reason, she wanted to cry. She didn't know if they were happy tears, sad tears or a bittersweet mix. She was wearing her mother's dress, marrying the man she used to dream about, and indeed, she could feel the warmth of her family around her. Her mother, even her sister… It touched her grief too intimately, but it shored her up, as well. It was such a strange feeling.

Helga was wearing the robes and doily again, and her stern face was in place, almost like a mask.

She knew the woman spoke, but it was as if there was a kind of disconnect between her ears and her brain. Between her brain and everything, in fact, but the man who stood next to her. He was so confident and serene. So totally sure of himself.

Gina wondered if she were the only one who was afraid, whose knees were jelly and whose insides were all twisted up.

She wondered if he felt any of the same doubts, fears and hopes as she did.

This was nothing like how she'd imagined getting

married, but it was okay. It wasn't a real marriage. It was a just a contract. A simple piece of paper that bound them together for the sake of Amanda Jane.

That was how she had to think of it. Otherwise, it would break her heart. She'd dreamed of more for herself.

But maybe this was enough for now. It was enough to know that Amanda Jane would be cared for. Enough to know that she'd have two loving parents. She deserved that.

She was determined not to start this new chapter in her life with doubt and fear in the forefront of her mind. Gina had to remind herself it was okay to be hopeful, it was okay—vital even—to find something to be happy about.

Gina took a deep breath and looked up at this man with whom she'd entered into this contract. It was the right thing.

So that made it a good thing, right?

When he descended for the obligatory kiss, any thought she had of denying him or presenting her cheek fled. This was her husband—for better, for worse. For pretend and for real.

When their mouths met, even for just the casual brush of lips, sparks ignited and exploded into something more.

"For a second there, I thought you were going to say no," he whispered.

"I'm here. It's done. It's real," she said, more to herself than to anyone else.

"Are you ready to meet the press, Mrs. Hollingsworth?"

"I am," Amanda Jane piped up. "I have on my prettiest dress and my clackiest shoes."

It was utterly surreal and Gina would be glad when things returned to normal. Or perhaps better to say, when they found normal.

She wondered if this was how the princess and the ranger felt, with cameras and microphones shoved in their faces.

Gina wasn't prepared for this part. There'd been a bit of it at the fund-raiser event, but it hadn't been this crass, this…immediate. She wanted to hide Amanda Jane. Wanted to keep her from them, but she chattered happily and showed them her shiny shoes and her dress.

She managed to smile and wave, but was utterly grateful when Gray stepped forward.

"See, this is why we have him," Reed whispered in her ear.

"That's enough questions for the happy couple. They're leaving on their honeymoon and I'm sure you don't want to disturb them."

They took that as their cue to exit and while there were some who tried to question them on the way to the car, it was simply a matter of ignoring them until they were secured in the limo.

"Where are we going on our moon-honey?" Amanda Jane asked, crawling into the car.

"You mean a honeymoon?" Gina asked.

"Grams said something about sweet mooning."

Reed grinned. "Well, that's something that people

do when they get married. They don't generally take Amanda Janes with them."

"Oh." She seemed to consider this for a moment. "If you promise to take me to Sippin' Cider Days when you get back, you can go without me."

"We don't want to go anywhere without you," Gina rushed to reassure her.

"Isn't that what mommy and daddies do?"

"Sometimes. But we do what we want to do, how we want to do it." Reed fielded the question deftly.

Gina had to admit, he'd gotten good at this. He'd taken to it so easily.

"But it's okay to want to do it like everyone else, too, right?"

She couldn't help but be pleased that she'd stumped him with that one. "I suppose it is. Only if you can balance fitting in with good sense."

"Good sense," Amanda Jane repeated like a mantra.

"I thought we'd stay home for our mooning honey. Have a sleepover with popcorn?"

"And unicorns?" she asked doubtfully.

"Unicorns can come." Reed shrugged.

"I mean, can we watch the unicorn movie?"

"Whatever you want."

"Okay. But I still want to go to Sippin' Cider Days."

"We'll go to all the days," Reed promised her.

She sat back against the seat and curled one hand into Reed's and one into Gina's and swung her legs contentedly.

CHAPTER FIFTEEN

WAKING UP WITH nowhere in particular to be on a Saturday was foreign to Gina. She felt as though there had to be something to do. There was some minor unpacking, but she'd put most of her things in storage and had donated the rest.

She liked that they'd spent their first few nights together as a family unit, focused on Amanda Jane. That was how it should be. That's why they'd done all of this—for her. So it was only right that their time together be about the child and not about the heat between them.

It was a relief actually, to not be afraid of pouncing on him like some sort of rabid animal in heat.

The best part was that Amanda Jane seemed to have settled in with no problem at all.

A small face peeked up over the edge of her bed, interrupting her thoughts. "Wanna go on a picnic?"

Amanda Jane was already dressed and had an empty picnic basket at the ready.

Gina was kind of enjoying not having to move anything, but it was nice to be able to tell her niece yes instead of telling her that she had to work, she had to rest or she had to study.

"Yes."

"I'll get Daddy."

For all of her constant thinking about him, she'd forgotten that he was now a part of everything that Amanda Jane did or wanted to do. She kind of missed the one-on-one time, but she supposed that having a dad was something Amanda Jane was still getting used to and enjoying.

"Okay. Let me brush my teeth and get dressed."

After getting ready in a pair of shorts, a T-shirt and trainers, she went downstairs to find Reed and Amanda Jane waiting for her.

Reed was wearing a pair of jeans that should in no way ever be legal on a man. They reminded her of things that she shouldn't be thinking about—like just what exactly was under that zipper.

Above the waist wasn't any safer. He was wearing another of those damn shirts with the guy on the horse stitched on the chest. The way it accentuated his shoulders, it just wasn't fair.

"Hey, sunshine. You ready to go?" He cocked his head to the side.

"I didn't know we'd decided where we were going?"

"I thought we'd take the new walking trails and go downtown. Maybe take Amanda Jane to the carousel museum and eat by the river?"

"That sounds really nice."

"I'll make the picnic," Amanda Jane volunteered.

"I'll help," Gina offered.

"No, no. No help. We're going to celebrate. I made

She tried not to think about the fact that she'd been picking up sticks and rocks and…Gina leaned back in the grass again.

"I kind of like this grass-angel thing," Gina said.

"Me, too."

"Thanks for taking a day off."

"I work when I need to. I didn't come through all of this to not live the life I fought for, you know?"

"Yeah, I think I'm just learning that. When I woke up this morning, it was so weird not to have anywhere to be. I felt out of place."

"I think a donut will make it feel all better."

"Is that your official course of treatment?" Gina teased him.

"You're going to be the doctor, you tell me."

"Probably not."

"Fine. Then, as a risk/reward scenario, invest in the donut. It will pay out in bliss."

She laughed and he pushed a donut toward her. Gina struggled and turned her head, trying to get away from him, but the moment the sweet bread touched her lips, she opened for him.

His fingers grazed her lips as he pushed the bite inside and Gina nipped at his fingertips before she could think better of it.

The intensity on his face was suddenly dark and heavy, and it made her squirm. She didn't want to feel this way, but she didn't want to fight it anymore, either.

If she could just let go, maybe this happiness, it would stay. For all of them.

After the donuts had been ravaged, and Amanda Jane

took their trash to the bin, Gina saw a look on her face that cut her to the core.

She was crying.

Gina rushed to her and guided her back to the blanket. "What's wrong, honey? Did you hurt yourself?"

Reed reached out for her and she wound her small arms around his neck.

Gina watched as Reed's expression melted through a series of emotions. Concern, sadness and then something else she couldn't name. He closed his eyes and rocked the girl in his lap.

She leaned in and rubbed her hand down Amanda Jane's back in a soothing motion.

"I just don't want this to end. This is perfect. Please don't go away."

Her words cut Gina more deeply than her tears had.

They couldn't afford to screw this up.

"I'm not going anywhere," Reed swore.

"Do you promise?"

"To the moon and stars, kiddo."

Gina just hoped he would keep it.

CHAPTER SIXTEEN

GINA WAS RELIEVED when things fell into a routine.

When Reed came home, everyone made dinner together. He had a personal chef in the city, but the very idea made Gina uncomfortable. In the beginning, she'd starting preparing meals, easily falling into the caregiver role. But Reed liked helping and so did Amanda Jane. It had become one of their family rituals. Gina liked it because there was no pressure. They'd tried a few new things and when it didn't work out, it wasn't a big deal. They'd throw it out and order takeout.

Their rituals, just like their definition of family, were all their own.

And as before, nothing else had been said about the spark between them. Amanda Jane's fears about losing them, losing this new dynamic that had blossomed between all of them, trumped whatever she and Reed might want personally. That was something that didn't even have to be discussed.

She wondered if it was the universe trying to tell her that they didn't belong together. It seemed as if every time something happened between them, Gina was reminded why it shouldn't.

But that didn't stop her from daydreaming about him just as she had when she was a stupid teenager.

Now, her daydreams were twelve years into the future with Amanda Jane off to college and then whatever happened between them could sink or swim and it wouldn't affect her development and sense of stability.

The thought of never being touched or loved by a man until then was hollow and cold, but thinking of letting any man but Reed touch her was worse.

She was a wreck in her head, but on the outside, she'd managed to keep it together.

At least until Missy wanted to take Amanda Jane for the night to give them a break.

Gina didn't need a break. She didn't want to be alone in the house with Reed because she knew exactly where her mind would go and her flesh would follow. She'd end up in his bed—and she was afraid of it, not just because of what it could mean for the future, but what it meant in the now.

Reed found her in the downstairs living room after Missy had picked up Amanda Jane. "Hey, so we're free tonight. I think we're supposed to be excited about it and go see an R-rated movie or something."

She grinned. "I kind of liked watching cartoons."

"Me, too."

"This is still pretty weird," she blurted.

"Yeah, for me, too." He nodded. "It's almost like Mom's gone so we should get in trouble or something. But I don't need any trouble."

"Me, either," she agreed, but wondered if they were

talking about the pretend scenario with the cat away and the mice will play, or something deeper.

"So we've agreed not to get in trouble. How about dinner and some TV?"

"Yeah, I think we can swing that. Maybe we could get a little wild and order Chinese?"

"We're partying hard there." The corner of his mouth turned up in a grin. "You know, that's really all I wanted when I was a kid."

"Right now? Today?" She nodded. "Yeah. It's hard to believe that something like this is what we dreamed of. Most kids have way cooler dreams than that. Even Amanda Jane wanted a pony."

"I really think we should revisit that."

"A pony? Are you kidding me?"

He shrugged. "Why not?"

"You've been set on this since day one. Did you want a pony?" she teased.

"No, but you did."

"Of course I did. All little girls want a horse or a pony. I think it's hardwired into the gender." She laughed.

"And we can give that to her. It may be extravagant for other people, but it's not for us. It would teach her responsibility if she had to care for it herself, clean its stall, put out hay. Lessons would be something that would get her involved with other kids and when she's a teenager, she'll be more interested in animals than boys. Where's the downside?"

"I don't know. It just seems…like you said, extravagant. But I guess it's really not when you say it like that. I can't help but think of Nora Rochette, remember her? She always wore designer clothes, fake-baked and was always going on and on about her stupid horse."

"Nora Rochette wouldn't have given me the time of day, not even to tell me to eat shit and die, back then."

"She only talked to me because I was on her SAT/ACT study team. I think she married some congressman."

"Better him than me." Reed shuddered.

"So did I just agree to a pony?"

"Sort of. But you for sure agreed to takeout and a movie. Or maybe a few episodes of a new series."

"A series? That's practically a relationship. I mean, we'd be committed to the whole thing once we start," she teased, and realized she meant more than just watching television.

"Kind of like where we're at now, huh?"

He was right. "I guess so. Only if we don't finish a series, it's not a matter of life and death."

"I think it depends on the fandom, my dear."

She laughed again. That's what she liked best about this version of Reed. He made her laugh all the time. "Okay. Let me get into something more comfortable." Gina waggled her eyebrows, teasing him.

"I'm pretty sure that your idea of something more comfortable and mine are vastly different animals."

What she liked best about this banter was that even though there'd been some seriously hot tension between them, this was all in good fun and there was no pressure here. It was as if they were just Reed and Gina, pals, the way it used to be.

"See, we get left alone and we get in trouble." He shrugged as if he just couldn't help himself.

"You mean like this?" She poked him in the side.

"Oh, really?" He grabbed her, but he didn't tickle her. Instead, he froze and they were trapped in the moment.

That easy banter disappeared and she'd been wrong for ever thinking they could be just Reed and Gina. Just pals. Because she would always want more from him.

She lifted her lashes and stared into the pools of his eyes. Gina wanted to drown in them, drown in him. She imagined it would be like submerging herself in water, that cool embrace as she was rocked gently down to the bottom. The insulation from the world above where every sound, every sight, every sensation was dulled by the bliss of the deep.

His arms came around her and it was anything but cool and peaceful. He was so strong, so warm and vital, that she melted and burned, her insides languid. But her emotions were a roiling volcano and her pain, her need, it was all hot lava.

For the first time, Gina didn't feel that she had to do everything on her own. She didn't have to stand tall and hard against the world, she could lean just a little bit.

Guilt surged for liking the way his hands felt on her, the masculine scent of his expensive aftershave and the illusion of safety in his arms. She'd never had this before and she wanted it.

Gina wanted it more than easing the guilt she had about Crys, more than she wanted to guard her heart against Reed and the inevitable shattering of the thing—

more than anything she wanted this moment between them to last forever.

Although she knew nothing could last forever. Not the sating of flesh, or daydreams made real, or the solid, concrete support he offered. It was all a moment's blush, and like any exotic bloom, would wither and die.

Cold guilt made another splash down her back.

"It's okay, Gina. Everything that you're feeling is okay."

"You don't know what I'm feeling. How can you tell me it's okay?" She pulled back and looked up at him, their lips only a breath apart.

"You're feeling relief, sorrow, guilt…"

His voice seemed to touch each emotion, causing it to ring through her like a bell. But he didn't come close to the one feeling that elicited the most guilt and shame—the need for his hands on her body, the way she was tempted to close that space between them and taste his lips again, the way she just wanted to drown in him and forget everything.

Because part of living was experiencing life and she wanted to experience Reed Hollingsworth to the fullest. He was something she'd always wanted and the thought of being so close, but never really knowing him, touching him, she didn't want that regret.

When it was her turn to face the long dark, she didn't want to be thinking about all the things she wanted to do, all the experiences she wanted to have and find she'd missed them all.

But every time she thought she could turn her face that fraction of an inch, she thought about Crys again.

It was a poignant image that she had of her sister, if not a bit melodramatic: her hair spread about behind her like a halo…

Yet, that image made her sister into someone she wasn't. Being close to death didn't absolve all of her sins as much as anyone might wish it would. While it wasn't Gina's place to judge her, that little voice in her head told her—no, screamed at her to reach out and grab at life with both hands because this tableau could easily be herself.

All manner of situations, fractions of a second, those things could easily change her very ordered life to one of chaos and loss. She couldn't control everything, so why not surrender? Why not just once reach out and grab hold of something dangerous just because she wanted it?

"Gina," he said again, but this time, it was most definitely a plea.

A plea for what, she didn't know. A plea for her to stop, or a plea for more? She'd tangled her arms around his neck, and climbed into his lap like she had before— when they'd kissed.

She'd been so lost in "should" and "could" that her body had made the choice for her and she wasn't inclined to argue. Not now, when she felt so lost in the dark. His touch was a candle, a guide home.

"Please don't tell me no."

"You're vulnerable. I don't want to be what you regret." He whispered against her mouth, his breath ghosting across her lips in the mockery of a kiss.

"I am vulnerable, Reed. I'm so alone. I always have

been. And I'm tired of being someone—something—apart from the rest of the world. Give me this." She brushed her lips across the blade of his cheek. "Give me *you*."

His hand fisted in her hair and he tugged her back so that she was forced to look into his eyes. She would've fought, she didn't want to have to look at him if he was still going to tell her no.

"You've always had me, Gina. You don't have to do this to keep me. I'm not going to leave you, and I'm not going to fail you. I swear."

The intensity of his words made his declaration something more than he meant it to be. She knew he tried to reassure her, to wind down whatever had sprung so tight and ready inside of her. But it only wound her tighter, amped her need.

"When you look at me like that, Gina, I want to give you everything. Even when I know what you want isn't what you need." His voice was low, like the crunch of gravel.

His lips were so close, so perfect, and they were what was going to save her.

"I can decide what I need."

He tilted his face up a fraction of an inch, just enough so that their lips barely touched. "What about what *I* need?"

"What do you need?" Electric jolts shuddered under her skin at the contact, insides alight.

"To know I won't be a mistake. That you want more from me than this moment."

It would be so easy to tell him that she wanted forever, but did she? No, she wanted right now and she didn't want to think about forever. Forever was terrifying, forever was a chain around her neck.

"I need you." She didn't make him any promises, she couldn't.

He searched her eyes for a long moment and Gina could tell the instant he made his decision. The cornflower blue of his eyes was suddenly dark like the Kansas sky before it raged with a storm and the change had come over him just as quickly as the clouds rolled in off the prairie.

She gasped when he pushed her down on the couch and she found herself beneath him, his hard body weighing her down, grounding her.

Gina loved the feel of him, that weight of him that made it all so real. It anchored the sensations in her mind, reminded her that this was no fantasy. That she took what she wanted in the here and now—this was no dream.

She was going to lose her virginity to Reed Hollingsworth on a couch in his living room.

No, *their* living room.

God, she just wanted to shut her brain off. She didn't want to think about all the minutiae. For once, she wanted to feel and experience. She could analyze it to death later. Gina prayed to anyone who would listen that he didn't stop, didn't ask her if she was sure. Because then she'd have to think about the question and in turn, her answer.

All the reasons why she shouldn't and the singular reason why she should—because he was what she wanted.

The two things in life she'd ever dared let herself want—being a doctor and Reed Hollingsworth.

Before the part of her brain that made her always choose the safe path could kick in, before it could tell her that she could only have one or the other—Reed or a career—that she wasn't the girl who got everything she wanted, she hooked her legs around his hips and clung to him.

Being with him this way drowned out all those voices, forced them into compliance. Or maybe not even that…maybe it was simply that his touch caused her heart to pound so loudly, that was all she could hear inside her head.

She pulled his shirt up over his shoulders, her touch gliding over the hard planes of his back as she went. Gina was lost in the taste of him, the force of his kiss, his hand sliding up beneath the hem of her T-shirt to cup her breast.

If she thought his kiss was intense, his fingers were even more so. They moved over her flesh in turns as if she was some work of art he was committing to memory, using his hands as his eyes.

The friction between her thighs, the way he pressed into her and she arched up against him, it did nothing to assuage the ache. It only made her burn hotter.

She'd wondered why people did so many stupid things for that connection, a joining of flesh that was as simple as Tab A into Slot B. In her head, it had always been something clinical—a body function like any other. But now she understood. Gina would do anything to feel this with him.

It was as if her flesh wasn't her own, it was his. He was a dark master, moving her for their pleasure.

While she loved his kiss, there was something forbidden about looking into his eyes while he touched her. It was a trespass, but it was a bond, too. His fingers flicking over her rosebud nipple, eyes focused on her face watching her desire.

And it didn't occur to her to hide it from him.

In fact, she wanted to be even more exposed. She shifted so that he could peel her shirt from her and then he unsnapped her bra with one quick motion of his fingers.

"Christ, you're beautiful," he murmured and dipped his head to follow the path of his hands. "Perfect and soft, just like I knew you would be."

Reed knelt to the floor, peeling her jeans down her hips, and she shivered, not exactly afraid, but need warred with anticipation.

"I'm going to taste you."

He wasn't asking, but she wouldn't say no. Reed positioned her so that he could divest her of her panties, and hooked one thigh up over his shoulder.

She bit her lip, breath caught in her throat.

Then his hot mouth closed over her. She arched up off the couch, a sharp sound of delight torn from her. His hands anchored her hips and she thrust up to meet the caress.

Gina tilted her head so that she could see his face and his eyes were open, and their gazes held while his tongue pressed in wicked motions against her. Something built deep in her belly, something that managed to be both sharp and languid at the same time. It was hot, and smooth, like whiskey, but was something more than fire.

Reed's mouth moved over her, driving her higher and pushing her past all boundaries of bliss she'd ever known. That tension burst into pleasure and as the aftershocks rocked her body, he pulled away.

"Reed," she breathed.

He didn't speak, didn't ask her the question that hung between them. Instead, he kissed her forehead and went upstairs alone.

CHAPTER SEVENTEEN

REED SAT ON the edge of his bed, contemplating what had just happened.

Or what hadn't.

He'd been offered everything he wanted on a silver platter and he'd pushed it away with both hands.

No, that wasn't true. It wasn't everything he'd wanted. It was almost everything he wanted. He didn't want to be a mistake and he didn't want to be a throwaway ever again.

His cock throbbed and there was a part of him that rebelled at the thought of passing up a night of passion with Gina. He ached to bury himself into her sweet sheath.

God, when he thought about the way she'd arched under his tongue and fingers, the pretty little sounds she made when she was begging him for more, he wanted to give her everything and more.

But he had a feeling that he'd be trading one addiction for another. He'd never have enough of Gina and when she was done with him, it would break him and he didn't know if there'd be any fixing himself this time.

His door creaked open and Gina stood there, hair wild, cheeks flushed and only a T-shirt and panties.

His mouth went dry.

"What the hell was that, Reed?" she demanded.

He licked his lips, tasted her and closed his eyes. He couldn't tell her no again. Reed had been so sure she'd just let this go. She wouldn't push, but she did. She was there, standing half-naked in his doorway.

"I told you, I don't want—I can't—be a one-night stand."

"Don't you want me?" she asked, her voice small.

"Of course, I want you. I've always wanted you. Don't you understand?"

She walked toward him slowly, and it was like watching his own doom—beautiful and elegant—wash over him in a wave. Gina put her hands on his shoulders and brought him close to her.

"Then take me."

"No."

It was as if he hadn't spoken. She pushed her hands through his hair and then sank to her knees to look into his eyes. Gina leaned ever closer until she brushed her lips against his.

"Yes," she said. "For both of us."

He didn't want to resist her, because in his heart, he still didn't believe he deserved what he wanted. That voice in his head that knew him best told him that he should take what she offered because holding out hope for more was reaching too high. This was as close as he'd ever get.

His fingers dug into her back, pulled her closer. Tighter. As if he could anchor her there in the moment and keep her forever.

It had been so long since he'd been with someone—years. He'd vowed not to be with a woman he wouldn't marry, that he didn't want to spend his life with. But that was the problem. He wanted Gina more than he'd ever wanted anything.

And here she was, offering herself to him. Asking him to be her first.

But not her only.

Yet, he failed to find the will to push her away. He dragged her onto the bed and she unfurled beneath him like some exotic flower, legs around his waist, hair spread out behind her.

She was the most beautiful thing he'd ever seen.

"I don't have any protection," he whispered. Reed hadn't planned on having any reason to keep anything in the house.

"I've been on the depo shot to lighten my cycle forever."

"There's more to consider than that." He searched her eyes.

"I know." She licked her lips. "You've been tested, right?"

"Yes."

She kissed him, pulling him down closer. "Then make love to me."

And that's what he was doing. He was making love to her. This wasn't a fuck. This wasn't a one-off, a quick culmination of a physical need. It was something more.

Somehow, he was naked. He hadn't noticed her hands, or his body's response. All he knew was that he poised at the edge of heaven.

Gina reached up and cupped his cheek with her palm, as if he were the virgin and she were the experienced one.

While he held her gaze, he pushed into her slowly, gently, allowing her body to adjust to his girth. Her lips parted and she gasped, but she didn't look away, didn't hide from him.

In this moment, they were connected as deeply and wholly as any two people could be.

When he began to move, he watched as her expression ran through a gamut of emotions: surprise, awe and pleasure.

Reed moved faster, thrust harder and she clung to him, burying her face in his neck. Her breath coming in tiny gasps against the shell of his ear.

"More," she begged him.

So he surrendered. He surrendered to his desire, to the friction and heat between them and to the fulfillment of a fantasy.

She clawed at his back, hips arched up to meet him and his kiss had swallowed her cries of pleasure when he reached his peak. Reed wanted her eyes open, wanted to make sure she knew where she was and who she was with.

"Open your eyes," he growled low, and soft.

Gina didn't hesitate. She opened her eyes and looked up at his face. He drove into her with purpose then and her sheath tightened around him.

He was looking into her eyes when he spilled inside of her, and he'd been right—it was heaven.

Reed pulled her into his arms, knowing that after this

had passed, nothing could ever be the same between them. He was pretty sure that the divine landscape he'd previously acknowledged in her arms would be his own personal hell. Because even in those last moments, he knew that this meant more to him than it did to her.

He was a Band-Aid, a painkiller. Something to stanch all the ugly things she felt.

And when he awoke the next morning, Reed knew he'd been right.

The space in the bed next to him was empty and his sheets smelled like her shampoo.

He needed to put her out of his head as easily as she'd put him out of hers.

Whenever he needed to clear his head, or he felt bad, he made money. He'd buy something and sell it. He'd invest; he'd move things around.

But today, he was going to try something different. What he was doing obviously wasn't making him happy so it was time to try something that might.

He wanted to throw money at the problem, in a sense. He wanted to do something good for someone else. There was a part of him that knew whatever his good deeds were, they wouldn't change the way he thought about himself deep down.

But it would make him feel better for a time.

He emailed Gray about making some anonymous donations to several cancer charities, for Gina's mom. And for a few minutes, there was a spark of warmth in his chest. He liked how that felt.

But nothing could bring out that spark like Amanda

Jane. He wanted to see her, know her, see the world as she saw it.

There was something so spectacular about her innocence, but she had this clarity, too. He thought she was the most amazing little person. He liked her perspective on things and he wondered how that would change as she grew. As the world touched her, molded her and showed her all the wonderful and terrible things it had to offer.

He wanted to keep her from the darkness, from the bad, but he couldn't. No matter how hard he tried. But he'd read somewhere that to appreciate the beauty of the stars, you needed the night.

That made sense to him. He could appreciate the stars so much more now.

And he could admit that their fire still scared him, humbled him and made him just a little bit raw.

But that came with the things he could accept, the things he had power over and the things he didn't. The best he could do was love that little girl with all his heart and do what was best for her.

His heart swelled and swelled until he thought he was going to burst. He didn't know he could love another person this wholly, this completely.

He dressed, wondering when would be too soon to call and see if she was ready to come home from sleeping over with Missy and Emma.

As he emerged into the kitchen, he heard her little voice.

Gina's, too.

He couldn't make out what they were saying, but he could see them through the glass outside on the patio.

Reed contented himself just to watch them for a moment. Just to take in the way the sunlight fell around them, like a big beacon.

Whatever happened between him and Gina, he supposed it didn't matter so much. As long as Amanda Jane was happy and safe. They could work through whatever this was between them because they both loved Amanda Jane more than themselves. With that kind of recipe, it couldn't help but work out.

GINA DIDN'T REGRET what had happened with Reed, but she wasn't ready to talk about it and she wasn't ready to be alone with him again.

She wasn't sure if it was because she knew she'd talk about it, she'd do it again or both.

Oh, did she ever want to do it again. It was the culmination of a fantasy, but so much more than that because it had been real.

Making love with Reed had been everything she'd hoped it would be.

Which made it dangerous.

She could fall in love with him so easily, but Gina couldn't let herself do that. She was already emotionally invested in one person who had been an addict. She didn't think she could survive two.

Reed was healthy and clean now, but what about if he wasn't?

The question should be when he wasn't. She'd seen it too often, read the stats.

And Crystal—God, Crystal.

Gina wanted to cry every time she thought about her, but she'd learned a long time ago that tears did nothing but give her a headache. They never fixed anything and most likely would make her feel worse. So she swallowed them down, swallowed all of her feelings and hoped they wouldn't come crawling back up from the dark to drown her.

When Emma and Missy came by to drop Amanda Jane off, Gina beamed and saw the perfect opportunity to save herself from facing the consequences of her actions, and to keep her mind off of Crystal. "I was going to take Amanda Jane swimming. Would you like to stay?"

"I have…to meet someone." Missy bit her lip. "But I think you should stay, Emma."

"You just don't want me quizzing you about your date with Sheriff Old School." Emma grinned.

"Oh, you have a date with Cowboy Hat and Boots himself?" Gina teased. "You'll have to tell us all about it."

Missy blushed. "It's not a date. It's…a walk."

"And a picnic, and hand-holdin' and country songs." Emma winked at her.

"It is not. He's going to help me with a thing."

"A thing." Emma nodded. "Is that what they're calling it?"

Missy blushed harder. "Stop it or I won't tell you another word."

"Fine. I'll just stay and swim and bother Gina all day."

Amanda Jane smiled. "Really, you'll stay? And you'll swim?"

"I don't really have a suit."

"I have one you can borrow and a T-shirt so you don't burn," Gina offered.

"Thanks."

"What's this? There's my princess." Reed swept Amanda Jane up on his shoulders and she giggled.

"We're going swimming."

"We are?" Reed said. "I guess I'll have to clear my schedule."

This had been a ploy so she didn't have to think about Reed and that definitely didn't include looking at him all half-naked and wet.

He swung Amanda Jane around and deposited her gently back onto her feet. "I have some things to catch up on and I'll be outside shortly."

"Promise?" she asked, eyes wide.

"Promise."

Gina felt like an utter ass. Amanda Jane was so happy to spend time with him and she'd begrudge that just because she didn't want to own her actions.

"We'll meet you outside." She turned to the little girl. "Go on. Go put your suit on."

She dragged Emma up to her room. As soon as they were inside, Emma leaned against the door. "So, you did it."

"What?" They couldn't be talking about the same what. It wasn't as though she had a tattoo on her forehead that said *I banged Reed Hollingsworth.*

"*It.*"

So, maybe she did, after all. "I did not."

"Oh, please. The tension between you has been hot enough to light a fire. But when he looks at you, that kindling is nothing but ash. You had sex. Admit it."

"Fine. We had sex." She swallowed.

"And?"

"And what?"

"And what?" Emma practically shrieked. "You're killing me."

"It's not a big deal. It was a one-time thing…"

"You are such a liar." Emma laughed.

"I just… I think I screwed up. I don't regret what happened, because wow." Just thinking about it made her blush and long to do it again. "But where do we go from here? I'm trying to become a doctor, raise a child…and where is the room for a relationship?"

"I don't know if someone failed to mention this to you, but you're already in a relationship. You're raising Amanda Jane together."

"Sex complicates things."

"It can. But sometimes, it's the right thing."

"I feel so guilty."

"For what?" Emma gave her a gentle smile. "For living? Your sister made her choices, and you get to make yours. You've spent your life taking care of other people and you've got years ahead of you raising Amanda Jane. It's hard and it's okay to do something for yourself. It's okay to have needs and it's okay to fill them."

"With Reed?"

She and Emma looked at each other and laughed.

"I didn't even make that dirty joke. I could have, you know," Emma said.

"You didn't have to. I heard it in my head."

She handed Emma a suit and after changing, they made their way down to the pool and waited in the shallow end for Amanda Jane. It was several minutes later when she came outside, dragging not only Reed behind her, but Grayson James, as well.

"I hate that man. It should be a crime for a man who is that much of a bastard to look so good without a shirt," Emma grumbled.

Gina had to admit that Reed's lawyer didn't look too bad in a pair of swim trunks. Surprisingly, he didn't look like a lawyer at all. He was scarred, tattooed, and his muscles were born of hard training.

"And he kissed you."

"No, he didn't."

"Yes, he did. Remember? At Frogfest?"

"I blocked it out."

"I wonder if he did."

Emma splashed her. "Stop playing matchmaker. I'm not ready."

"If you have your own man to keep you busy, you won't be bothering me about mine."

"Fine. I won't tease you anymore. Just don't, okay?"

"Okay." She put her hand on Emma's shoulder. "That was teasing, too, Emma. I'm sorry if it upset you."

Emma sighed. "I'm just being touchy. Sorry."

"Let's just have fun."

But Gina had a feeling that Emma and Grayson

could be good together. From the way he was eyeing her friend, maybe he thought so, too.

"Who knew it would be a party?" Reed shrugged.

She found herself drawn back in to watching him. The way his muscles rippled, the way the water beaded on his skin, the way his hair looked wet and tousled.

Amanda Jane jumped in and demanded Reed toss her up in the air again and again.

This was the life she'd dreamed of.

This was the life that should've been Crystal's.

She knew Emma would tell her to stop doing that to herself, but what would Crystal say if she could see her now? Would she be jealous?

Maybe she wasn't suffering anymore. Maybe she was in that peaceful place, that land of white and peace that her mother always talked about before she died. Maybe they were together and finally, Crystal wasn't hurting.

Or maybe she just wanted to think that so that the guilt for taking everything that belonged to Crystal. No, not just taking it, but for being glad to take it. For wanting it.

A warmth at her back, a hand on her shoulder. "What's wrong?" Reed asked her.

She looked up at him, saw concern in his eyes. Gina decided to be honest. "I was just thinking about Crystal."

He nodded solemnly. "I will always be grateful to her for giving me Amanda Jane, but I can't and won't wish she was here instead of you."

Reed dove under the water and swam toward Amanda

Jane. Gina wasn't sure if he was fleeing her, or what he said, or both.

She hated that warmth bloomed at his words. She was ashamed that it took her sister's suffering to get what she wanted.

But then another voice in her head made itself known. It was cool, calm and logical. It said that she hadn't sought out her sister's pain; Crystal had done all this to herself. Taking joy in the life she'd been given and the circumstances she found herself in wasn't wrong. Who knew how much time any of them had. Should she spend it all lamenting someone else's choices or should she grab on to her joy with both hands and hold it so tightly that no one and nothing could ever take it away from her?

That voice sounded a lot like Emma.

And maybe it was right.

She looked for her friend and saw that Grayson had her cornered. Gina gave it just a minute to see if it was good cornered or bad cornered—and she lost her window of opportunity. Grayson had grabbed her and hauled her up in the air as if she was nothing but a sack of apples and tossed her shrieking into the deep water.

Emma came up spluttering with war in her eyes.

The man himself looked a little afraid, but to his credit, he laughed, daring her to come take her revenge if she could.

Maybe they would be good for each other and not just because Gina didn't want to focus on her own situation, but Emma had never been able to find a man who could give her what she dished out, and Grayson James was all of that and then some.

She'd bet that he was just as fierce in his personal life as he was in his professional life. Emma needed that.

"Looks like our friends are getting along," Reed said, as he brought Amanda Jane over on his shoulders.

"About as well as a cat and a thunderstorm," she teased.

"Everyone knows that when a boy likes a girl he pulls her hair or gives her something gross," Amanda Jane tossed in.

"Oh, really? And just how do you know this?"

"There are things a woman just knows," Amanda Jane replied.

Gina laughed, but Reed scowled.

"Are there boys giving you gross things or pulling your hair?"

"No, Daddy." She laughed. "And I won't let him unless he's a prince. Like you."

Watching the emotion that came over Reed's face at Amanda Jane's proclamation twisted her heart and her guts. She saw all of his hopes and fears written so plainly that she felt it was almost a trespass to see them.

But this moment, it wasn't something she ever expected Amanda Jane to have—a present father figure who adored her more than his own breath.

Reed was flawed, broken and imperfect—but somehow, that made him utterly perfect.

That moment was when she knew she was screwed. If she'd had any doubts as to what her feelings for Reed were, they'd just punched out from the darkest corner of her heart to fill her entire being with warmth.

She was still in love with him.

No amount of avoidance or deflection was going to change that.

In that moment, she saw a future. Instead of being a wispy dream or teenage fantasy, it was solid and whole.

Years down the line, together in this house, they'd be celebrating weddings, graduations, birthdays…they'd have more children together. Big family holiday dinners, romantic vacations…and every time Reed was gone for too long, or every time there was a change in his routine, even though she loved him more than her own life, she'd wonder if he was using.

This was her almost happily-ever-after.

She didn't want that, but she didn't know how to change it, either. Because even knowing that's how it would be, she still wanted him. Still loved him.

And if he did relapse, what would that mean for their children? For her? Would she be committing them to the same life she'd had? Terror knifed at her. She'd always sworn that no child of hers would know what that was like.

She should run away, take Amanda Jane…

He turned and smiled at her. "A prince like me, huh? He better be much better than me."

Almost as if he knew the bent of her thoughts. That smile, it melted all of her defenses, even when she knew better.

"Come see, Gina-bee. We'll have an underwater tea party."

Amanda Jane reached out her arms and Gina took her, hugging her closer.

"Okay, on the count of three, hold your nose and we'll sit on the bottom."

Amanda Jane took a deep breath and the expression on Reed's face as they slid under the water together was one of a pained knowing.

They sank down and Gina struggled to keep them down until Reed was gone. She mimicked drinking tea and Amanda Jane did the same, pouring and making silly faces. The chlorine burned her eyes, but she made faces in return until they came up for air, giggling.

The only thing she loved more than Reed Hollingsworth was his daughter.

CHAPTER EIGHTEEN

REED KNEW SOMETHING had changed with Gina, something other than their hot night together. Only he couldn't put his finger on what.

There was a weight on her shoulders that hadn't been there before. He tried repeating Gray's words to him. That he wasn't responsible for everyone else, that he was trying to take on more than his burden, but he had the distinct feeling that this was his burden.

After the impromptu pool party, an exhausted Amanda Jane was now snoring in her room, and he knocked on Gina's door.

She opened it slowly, and when she looked up at him, he knew he hadn't been wrong.

"What did I do?" he asked.

The corner of her mouth curled up in a self-deprecating grin. "You didn't do anything."

"There's something bothering you and if I screwed up, I can't fix it unless you tell me." He wanted so desperately to make this work, to be the man she needed, to be the father Amanda Jane deserved.

"I don't think you can fix it." Her eyes were wide, almost innocent.

"Why don't you tell me about it?"

"Because it's going to hurt you."

Her words wounded him before they were even a weapon. It was like a casual touch of a razor blade creating a wound that didn't bleed until after the blade was gone. "Tell me, anyway. I can't stand the look in your eyes."

"And I won't be able to stand the look in yours."

"Let me shoulder some of the burden, Gina. It's been all yours for far too long." He wanted to be of use to her. This was where he proved that he was more than a bank account, more than a genetic contributor to Amanda Jane. This was where she would see he was good enough.

As if those were some kind of magical words, she leaned against him and wrapped her arms around his waist. He touched her hair, stroked her back until she sighed deep.

"You know, it's moments like this that I think I'm doing you such a grave disservice in my head."

"And other times?" He knew she needed to speak these words, release them because they weighed her down like irons.

"Other times I'm just afraid," she whispered into his neck.

"Of what?" he prodded. Reed knew what she was going to say and there was certainly part of him that didn't want to hear it. There was no reason to go digging for the knife to put in her hand.

But the man he wanted to be, the man he was trying so hard to become, he knew this was what she needed.

Knew that they had to acknowledge their fears together before they could conquer them.

She stiffened, but he stroked her again, like he would a cat. "Lean on me, Gina. Let me in."

That was what he wanted, to be allowed inside the circle. To really feel as though they were in it together. As it stood at the moment, he felt as if he was here to prove himself. Not that he wouldn't do the same in her position, but she needed to give him something that showed him that one day, she'd trust him. One day, they'd be a real family—whether they were in a romantic relationship or not.

And if not, if she couldn't do that, they needed to talk about what their choices were.

"I saw a future with you today."

He closed his eyes, because he knew exactly where she was going. Reed eased inside the room and closed the door. He didn't want Amanda Jane to wake up and hear their discussion.

"You saw a future that you didn't like." He prompted her to continue.

She tightened her embrace, as if she knew her words were going to push him away. "Part of it was really good."

"And the other part?"

"The other part was all doubt and fear."

"You can say it, Gina. You should say it. It might hurt me, but it's the truth. We shouldn't hide from the truth or be sorry for it."

"If you know what I'm going to say, why do you want to hear it?" She looked up at him.

The conflict in her eyes solidified his position in his own mind. "Because *you* need to tell me. I can say with absolute surety that I don't want to hear it, but that doesn't make it any less true, does it?"

She touched his face, as if that would somehow soften the blow. "I saw a future with you. I saw years together in this house. I saw us…together."

"Together?" He cocked his head to the side.

"I saw us having children. Holidays. Birthdays. Grandchildren. And I saw the fear tinge everything. That no matter the life we build together, you will always be an addict. I'll always wonder when everything is going to come apart and when you're going to use again. Because that's what addicts do."

Hearing that she had so little faith in him was more than a knife, more than a wound. It was something soul deep that he couldn't begin to quantify.

"I'm sorry," she added.

"I'm not going to tell you I've changed. I'm not going to tell you I'm well. But I will tell you that I love Amanda Jane more than anything. I love her more than anything I could ever put in my veins."

When she wouldn't look at him, he said, "It's okay if you can't believe that yet. This is all still new for both of us. But I'll prove it to you." *And to myself.*

"Will you stay here with me?"

He pulled her down on the bed with him and he tucked her against him, his face buried in the sweet apple scent of her hair.

"I know you're a good man," she said finally. "Otherwise you wouldn't be here with me now. You wouldn't let me take a razor to you and ask for more. I'm sorry that I can't trust anyone. I'm sorry that I'm cruel."

"You're not cruel." That's what made it hurt more—it wasn't an intentional gutting. It was just the nature of the thing. If she'd set out to cut him, he could guard against that. He had armor for that. But this was just how she felt, and she couldn't change that.

He shouldn't have let things go this far with her. He'd be much better off alone in his room thinking about what making love to her would be like, and keeping her at a cool distance. Then, all of his self-doubt would be in his own head rather than echoing in her voice.

Somehow, it was easier to overcome those things when he thought them alone. He could write them off as his own fear. But hearing it from her…it made the possibility of failure more real. He didn't have anyone who believed in him but Amanda Jane.

And he felt that maybe he needed to protect her from herself.

After all, if she put her faith in a man like him, she was bound to need more looking after.

"Your heart is beating so hard, I can feel it against my back."

It beats for you. It beats for her. All things he wanted to say, but didn't.

She rolled over on her back, his hand over her heart. "Mine's racing, too."

"Why?" he asked.

"You."

"Are you afraid of me?" he asked slowly.

"Afraid of what you make me feel. Of what you

make me want. Of the hope that's been crushed so many times, I don't know how it ever puts itself back together."

"I'm not going to fail you. You'll see." In that moment, he meant it. In that moment, there was nothing that could stop him.

"What about if I fail you?" she asked.

"Not possible."

"You sound so sure. I feel like I've failed you already. Relationships have to be founded on trust and that's something we don't have. Not yet. We have heat. We have fire, but a flame can't burn forever and I don't think I can turn back now."

"I am sure, Gina. You've always been the one to depend on. Always." So many things roiled up inside him in a bittersweet brew.

"When you're close to me like this, all I can think about is touching you."

"It's good to know I'm not the only one," he teased, trying to lighten the moment, but it didn't work. It only intensified the tension between them, only added kindling to the fire burning between them. The one that she was so sure would burn out. Reed was sure it would consume him whole before that happened.

She shook her head slowly. "No, it's all I can think about when you're not close, too."

"Then touch me." He knew better. He'd regretted sleeping with her before and he'd regret it again. Reed wanted this with her more than anything, but he wanted it to be because she felt something for him. Not seeking comfort, or fulfilling desire, but that something deeper he knew wasn't there.

She pushed her hands up under his T-shirt, over his chest, his back, his shoulders. He liked how she looked at him, the way her hands felt as she explored him. Gina tugged his shirt up over his head and rolled so that he was on his back and she straddled him. She bent to kiss his neck—his chest.

Her mouth was hot and decadent, traveling down his torso. She seemed to take great delight in the abs he'd worked so hard for, her fingers lingering at the waist of the soft cotton lounge pants he wore. As if she were afraid to go lower, as if she wasn't sure of what he'd do. Or what she'd find.

His fingers closed gently around her wrist and he guided her hand lower. He knew better, he did. This wasn't the answer to their problems, but if pleasure was their only other common ground, he'd take it.

She cupped him through the thin material, stroked her hand over him. He arched his hips up into the caress, and she tugged his pants down and took him into her mouth.

He was now sure this was hell. It felt so good, it had to be a sin. Or that's how it would feel later when he thought about it. She needed comfort and this was how she got it from him. Oblivion in sensation, in pleasure. She was drowning out the rest of the world and using him to do it.

At one time, Reed would've been glad to be that for her, but he didn't want to be a coping mechanism—even if it felt this good.

But even as he had these thoughts, he was filling his hands with her breasts, tasting her skin, flicking his tongue over her nipples, pulling off her panties…

"Can we try it this way?" she asked, breathless. "It was so good when we were kissing and—" Her eyes widened as she eased down on him. "I'm so full, I feel like I'm dying and being born at the same time."

It was hard not to lose himself in a woman who said those kind of things. Made him forget about his other needs and thought only about his hard cock buried deep inside of her.

He grasped her hips and rolled her forward, firm and slow, so that she felt every inch of him.

She splayed her palms on his chest, gasping. "I want to feel this forever. I never want it to stop."

Gina moved against him, following his lead. She leaned down, her breath warm on his lips. "I'm tender, but this is good. It hurts, and I like it. Because I know it's real." She kissed him and he ravaged her mouth, tasting all she had to offer him.

His hands roved over her body, mapping and memorizing her every curve. He took control of the encounter, drawing them both up so that he leaned back against the headboard and he cupped the globes of her bottom to guide her motion.

He moved her at his pleasure, taking what he wanted from her because he'd already given all he had to give. She seemed to want him to take, to bend her to his desire, and he was done denying himself.

She braced herself on his shoulders and followed the rhythm he'd set that pushed them both ever closer to culmination. She clawed at his back again, and found that like her, he liked that bit of an edge.

For the same reason: because it made it real.

He thrust up into her while using her hips to pull her down to meet his motion and when her sheath walls shuddered around him, squeezing and pulling him ever deeper while she gasped and came undone in his arms, he let the orgasm take him.

They rode the last waves of their passion together and when the storm had passed, she leaned her forehead against his. "I never knew anything could feel like this."

She slid off of him, but settled against his shoulder with a contented sigh.

"Me, either." He could feel her eyes on him.

"Really?"

"Yeah, really." He didn't have the numbers that Gray did, but he'd been around enough that he knew that all women had the same parts, and that no matter how they got to that end place, the result was usually the same.

Except with Gina. It was a hundred times more intense.

She burrowed against him. "You'll stay tonight?"

"Yeah. I'll stay."

"I want to build a blanket fort, eat cookies, have us make love in the fort and never come out."

She was hiding again, but this time, he'd let her. "That's going to be a filthy blanket fort." He allowed his mind to entertain just exactly what all of that would entail and he found he could be quite content in a blanket fort with Gina and cookies.

"I know. And I don't care. We're going to stay there."

"Are we now? What happens when we run out of cookies?" he teased. Reed needed to lighten the tone. He wasn't ready to admit the intensity of what he felt for her.

"I guess someone will have to venture out for more." She burrowed some more. "Or I guess we'll just have to talk about this."

"Yeah. We should." Damn it. She was right, but hiding from it didn't make it go away.

"I knew you were going to say that." She sagged.

"Is it so horrible?" He'd asked a question he didn't really want an answer to.

"No. I'm just afraid. I have feelings for you, Reed." Her confession made it sound as if it was the worst thing that could've happened.

"I should hope so." He pushed a lock of hair behind her ear. At least there was that, he wasn't alone in this. That would've made it so much more awful.

"But I keep thinking, what if this doesn't work? We're still going to have to be together under the same roof for the next twelve years."

"Yes," he agreed. Reed tried to imagine having her, losing her, but still being so close, still living under the same roof. It would be agony. It was best to slice this open now, to tear out all of those things that wound them up together.

"And I make up my mind that we're not going to do this again, that we shouldn't, and then I can't stop touching you. I have no self-control."

Neither did he, because the thought of severing those ties to her made him feel a loneliness like nothing he'd ever felt before. A kind of grief. "Do you want to stop?"

"No." She sighed. "Yes. I don't know."

He steeled himself. "What do you want? Not what *should* you want. But what do you really want?"

"The answer to that, Reed, has always been you."

"Then m—" He cut himself off before he could blurt the words that were on the tip of his tongue. They were not the right words, they were not the right time.

He'd been about to tell her she should just make their marriage real, but that was insane. He didn't know if he was ready for that kind of commitment. His stupid tongue needed to start obeying him. They were doing everything wrong. He wasn't going to get that wrong, too.

Because what if she said yes? What if they tied themselves to each other and it all crashed and burned?

"What?" She looked up at him.

He thought again how beautiful she was. "Nothing that can't wait." For as much as he had all of these feelings that burned hot and bright, a true marriage was a giant step that neither of them were ready for. They'd only had one date.

"So that's what you have to say to my confession?"

"What confession? That you want me? You just had me," he teased. "But you've always got me."

"Always?"

"Yeah, always." He had a feeling that his idea of always might end up being longer than hers. She wanted him now, now that things were fresh and he was whole. But what about when he wasn't? What about when he wasn't the savior, when he was just the guy she knew in the trailer park all those years ago?

It seemed as though Gina had her own doubts and while he didn't want her to be upset, it comforted him that he wasn't the only one who felt as if he was set adrift. "Whatever we build here is ours and no one can take it from us, but us."

"I wish I could believe that."

"I wish you could, too."

She didn't speak any more after that and it wasn't long before her breathing became deep and even.

This time, it was he who untangled himself from her in the early hours of dawn. He needed to work, to think about the things he knew he could do right. He may not have known how to be a father, a partner or even a lover. But he did know how to make money. So Reed was going to work and think about what he knew, because numbers and percentages made sense in a way that feeling and emotion never did.

CHAPTER NINETEEN

WHEN GINA WOKE UP, he was gone, but it was just as well. She wouldn't have known what to say to him. She'd meant to fix things, meant to put their relationship back behind that line they'd crossed and retreat to a place that made sense.

She meant to put herself back in that place, too.

How was he supposed to know what she wanted from him if she kept changing the rules? She hated that she dragged him closer with one hand and pushed him away with the other. She didn't understand why he put up with it or why she kept doing it.

Aside from the fact she was playing house. That's all this could be. She was caught up in the rush, dressing up in her sister's clothes, but pretending to do it better.

Her phone rang and she saw it was Rob Ness, a doctor she'd worked with as an EMT. Part of her wanted to believe he was just calling to see how she was, but there was that knot of dread in her stomach. The one that told her something was wrong. Something bad had happened.

She debated not answering the phone. She didn't want to know.

But not knowing didn't change anything.

Gina answered the phone. "Hey, Rob."

"I can tell from your voice that you know some-thing's wrong. So I'm just going to tell you. Your grand-mother's been brought into County."

She gasped as the sound of her world imploding echoed in her ears.

"She's responsive. She's just had a fall, but you should come."

"I'll be there. Thanks for calling." Terror knifed her gut. Even though the doctor said she was fine, she knew that with falls in elderly patients, sometimes complica-tions waited a long time to manifest. She couldn't lose Grams. Not now. Not ever, she'd wished, but she knew it was inevitable.

She dressed quickly and got Amanda Jane ready to go. She didn't even stop to think about Reed. Not until Amanda Jane asked, "Can Daddy come, too?"

"Daddy has to work. Daddy doesn't need to come. Grammie had a fall so we're going to go see her, okay?"

"Like when I fall?"

"Sort of. Put your shoes on, okay?" Gina tried to keep her voice calm. Rob said she was responsive, that was a good thing.

She drove directly to County and headed straight to the ER, forcing herself to stay calm, to stay focused.

Rob met her at the door. "Look, nothing's broken. We'll probably keep her overnight for observation. But you know how hard chemo can be on bones. Makes them brittle. I want to make sure we don't miss any-thing."

"Chemo? What are you talking about?" He had

to have the wrong chart. Her grandmother wasn't on chemo. "No, no. It was my mother who—"

The look of pity on his face cut her off. "She didn't tell you."

"Oh, my God." Fear and panic slammed into her all over again, but this time it was rancid and dark—it threatened to drown her. The small hand in hers kept her sane. Kept her from coming apart at the seams. "What are we looking at?"

"She's in recovery, Gina. It looks good. It looks really good. But you might want to think about getting tested. She had BRCA-1. The genetic marker for hereditary breast cancer. You should get everyone tested." He looked down at Amanda Jane. "And you should talk to your grandmother."

"I… Test us now. Can you do that? Right now?" She had to know. The possibility that Amanda Jane might face this same future was too horrible to comprehend. But if they could test for the gene, there were steps that could be taken early.

Rob pursed his lips. "This is really something that should be handled by an oncologist or a geneticist. But I can order the test, if that's really what you want."

"Yes."

"I'll have one of the girls bring you some paperwork. Maudine is in room three."

Amanda Jane's hand tightened around her fingers and they went in and saw her grandmother.

She was perched on her bed, her light blue hair perfect, because Gina had just realized it was a wig. And she had Helga Gunderson on one side of her and Ethel Weinburg on the other.

"Looks like someone is in trouble," Ethel said when she saw the stormy look on Gina's face. "I'll leave you two alone."

"Well, I won't," Helga snorted. "I called the ambulance. And I told her she was being a turd by not telling you."

"They all knew? All of your friends knew but you didn't tell me?"

Maudine laced her fingers together. "I didn't see the point in getting you all riled up over nothing. I figured I'd rile you up when it was something to be riled up about. Except for this little setback, I'm obviously fine."

"Cancer isn't something to be riled up about? My mother died of cancer. And what about Amanda Jane? What about me? Dr. Ness said you had the BRCA-1 marker. Don't you think we'd want to get tested? I'm so angry with you right now I could scream."

Amanda Jane's grip tightened again.

"I didn't want to tell you. That's my decision. I didn't think you needed anything else on your plate. Whether you like it or not, that was my choice to make."

"No, no it's not. Not when it comes to something like this." Gina was so angry she could chew nails and spit bullets. Everyone knew she got her temper from Maudine—very slow to burn, but when it did, there were going to be fireworks.

"No one is going to ask how I'm feeling now?" Maudine sniffed indelicately.

"No," Helga said. "You're being a stubborn cow and

need to be taken to task. Even playing the invalid as you are."

"I am not an invalid." Maudine wiggled to get out of the bed.

Helga grinned. "See, you're fine. All fire and sass. Nothing wrong with you."

"I am going to punch you in your shiny new teeth tomorrow," Maudine said without any sincerity.

It was then she realized Amanda Jane was crying.

"I don't want to be here. I wanna go. Let me go. Please, I wanna go," she started to sob. "I want Daddy. I want my daddy." She clung so tightly to Gina that she thought her little fingers were going to break.

"He's at work, sweetheart." Gina was at a loss.

"I don't want to have cancer. I don't want the test. I don't!"

The way her thin back shuddered under Gina's hand made it clear that Amanda Jane didn't care if he was at work and Gina knew that Reed wouldn't care, either.

He'd care mightily that she'd brought her without consulting him, but he would come.

"I'll call him." She hoisted the little girl up into her arms, staving off her own grief. She had to be strong for Amanda Jane. She had to be the rock, she had to be the immutable. Even though inside, she was torn.

With her other hand, she pulled out her cell phone and dialed Reed.

"What's going on?" he asked.

"Amanda Jane needs you."

"Where are you?" His voice was calm, and if she

hadn't screwed up, it would have been a balm to her. Instead, it only set her on edge.

"County." She knew he was going to be angry when he found out exactly how everything had gone down.

"What happened? Is she hurt?"

She should've thought about what talking about this in front of Amanda Jane meant. Even though she acted very much like a grown-up, she wasn't. She was a child. And she should've talked to Reed. He was her father.

She'd screwed up big-time.

"No, it's my grandmother. She fell. We're at County and Amanda Jane is freaking out."

"Why? Is Maudine really hurt?" Concern tinged his voice.

"No, she has cancer. Hereditary and Amanda Jane overheard that I wanted to have us both tested and—"

"I'm coming." He hung up the phone without waiting for another response from her.

She carried Amanda Jane out to the waiting room. She wanted to take her home, wanted to be somewhere familiar, somewhere safe. But her hands were shaking and if she was honest with herself, she needed Reed, too.

His strong, steady presence. His smile. His arms. It would make it all better—make it all okay. He wouldn't be able to erase the loss, but he'd fill in the gaps, he'd make the crash softer.

The nurse came out with the paperwork after Amanda Jane cried herself to sleep and she signed it one-handed. The nurse took the draw while the child slept. Even though she may not have wanted the test, that wasn't something that would go away if it wasn't acknowledged.

Much like the distance between her and Reed. They had everything between them, everything but the thing that was the most important.

Trust.

She sat, rocking Amanda Jane as she slept, wondering how she was going to fix the mess she'd made. And what she'd do if they both tested positive for the gene. Fear, hope, so many things were tangled all up together and she couldn't begin to unravel the thread.

Reed made it in record time. He took Amanda Jane from her and even though it was obvious that's what she needed—wanted—Gina's arms were barren without her. She didn't want to share her. She needed Amanda Jane as much as the girl needed her.

"I'm here, honey." He stroked her head and back. "I've got you."

"Don't leave me, Daddy." She whispered the words, groggy with sleep.

"Never," he swore.

The words were a dagger in her own heart.

He rocked her gently and her little fists clutched the lapel of his jacket as tightly as they'd clutched at Gina.

"So you didn't think that maybe this might be too much for a little girl to shoulder? That maybe you shouldn't talk about things like testing her for a cancer gene without talking to me about it first?"

"I…" She lifted her chin. "I did."

"And you're not sorry for it?"

She was. Standing there under his gaze, she wanted

nothing more than to take it back. To have called him. Of course he would've wanted her to be tested. He would've wanted them both to be tested. But he'd wanted to be here, and it was important that he was here—as evidenced by Amanda Jane's reaction.

"Can we not talk about this now?"

"We don't have to talk about this now. But we will talk about it."

"Way to make it about you when my grandmother is sick," she spat. Even as it came out of her mouth, she regretted saying it. She knew that wasn't what he was doing. She was too open, too raw, too weak. In trying to defend herself, she was just making things worse.

"Is that what you think I'm doing? In case you hadn't noticed, this isn't about either one of us. It's about her." He nodded down at the quivering bundle in his arms.

"I'm sorry," she whispered. She felt so awkward, out of place. There was nothing for her to do with her hands. Her arms. She'd never felt so…alone.

"Did they call you?" Emma interrupted them from the doorway. She looked harried and scattered. "They called me, too. Something about your grandmother? I'm on her contact list."

"Yes." Gina shook her head.

"Are you okay?"

"I don't know. Amanda Jane wanted Reed. So I called him."

Emma pulled her close for another hug. "You mean you didn't… Oh, honey."

"I didn't… I wanted… I…"

"You, you, you what?" Emma repeated back to her and cast her a knowing glance.

Gina realized that was the problem. All she could talk about was herself. She'd thought that she was this paragon of virtue raising her sister's child, not taking things for herself—but all of this had always been for herself. A way so that she didn't rot in the shadows. So she was important. So she was someone.

She was the good girl gone better. That was her role.

Reed had threatened that.

She didn't like herself very much in that moment. Not at all.

"Let me take Amanda Jane," Emma said.

"She wanted Reed," Gina said dumbly.

But when Emma reached for her, the girl went willingly into her arms. It seemed that Amanda Jane wanted everyone but Gina. Maybe she could feel the turmoil that roiled inside of her.

"Reed—"

"We're not going to do this here," Reed said in a clipped tone.

"You don't have to do anything. Why don't you just go get some coffee and bring Amanda Jane a hot cocoa?" Emma offered.

"I know where they keep the good stuff." Gina walked down toward the cafeteria and hoped that Reed followed her.

"This wasn't okay," he said, his voice calm and steady.

"I know." She did, she'd known it while she was doing it. It wouldn't have hurt anything for her to just tell him.

"And you did it, anyway."

She stopped to face him. "I did and I'm sorry. *I'm so sorry.*"

"Why didn't you just call me?" He searched her eyes. "To what? Prove that you didn't need me?"

That was exactly why. She hated how well he knew her. Even more, she hated the pain that flashed in his eyes when he read her answer in his.

"I don't care if you need me or not."

"Don't you?" she dared.

"No." His voice was clipped, cool and composed. "Compared to that girl in the waiting room? Not one bit. If you'd have been thinking of her instead of yourself, you would've come and talked to me. We could have decided together—"

"And where have you been for the first six years of her life? Why is it suddenly okay for you to just show up and think that you're entitled to make any choices for her just because you contributed some genetic material?"

His expression closed like the gates to some fabled city. They locked her out, showed her nothing of the man underneath. That was how she knew she'd wounded him.

"If I'd known…"

"If you'd known you'd what?" she spat, unable to hold back. "You'd have gotten high some more? You'd have come back to this town thinking that she needed you? You'd have worked some crap gas station job until you realized you couldn't take care of anyone, let alone yourself, then you would've started dealing. So don't tell me what you would have done, Reed. Because you wouldn't. The only way that you're the person you are now is because of what happened to you. If you'd have come back before that, Amanda Jane and Crystal both would be statistics."

The venom that came out of her mouth now, she couldn't believe how easily she took aim at the soft places under his armor and how cruelly she lobbed the spears.

"Whether you like it or not, I'm her father. Maybe you've taken care of her, good care of her up until this lapse in judgment, but you're not her mother."

"No, her mother is dead. My sister is *dead*."

"Why do you think you're the only one allowed to feel pain?"

"I don't." Only, maybe that was how she'd behaved. She wasn't ready to see that.

Because she'd built it up in her head that it was Gina he wanted, not Crys. It was how she'd always wanted it to be. For him to have wanted her, to think that she was too good for him, too pure. That maybe she'd go on and do something better and he'd settled for Crys. That was really what was going on in her head.

She hated being forced to see this side of herself. It was ugly and wrong. She loved Crys. She loved Amanda Jane.

And she loved Reed.

But this wasn't how things were supposed to happen.

She'd been so sure if she just did everything that she was supposed to, if she was good enough, that everything would work out to some happily-ever-after. Gina realized that she'd only been playing at being jaded the same way she'd been playing house.

"I'm sorry." She deflated and leaned against him. "I'm so sorry."

For a moment, she didn't think he was going to return the embrace.

"Please don't shut me out. Don't leave me out here alone. Not now."

His arms tightened around her and she buried her face in his chest, inhaled the safe, familiar scent of him.

"I can do better," she said.

His fingers curled around the nape of her neck and he didn't say anything.

She touched her lips to his cheek, to his mouth, looking for some connection, some reassurance that everything was okay between them. But it wasn't.

He released her and put an obvious, calculated distance between them. "This isn't how it works."

"I don't understand."

"Whenever you feel something that you don't like, or don't want, you come to me. You want your hit so you don't have to feel it."

She wrinkled her nose. "You're saying that you're my drug? Please. That's a little arrogant, don't you think?" Her tone was sharper than she meant, but his rejection stung. It seemed that it was still like when they were kids. She was always chasing and he was always running away.

"Not me. I think it would be like this with anyone for you. Sex is great. Touch feels good. And when you're screaming and clawing your way toward bliss, you don't have to think about what's wrong, what's ugly or what hurts. All you have to do is fly."

"Screw you, Reed."

"I don't think so. Never again."

Her eyes widened. "Why would you say that to me? We were building something and you're going to throw it all away because I made one mistake? I said I was sorry. I don't know how many times I can say it that will make you believe me."

"I believe that you are sorry, but that doesn't erase what you did. Sorry fixes everything? That fixes what you said to me? That makes it okay that you want nothing from me as a parent for Amanda Jane except to write the checks."

"You were the one who insisted we move in. You were the one who demanded I quit my jobs. You were the one who tried to buy her a pony. How does that have anything to do with me? Or this? You did that."

"And you said that you didn't want to need me."

"I don't understand." Gina was lost and hoping desperately he'd lead her to what he was trying to tell her. She wanted to understand. She wanted to get it right.

"No, I don't guess that you would."

He turned on his heel and headed back the way they'd come, leaving her standing there, broken and alone. Just like she always feared.

CHAPTER TWENTY

REED WOULD HAVE almost given her everything, but he could see now that she couldn't be trusted with it—his heart. His hope. His future.

Because she didn't want it. She didn't want to need him the same way he needed her.

She didn't want anything he had to offer her.

But she wasn't going to keep him from Amanda Jane. She could do as she liked, until it came to his daughter. That was just it; it was obvious that Gina didn't think of him as Amanda Jane's father. He was just this interloper who happened to have what they needed to get by.

He'd begun to think that because she'd turned to him time and again that she'd started to rely on him, trust him—need him.

But it had all been dress-up in his head.

She'd never trust him.

And she had no reason to.

He was good enough to fuck, but not good enough to trust with anything important. Like her heart. Her well-being.

His daughter.

He took a deep, fortifying breath before going back into the waiting room. Amanda Jane was already upset.

She didn't need to see him upset. He could be strong for her.

When he went back into the room, she was sleeping on Emma, her first and middle fingers tugging on her left ear.

The sight of that kicked him hard in the solar plexus. It made him think of all those moments he'd already missed and why.

Maybe they'd been right to keep him away.

That thought rang with such clarity and truth and it threatened to drown him with it. His eyes burned and his chest pulsed, as if there was something trying to crawl outside his rib cage. He could only imagine that it was his heart.

"Is she sleeping?" he managed to ask, because he didn't know what else to say.

Emma nodded and shifted, moving as if to hand her back to him.

Suddenly, it was too much. Crys hadn't trusted him with their daughter, Gina didn't trust him, these people didn't want him here. So why was he fighting so hard to stay?

He shook his head. "I can't."

Reed fled the hospital as though the hounds of hell were nipping at his heels—and maybe they were. Their jaws were made of his past sins and their teeth of his regrets.

No, not his regrets.

His hopes.

There was nothing crueler than the sharp stab of hope, especially when it was in vain and he knew it.

This was what he never wanted to feel again, this was what he couldn't stand digging into his soft places.

He wanted to be numb to it, wanted it to fade into some dusky oblivion where the pain wasn't as sharp and his lens not so clear. It wouldn't hurt as much if he couldn't see it, if he wasn't aware of every minute detail of his shortcomings.

As he walked, he thought about the needle and that was a bear he couldn't fight. But a few shots of hot whiskey relief wouldn't be amiss.

Fuck it.

Fuck it all.

He found a bar and went inside. It was one of those back-alley entrances and the bar was above one of those kitsch-charm downtown antiques shops. But upstairs it was all hardscrabble bikers and hipsters pretending to be cool.

Reed bought a double, but then said, "Just give me the bottle."

He took it to a dark corner of the bar, away from the jukebox, away from the pool tables, away from everyone who'd get some wild hair to talk to him. He didn't want to talk—he wanted to drown.

But only for a little while. Only until he could breathe.

He supposed that made no sense to anyone but him. The boa constrictor around his chest would release her hold when he'd numbed himself just a bit. Just enough to get her to let go so he could exist in his own skin.

For Reed, that was the worst place to be.

No matter how high he climbed, he couldn't shed the

image of being poor white trash from the wrong side of town. It wasn't just Gina who made him feel that way or anyone else—it was himself.

He'd tried to outrun it, outspend it, outdo it. But he never could. That label was tattooed on his forehead and followed him like a ticker tape parade wherever he went.

Amanda Jane didn't need that.

Gina didn't need that. Gina had shed hers like a skin, like the skin of the snake that wrapped around his neck and chest, that choked the life from him. That stuffed him full of hope all the while it sucked him dry.

He could leave them and they'd be better, he decided. Everything would be better.

Promise you won't leave me, Amanda Jane had said.

The girl was six; she didn't know what was good for her.

But he did. What he was doing right now was a choice. He was choosing to drink, to numb his pain. And that was not the man he was now.

He handed the bottle to a group sitting by the door on his way out.

Reed had been given a chance to have the life he'd dreamed of and the first time things got rough, he'd fled, hidden.

She was right not to trust him.

Gina was right.

He was going to tell her so tomorrow. He'd give her the money, the house and whatever she wanted. He'd go far away where he couldn't taint anything else, where he couldn't wreck anything else.

Screw you, Gina had said.

Yeah, he'd screwed himself this time.

GINA COULDN'T DO this again.

She wouldn't.

She was thrust back in time to sponging Crystal's fevered brow, all the nights she'd spent making sure her sister didn't aspirate her own vomit, waiting up for her wondering if this would be the night she never made it home and they'd find her in a ditch somewhere, needle still in her arm.

Or they'd never find her.

Someone would take advantage of her, she'd end up running with the wrong people.

After their mother died, she used to stay awake at night and watch Crystal sleep, just to make sure she was still breathing.

Just to make sure that she wasn't going to die too and leave Gina all alone.

She could almost stand to do it if her vigil had done any good. If staying up and watching Crystal's chest rise and fall with steady breath would've kept that breath in her body. Would have somehow anchored her.

But it didn't.

There was nothing she could do. All she could do was keep her vigil, waiting to bear witness.

Gina had had enough of bearing witness, of watching those she loved die, lives wasted. She wouldn't do that to herself again and she wouldn't do it to Amanda Jane.

Don't leave me.

Never.

He couldn't keep that promise. No one could. A person shouldn't be allowed to speak of things like promises and hope when they couldn't follow through.

When he finally came through the door, his eyes were haunted and dark. But he was one-hundred percent Reed.

Maybe she had judged him too harshly.

He went upstairs and closed the door. It took her about a minute to decide to follow him.

"Are you okay?" she asked, sitting down on the edge of the bed.

"Yeah."

They sat together in that awkward, dark silence for a long time.

"I'm sorry," Gina said finally. "For everything. Maybe I expected too much."

"Are you sorry for expecting too much or for making decisions about my daughter without even talking to me?"

She cringed and turned her head. She deserved that. Being sorry didn't change the fact that she didn't trust him. Gina knew she'd been in the wrong even while she was taking action, but that hadn't stopped her. She'd been so afraid to trust in him, afraid to surrender control. Afraid to give him what was rightfully his, a say in his daughter's health and well-being. Her fear didn't outweigh that, no matter how much she wished it did.

"For everything," she said finally.

"I'm sorry, too. I didn't expect you to be waiting up for me." He was quiet for a moment. "Actually, I didn't expect you to be here at all."

His words were telling. Another proof, as if they needed it, that they didn't have the foundations they needed not just to build a relationship, but a solid family unit. "After you left, I didn't know what to do. I was so afraid for you. For me. For all of us."

"I know. I shouldn't have done that. Did Amanda Jane get to bed okay?"

"Yeah. She's in bed now. Didn't even wake up when Emma put her down." For that, she was thankful. She didn't want to try to explain where Reed had gone and that she didn't know if he was coming back.

"How's Maudine?"

"Resting comfortably, if unwillingly. She has her whole crew of the Grandmothers keeping her company and fetching things."

"Things will look better tomorrow." He nodded slowly and leaned back on the pillow.

"Yeah. Tomorrow," she echoed. That magic place where all good things lived.

She lay down next to him and stroked her fingers through his hair. He lay still, stiff, like a dog who'd been kicked too many times to enjoy the petting. Gina smoothed his hair from his brow softly.

"I remember the last time you took care of me," he said finally.

"You do?" she asked, as if she didn't quite believe it.

"Yeah."

"The first time you tried to get that monkey off your back." She kept stroking. "You were so sick. I was sure you were dying."

"I thought I was, too." He turned in to her caress.

"Your hands were so cool and soft. That was the definition of heaven for me. Heaven through the gates of hell," he said quietly.

She didn't realize that's what she meant to him. "You didn't have to suffer if all you wanted was for me to touch you."

"Yes, I did. I'd have wrecked you then. Ruined you."

"Don't you know that's what you're doing now?" she whispered. "What you've been doing since you came back?"

He stiffened again.

"I love you, Reed. I love you so much it terrifies me." She hadn't meant to say it, hadn't meant to put that on him because if he didn't feel the same, it was a burden.

"Because of nights like tonight. That's why you're afraid." He made no mention of his feelings for her, if he ever had any. But that was okay. She knew he felt something for her; he had to.

"Yes. And because you said that it'll all be better tomorrow. That you'll fix it. I know you can't do that, but I still believe you will." She leaned her forehead against him.

"I will this time."

"Do you remember when my mom died?" This probably wasn't the best time to bring this up, but it was there on the tip of her tongue, begging to be breathed out into the world.

"Of course. I'll never forget that night."

"You held me all night on the couch. You stayed with me and took care of me, too."

He didn't speak.

"I think that's why I always look to you when I'm hurt and upset. When you weren't here, I had to handle things on my own and I could. I did. But with you here, it's like that night all over again. I think I forget that you need that from me, too." She sighed. "But you can't run away from me every time we have a disagreement. What's it going to be next time?" She was afraid that everything was going to crash and burn.

"I told you, tomorrow."

"What's so magical about tomorrow? It never was for my mother. For Crystal. For me. Why does it get to be special for you?"

"Gina, I'm done talking about this now."

She inhaled. "I guess I need something to be fixed now. I feel like I can't be comfortable in my own skin until it is. Until I have some stability. You know, like I was saying about my mom. You're that for me, so please…"

He rolled over and looked at her.

The expression on his face told her that maybe she'd misread everything. He hadn't said he'd loved her back. He hadn't made any confession of his own. He just wanted her to stop, to be quiet and leave him alone.

Then he softened, pulled her close. "You're okay, Gina. Everything is okay."

She nestled against him and everything was right again. Everything would be okay. All of the comparisons she'd made to Crys faded away in the wake of his closeness and the security she felt.

"This was why," she said, hoping he'd understand. This was physical proof of why she'd tried to push him away. She needed him and she couldn't afford to need him.

"I know. Didn't make it cut any less or make it any more okay."

"I've been talking about making this better for me, like all I had to do was say I was sorry and it was all fixed. How do I make it better for you?"

"Put your hands on me again. Stay with me tonight."

Gina reached out and caressed his cheek, smoothed her thumb over the blade of his cheekbone, smoothed his hair.

When she was younger, she dreamed of moments like this. She'd gotten exactly what she wanted, only it was like the story of the monkey's paw—a couple wishing for a million dollars only to have someone they loved die to get it. She should've specified the circumstances in which this was her version of happily-ever-after.

But maybe this was okay. Maybe they'd work through it and be a family. After all, all they had left in the world was each other and Amanda Jane.

"I'll always stay with you."

"You told me not to make promises I can't keep. I'm going to say the same to you. Don't promise to stay when you can't. When you shouldn't."

She had the feeling he was going to do something they'd both regret. He was as much as warning her he was going to fail her. Fail Amanda Jane. "Let's not talk about that. Let's talk of good things. I don't want to sleep with any sour words on our tongues or sour thoughts in our heads."

"How about something sweet, then?" He kissed her gently, tenderly. A wealth of emotion was in that kiss.

At least, that was the way it felt to Gina.

She surrendered to it easily, gratefully.

His arms always felt so good. So right. As if this was where she belonged and nothing could hurt.

He pulled back, looking at her, searching her face for some answer to his questions, some sign. She knew then what it was. He loved her.

"You don't have to say it."

"You won't believe me tomorrow, so I do have to tell you. I love you, Gina. I've always loved you. But I've always known that you're out of my league."

She wondered why he thought she wouldn't believe him tomorrow, but Gina pushed it out of her head. She wanted to think about now, wanted to think about his hands on her, his lips, and that he loved her.

Gina had never had a love all her own, and it was scary and beautiful at the same time.

She had emotional whiplash and everything was all jumbled up together inside her guts.

"That's all I've ever wanted."

He drew the pad of his thumb across her cheek. "You wanted to be a doctor."

"I do. And I have both. I can't help but think girls like me don't get happily-ever-after. I mean," she confessed.

"Because if you were thinking straight, you'd only want to be a doctor."

"How can you say that?" She turned her cheek into the caress, loving the way his hands felt on her.

"This isn't the life you want."

"Yes, it is," she cried.

"You said so yourself. You said you can't do this again. You said that you could see our life together, but that there would always be this doubt. It would suck the joy and love right out of you, sweetheart."

"Isn't it my choice to make?"

"It's our choice to make."

"You don't want to be with me?" She hated how small and weak she sounded. Gina wanted to be a lion, she wanted to roar, she wanted to demand that he be brave with her.

"My heart has been yours for all of my life, Gina."

"You didn't answer the question."

"And I'm not going to. Not until tomorrow."

She sighed. "Again, I ask, what's this magical tomorrow?" Her voice was a lot gentler than the last time she asked. There was no anger behind her words, just a curious sort of bittersweet pain.

Gina wasn't stupid. She knew he was going to plan some grand gesture that would suck for both of them, but it would make him think he was doing the right thing. She wanted to talk him out of it, tell him that whatever he was planning, no. Just no. They'd figure this out together.

She spoke again. "I've decided that I don't like tomorrow. I'm not going to do it."

"You're not going to do tomorrow?" He pulled her closer. "How would you avoid it? Tomorrow is the best thing that can happen to any of us."

Crystal wouldn't have tomorrow even if she wanted it. So that wasn't something she meant. "I don't know what I'm saying." She shook her head. "I just don't want you to throw this away between us because you think you're saving me. I don't need you to save me."

"Then what do you need from me, besides my money?"

"Don't be stupid."

"That didn't answer the question."

"What if I say that I won't answer the question until tomorrow?" She thought she'd already answered the question, but if he still didn't know what she wanted from him, hearing her say it wasn't going to clear it up any. To Gina's way of thinking, she'd already said it a million times, in a million ways.

"I'd say that's okay."

No, damn it. It wasn't okay. "Words are just hot air, Reed. It's actions that matter. That's what counts."

"Words matter, too. Words are the sharpest of swords and cause wounds that never heal. Bones will mend, sometimes hearts do not."

Something in her twisted. "That's actually rather pretty."

"Yeah, here I am, the poet." He brushed off her compliment.

"Yeah, there you are." She brushed her lips against his. "Don't hide from me. I know that you've got a gentle heart, Reed. You always did."

He snorted, but didn't turn away. "What good has a gentle heart ever done me? Or anyone else?"

"It made me love you."

"That's probably not a good thing."

"Why do you keep saying that? Like you think that

you're not worthy of love? But that's what you wanted, isn't it? To be seen as the person you are? I do, Reed."

"That's the shit of it, isn't it?" His eyes were hooded and dark. "I think that you do and I can't have you or this because I see you, too. I see who you are. I see who you can be."

"I like who I am right now."

He closed his eyes for a minute and took her hand. "Maybe this is that moment of drunk clarity, you know? Where everything blurs, but then comes into sharp focus that's so HD that it's surreal."

"What do you mean?"

"You don't think that being with me would change you? Or do you think that you're going to change me?"

"We'll change each other."

"But not for the better. I keep hearing what you said to me. Those words about what our future will be like and you're right. You will always wonder."

"Reed…"

"Yeah, you would. And you'd be right to. Then you'd feel guilty for not trusting me, but that wouldn't stop you from always wondering. You know how much that wears on a person, on your heart, on your soul. On the love that you have for them."

"Fear isn't noble."

"There is a difference between fear and knowing. Between preservation and annihilation."

"That's a little overdramatic, don't you think?" She continued stroking his cheek softly, trailing her fingers through his hair.

"No, I don't. Loving me will break you. For a minute, I thought it would be okay. I thought if you'd just love me…and now you do and I know that I can't have it. Not if I give a damn about you."

"I thought this was our decision to make together, but it sounds like you've already decided."

"Gina." He sighed her name.

"Reed," she returned.

"It's too much for me, okay?"

She reared back. "Too much for you? No, that's not okay. What are you talking about?"

"I'm talking about all the pressure to be good for you. To be perfect. To be what I know you need. I can't. I just can't."

"I'm not asking you to be anything more for me than what you need to be for Amanda Jane. Are you leaving her, too?"

"I don't know."

Fear mingled with rage, but simmered with pain. "You're drunk."

"No. I'm being realistic. We fought today. And what did I do?"

Her lip quivered, but she refused to give in to tears. She didn't speak, she didn't know what to say. Even if she'd had the words, she was too angry to speak them.

"I fell. I crashed. I ran away. *I failed*." He tried to push a lock of her hair away from her face, but she pulled away.

"So what? We all fail. I failed Crystal. Now I'm failing Amanda Jane. We both are if you walk away. You don't want to be with me? I won't say it's fine, or that I don't care. But I'll get over it." Her heart protested that for a lie. "But if you leave Amanda Jane, she won't get over it. She's wanted a father for so long and you let her trust you, you let her believe in you. Don't you dare do this."

CHAPTER TWENTY-ONE

SHINING THE LIGHT of truth on himself was ugly and hard for Reed. He'd convinced himself that he could be a father, a partner—maybe even a husband.

But after what had happened today, he knew that wasn't true. If he loved Amanda Jane and Gina, the best thing he could do for them would be make room in their lives for someone who could be all of the things he wasn't.

He'd finally gotten someone to love him for who he was and because he loved them back, he knew he couldn't let them settle for a man like him. Reed wished he knew how to explain to Gina that it wasn't fear. It was the knowledge he had of himself—a home truth as her mama used to say.

If someone like him, no matter how much money he had, wanted a place in his daughter's life, Reed would do anything he could to excise him like a cancer. And that had to include himself. This was the best way he knew how to be a good father—to let another man do it. A man who would love Gina, love Amanda Jane and not only love them, but be worthy of their love in return.

"I wish I could make you understand." He needed to tell her to go, but he couldn't make himself. Reed wanted to look at her as long as he could. "I'm going to move back to the city. I'll have the deed to the house transferred to your name."

"I don't want the house." Her lips were set into a thin line.

"Yes, you do. You want a safe environment for Amanda Jane." He should've known that she wouldn't understand. That she'd made this difficult.

"This is *our* house, Reed. Don't you think she's going to feel your absence? I can't—" She shook her head.

"Then I'll buy you another house."

"We don't want your damn money," she snarled.

"No, but that's all I can give you that's worth a shit." The confession was torn from him.

"You know—" she scooted off the bed "—maybe you're right. If you'd leave me, us, right after her mother died, you're not the man I thought you were."

"If I don't do it now, I never will. And then you'll have that future that you didn't want." The future where she'd talked about spending her life with him. Children. Grandchildren. And never trusting him, always wondering if and when he was going to slip and fall.

Fail.

"Who says I don't want it? Nothing's perfect."

"You did. You said you didn't want it," he reminded her quietly. Reed pulled out the big guns. "What if Amanda Jane had seen me tonight?"

"So what if she did? Then she'll know you're not perfect. It's a lesson we all have to learn about our parents."

"I'm not good for you. Or for her. Don't make this harder on us than it has to be." Why wouldn't she let him do the right thing?

He watched as her face changed. "So much for tomorrow being magical."

Reed wanted to pull her close, comfort her, but he knew he was the reason for her pain. It tore him up inside, but better to hurt her now, like ripping off a Band-Aid, than to drag out and let it fester and rot like he knew it would. When the stardust in her eyes settled, she'd be wondering where her life went and how she ever could've wasted it on him.

He couldn't say anything else. He'd tried to clean up his mess as best he could, but the way she stood there so small, so breakable, it was as if every second was another slash of the blade against her skin. He didn't know how to fix it—and maybe he couldn't. Maybe time would be the best balm.

Though, he didn't see that time would ever mend his wounds. He'd love Gina Townsend for all the days of his life. And Amanda Jane—he ached at the thought of leaving her. His chest swelled with pride when he thought about her, how smart she was, how kind, how lovely. She was an amazing gift and he wouldn't spoil her.

Gina was a rare flower indeed to have been able to bloom among the waste she'd been born into. None of that would touch his daughter. He didn't care what he had to sacrifice to make sure of that.

"You're the one making it harder, Reed. You promised her, you bastard. You told her that you'd never leave her. How many times did you make that promise? If you didn't mean it, you shouldn't have said it. Don't you betray her."

The door creaked open slowly and Amanda Jane stood in the darkness, her blue eyes puffy and swollen, her small, ragged bear dangling from one hand. "Daddy's leaving?"

The expression on her little face punched up through his chest and into his heart. "Maybe for a little while."

She'd miss him at first, and then he'd just become something that happened to her. She'd move on. She'd forget—

Amanda Jane ran to him and crawled up on the bed. "You promised."

If she'd cried, it might have been easier. He could've chalked up tears to childhood hysterics, but instead, she just clung to him. Clung so tightly, that she thought she'd anchor him there with her. It was so adult, but at the same time, so very honest.

"Take me with you." Her voice was quiet, but much more adult that it ever should've had to be.

And the hand that had punched through his heart now squeezed it so tightly he couldn't breathe.

"I'll be good. I'll be quiet. I won't make a mess." As if being a good girl would right everything that was wrong. As if she could make everything right. She was so much like Gina.

"I know," he said, and rested his chin on the top of her head. "You're a very good girl."

Gina shot him a disgusted look and he knew he deserved it. God, this wasn't supposed to be so hard. He thought he was doing the right thing.

"If I was a good girl, Mama wouldn't have died. I'll

be better. Then you won't be sick. You won't die. Grammie won't die."

If the look of derision on Gina's face was any more intense, he would've burst into flames. He kept waiting for her to speak, to reassure Amanda Jane, but she sat in stone silence, waiting for him to fix it.

"That's not your fault, honey. You're—" He'd been about to say she was the best daughter ever, perfect, but then that was putting the same expectation on her that he'd found too heavy a burden on his own shoulders. He couldn't be the perfect father. He couldn't be the perfect anything, but then again, no one could. "You're just fine. Nothing you did could change what happened to your mama. Or to me."

"Then why are you leaving us?" If she'd been an adult, he might have thought she was being manipulative, but this was just a question from a child who didn't understand all the changes in her world.

Gina watched him expectantly.

"I have work. It's just for a little while." What was he doing? This wasn't helping anyone. This wasn't helping him, this wasn't helping her.

"It's forever. I know it's forever," the little girl cried and clung even more tightly.

"No, it's okay, Amanda Jane. I won't go." Even as he said the words, he knew they weren't the right ones. He was such a failure. He couldn't stand to see her in that kind of pain, that afraid. When all he had to do was say a single sentence and it would make it all stop.

"I want you to stay with me while I sleep."

He tucked her into the bed.

Damn you, Gina mouthed.

That's for sure. He was damned and so were they.

Gina turned and moved toward the door, but Amanda Jane stopped her. "You, too, Gina-bee. Stay."

"Honey, I—"

Amanda Jane looked up at her, a pleading expression on her face, and lay down on the opposite side.

"It should be like this," she said authoritatively.

Reed watched Gina over his daughter's head, and there were tears in her eyes, but he knew she was more angry than hurt. He didn't blame her. She had every right to be. He'd made promises he knew he couldn't keep.

Amanda Jane tucked her bear in next to her, and linked one hand with Gina's, one with his, and then joined them over her, wrapping herself in the place she felt safest.

Gina's glare bored into his head, but he couldn't say that he didn't deserve it.

He fell asleep like that, with Amanda Jane between them, and when he awoke, the bed was empty.

Reed padded downstairs to the kitchen and found Gina drinking a cup of coffee and reading on her e-reader.

He didn't speak. He wasn't sure what to say.

But she did it for him.

"Amanda Jane is playing in her room. We need to talk about last night."

Her spine was board-straight, and her eyes flashed fire.

"What's there to talk about?" This thing was broken and there wasn't any way to fix it, feelings aside.

"Oh, I don't know. The part where you're abandoning your daughter. You know what?" She stood and put her hands on her hips. "I don't care what happens between us. You don't want to be with me? Fine. We'll pretend all of that never happened. But you will not bail on Amanda Jane."

"It's the best I can do for her."

"No, it's not the best you can do for her. God, do you know that's what Crystal said to me? It's the best she could do—leaving us. Telling her sweet little girl that she didn't want her."

"That's not what I'm saying at all." He was horrified that she would think that, but maybe that was what it sounded like.

"Actions. Actions speak louder than any words you could ever say. It doesn't matter what you say. She'll just know what you did." She put her coffee cup down. "If you fight me on this, I'll take you to court for breach of contract. Both of our parts are all laid out in the document you had me sign. I had Emma go over it this morning. You. Will. Not. Leave. Her."

There was a part of him that was gleeful, happy that he couldn't do the right thing. Happy she'd fight him. He knew that was wrong, sick. Just like he was.

"If you feel that strongly about making a man stay where he doesn't want to be."

He shouldn't have said it, he didn't mean it. He was lashing out because all of this hurt too much. He couldn't get away from it. But the look on her face as his arrows struck true, it made him sick.

Reed didn't want to hurt her. He'd tried to love her. He'd failed at that, too.

"I do." She lifted her chin. "You made this bed. You lie in it."

She slammed out of the kitchen and went upstairs, stopping as she went.

God, the fire in that woman. It made him love her even more.

He decided to call Gray and see if she really did have him by the balls with the contract. Gray was the one who'd drafted it, and he was sure he could get him out of it.

Except that was the bitch of it. He didn't really want out of it. He just wanted to do the right thing. He wished that Gina could understand that.

He supposed maybe she did, but their definition of what the right thing was happened to be two different things.

He dialed Gray.

"Do you need bail?"

"No," Reed replied. "Why would you ask that?"

"Then I'm having breakfast. Let me call you back."

"Actually, it's about that contract."

"I thought that was all hammered out? *You* signed it. *She* signed it. It's filed. Done," Gray said.

He thought he could hear a woman in the background, but Reed wasn't sure. "What if I wanted to dissolve it?"

"You did not just say that to me. I didn't hear it."

"Why not?" Gray had never put him off before.

"Because I'm…busy. With someone I can't talk to if I heard that."

"You're always bus—Emma's there?" he said as the epiphany hit.

"I just got her to agree to breakfast."

"Emma knows. Gina said she went over the contract this morning."

"She most definitely did not. She's been with me since dawn. We went fishing."

"Fishing?" Reed wasn't sure he understood.

"You know. Out in a boat. With poles. Worms. Coffee. *Fishing.*"

"I didn't know you were into that." Reed breathed and laughed. "Well, here's the thing. I need to know if I can get out of it."

"I can get you out of anything," Gray said with pride. "But I don't know how easy it will be. Gina is determined to make you stick to the parameters?"

"Most determined." He found himself smiling, even though he knew he was chasing after his own heartbreak.

"Can I ask you something?"

"You're going to, anyway." He didn't really want to talk about it.

"Why do you want out?" Gray asked.

"Because I love them."

"That doesn't make any sense to me, man."

"I fucked up, okay?" he confessed. He couldn't bear to speak of his failure again.

"I'll be over." Gray's tone was grim.

"No, that's fine. Whenever. Enjoy your time with Emma. We can talk later."

"Look, I'm your friend too. Not just your lawyer. What happened?"

He didn't want to hammer over it again. "Things just got a little heavier than I expected."

"Far be it from me to judge you, but do you know that you sound like the biggest douche bag right now?" Gray said.

"Yeah. But it's for a good reason." Wasn't it? What had happened… Maybe he was being an asshole. Maybe this wasn't about him at all, but he was trying to punish Gina for not living up to the ideal he'd built in his head. She was a real woman with faults and weakness. It wasn't fair to hold her to a higher standard.

He thought that he knew himself, but maybe he didn't. Maybe not as well as he thought.

"No, it's not. I'm coming over. Right now." The line went dead.

That wasn't the reaction he'd been looking for. He'd hoped Grayson would go piranha and untangle him from this, but that didn't seem to be the case.

He put his head in his hands.

Why wouldn't anyone let him fix this? Why couldn't they understand this had all been a mistake to start with? He knew leaving would hurt Gina, hurt Amanda Jane and most of all, it would hurt him. It cut him so deeply, the thought of not being with them, not seeing them.

But after last night, he knew he couldn't be trusted.

Maybe if even his lawyer was trying to talk him out of it, maybe it was a mistake, after all?

He kept thinking about Gina, about the fire in her eyes, the pain…

Reed was still sitting there in the clothes he'd worn

last night, hair mussed and bleary-eyed, when Gray came through the door. He didn't bother to knock. Surprisingly, he had Emma in tow.

She was wearing shorts and wading boots. "Not one word from you about the boots." And she tromped up the stairs. "I'm getting Gina and Amanda Jane and taking them out."

"When did you two become a unit?"

Gray paused. "We're not a *unit*. We're friends."

"You. Friends. With a woman?" Reed didn't think his eyebrows could get any higher. Grayson wasn't the type to be friends with a woman. He liked women, to be sure. Just not more than once.

"Screw you, Reed." Gray rolled his eyes. "Come on. Let's go get some breakfast since you interrupted the catching of mine."

Reed allowed himself to be pulled out to Gray's car and they found themselves at a hole-in-the-wall diner outside of Highway 5.

It was one of those places that would either be the best food you'd ever had, or the worst and you'd find yourself in an emergency room two hours later begging for death.

But those were his favorite kinds of places. He liked the realism and it reminded him of where he came from, but in a good way. Not all that he was lacking, or all the ways he'd failed, but all the ways it could be good, too.

Like the food.

It was a roll of the dice and sometimes they rolled in his favor.

"So tell me why and how you've lost your mind," Gray said after they'd gotten their coffee.

"I think I just got some clarity."

"That you couldn't have had a few weeks ago when you started all of this? Come on. It's not like you to run away."

That rankled. "I'm not running."

"Aren't you?"

"No." Wasn't he?

"Really?" Gray eyed him.

"No. I just realized I'll never be better than this."

"Christ, man. We all have our faults. We all have our failings. Do you think Gina is perfect?"

"Yes." Even though he'd told himself she had her own weaknesses, he never could see them. In his mind, if she hadn't told him, hadn't consulted, it was because she found him lacking. That's where all his pain was coming from—because he believed she was right.

"Oh, hell. You're screwed, you know that, right?" Gray nodded emphatically. "She's obviously not perfect if something she did made you angry enough or hurt you enough—"

"I don't want to deconstruct my feelings." Reed took a gulp of the black brew.

"Maybe you don't want to, but if you don't, you're going to 'deconstruct' your whole life. You've got a good thing going. You've been happy. Have you told her you love her?"

Reed didn't even bother to deny that he was in love with Gina. "Yes."

"And? You're killing me here."

"And she loves me. That's why I know I'm bad for her."

"Oh, come off it. Really? I'm going to save you from yourself? She's a smart woman. She's been taking care of herself and your daughter for a long time. That's a cop-out."

"It's the truth," he said vehemently.

"It's the truth that it's a cop-out? Yes." Gray nodded.

"Stop debating with me and just fix it."

"I'm trying," he said, as if it were the most obvious thing and Reed was too slow on the uptake to comprehend it.

Reed narrowed his eyes.

"Look, are you sure this is what you want to do?"

No, he wasn't. But he knew it was what he should do. "I just want to do the right thing for her and Amanda Jane."

"Don't you think being present would be kind of helpful?"

"No, I don't."

Gray gave him a look of utter contempt. "Breaking a little girl's heart isn't going to help anyone."

Reed's guts were twisted from the inside out. "I love them."

"Then be there. Be a father. Be a husband."

He finally found the words he'd been looking for. "I'm afraid. I don't know how."

"Of course you are. If I was in your position, I'd be pissing my pants."

"I'm afraid that my daughter will see me as the way a man should be. If I stay in her life she'll end up with someone like me." There was nothing worse than that to his way of thinking.

"Is that so bad? You pulled yourself up out of nothing. You built an empire. She has all the advantages now. So just imagine the things she can do."

He and Gray came from the same dark pit, but Gray used every hash mark against him as a ladder to climb to something better. He was one of those people who was convinced he'd win no matter what odds were in his way.

"I don't know how to do this."

"Who does?" Gray shrugged. "You've been bottled up since I met you. Always worried about someone stealing your hoard and now you have someone you want to give it all to, but you won't. This makes no sense to me. It's okay to be happy, Reed."

"Is it? There's a part of me that thinks if I'm happy, that it'll somehow bring my good fortune to the attention of the universe and the powers that be will realize their mistake and snatch it all away."

"So why not enjoy it while you have it rather than throwing it away?"

"I don't want to break her."

"Gina or Amanda Jane? You know, it doesn't matter. They're both made of stronger stuff." He ate a piece of bacon.

Reed looked at the food in front of him and thought about rolling the dice, not just for the meal, but with everything else he'd been given. If only he hadn't run away from Gina last night. Even if he wanted to stay, he couldn't take back the words he'd said. He shouldn't.

Because no matter how he felt, he couldn't stop thinking about what she said about their future together. About no matter how happy they were together, she'd always wonder. He didn't want that for her or for Amanda Jane. And it didn't matter how good he was, if he never stumbled again, and still, it would be there in the back of her mind—a lurking darkness that shadowed everything.

"You know, if you really want to make her draw her line in the sand, you could propose a real marriage. Tell her to make it real, or you're out."

"Excuse me, what?" Reed coughed and barely managed to swallow.

"She wants to push, you push back. She wants you to stay, she wants you to keep to your end, ask her to put her money where her mouth is." He chewed as if he hadn't just suggested the apocalypse.

"She just lost her sister. This isn't really the right—"

"It's the perfect time. Because it sounds to me like Crystal gave you all each other. This was what she wanted for all of you. And if you're serious about getting out of the contract, make her see why she should let you."

"I still don't understand your logic."

"If you're good enough to be Amanda Jane's father, you're good enough to be Gina's husband." He shrugged.

He shoveled a bite of egg into his mouth. "A real marriage? I don't know."

"It will make your point."

"And what if she says yes?" The thought both thrilled and terrified him.

"Then you'll still get what you want, only this time, it'll be what you really want. Not what you think you're supposed to want."

Gray's words startled him because really being married to Gina was exactly what he wanted. "This is insane. I can't—"

"Just think about it."

That was the problem. He had thought about it. So had she. They'd come up empty. "Is that what you would do?"

"Hell, no. I'd have sued for sole custody. But I'm a hateful bastard." Gray grinned. "I know that girl loves you. If you let yourself, you might just get everything you ever wanted."

Reed seriously doubted that kind of thing had ever been in the offing for him.

But not Gina. Not Amanda Jane.

Only, there was this new track in his head and it wasn't as loud as the other one, but it asked him what if he really was what they wanted? What if it was Reed they'd been missing?

CHAPTER TWENTY-TWO

GINA WISHED THAT she could be more like Reed. That it could be so easy for her to forge ties and to break them. He was willing to throw everything away and not look back.

When she'd told him that she didn't care about how things went between them, that had been the biggest lie she'd ever uttered and it had tasted the most foul on her tongue.

A knock on her door startled her. "It's me," Emma said.

"Come in."

"Say nothing about what I'm wearing," her friend warned.

Gina looked her up and down. "I'm sure there's a story there somewhere."

"There is. But today isn't about my story. It's about yours and Reed's. And Amanda Jane's."

"He called Gray." She narrowed her eyes.

"Yes, he did. And you lied to him about me reading the contract."

"I did. I'm sorry. I just… I didn't have anything to bargain with and he was slipping away." She held up her hands.

"Gray took him out for breakfast and now, I'm going to take you and Amanda Jane to Sweet Thing. There is nothing that donuts can't fix."

"I don't really feel up—"

"Wasn't asking." Emma shook her head. "Either put on your shoes, or I'll do it for you. You've been spending a lot of time here and you need to get out. See people."

"Yeah, see people talking about my sick grandmother, what a hard time I've had of it, what a hard time we all have…" Gina shook her head.

"Oh, honey. I think you'd be surprised. Trouble has a way of erasing your sins, especially in a town like this. I promise." Emma nodded. "Betsy was just asking after you."

"That's Betsy. You know she's so nice she could put a saint to shame."

"It's more than Betsy. You just wait until the cars start their trek up Knob Hill. You're part of Glory. You're more than the poor kid done good."

Sometimes she hated how easily Emma could see through her walls. She didn't have to tear them down, she just had to look and they crumbled on their own.

"I've always felt like that's what they want me to be. So I'm a story, not a person." She was always reminded of the way that her teachers would look at her, their eyes shining, as if she was some kind of trailer-trash unicorn. She was always "that poor girl" until she became the one who would make a difference and it wasn't that she didn't want to make a difference, of course she did. She just felt the weight of their expectation.

"Of course you're a story. You're hope. Look at all

you've done. You might inspire someone else." Emma hugged her. "I know you inspire me."

"Now you're going to make me cry, stop that." Her face prickled.

"Only if you agree to come out to Sweet Thing with me."

"Fine. I'll come to Sweet Thing."

"Good." Emma grinned. "I'll go surprise Amanda Jane."

She stuffed her feet into her tennis shoes without untying them and followed Emma to surprise Amanda Jane.

Instead of playing, she was thumbing through a pop-up picture book of fairy-tale castles. That was something new that Gina hadn't seen before.

How could Reed think he wasn't a good father?

Maybe because you didn't tell him he could be a good one, a voice whispered.

Maybe if she'd had a little more faith in him— She cut the thought off at the knees. No, he shouldn't need her validation. Should she worry that every time she disagreed with him he'd run off looking for some way to kill the feelings inside him?

She cringed at herself, knowing it was more than that. Gina hadn't given him any support or any trust and that was crucial because he didn't trust himself. She should've acknowledged that he was trying.

And deep down, she knew all this talk about leaving them was him trying the best way he knew how. His words were sharp, the swords cut deep, and even when he tried to wound her, the crux of it was that Gina knew he thought he was doing it for her.

For Amanda Jane.

With a little room to breathe, she could see that.

But that didn't stop it from hurting. It didn't stop that fear from rising up to choke her and reminding her in no uncertain terms that she did not have control of anything.

It seemed that their demons just didn't play well together.

That's all a person could hope for really, that when you spend your life with someone that maybe your dark parts could fit together as well as your light. That your demons could play together as well as your angels.

Theirs just didn't.

They were both too broken.

She looked at Amanda Jane. She was the glue that could hold them both together—if he wanted to. If he'd just try.

"Did Daddy leave?" she asked quietly, looking back and forth between Gina and Emma. Her eyes were so large and clear, it was as if she was just waiting for them to come tell her that she'd been abandoned again.

"Just for breakfast with our friend Gray."

She managed a small smile. "That's a silly name. That's a color."

"His name is Grayson," Emma supplied.

"I like that much better." Amanda Jane nodded and put the book down. "Are we going someplace? That would be like someone calling me Mandy. I don't like that." She switched back and forth between subjects as kids tended to do.

"Breakfast with Miss Betsy at Sweet Thing," Emma supplied.

"Frosted frog legs?" she perked.

Emma raised a brow. "If that's what you want."

Amanda Jane nodded emphatically. "Can we bring Daddy some?"

All that child could ever talk about was her daddy. Gina sighed and decided that maybe Reed didn't know that, but he needed to.

"Of course we can."

"I liked us all sleeping in the same place. Can we do it again?"

Gina's face heated and Emma turned her head slowly, obviously making an effort not to give herself whiplash. Her brow was raised.

"I don't know about that. How about we have the frosted frog legs and worry about the rest later?"

"Okay." Amanda Jane went rummaging for her shoes.

When she disappeared into her closet, Emma said, "What was that?"

"I'll tell you later." She wasn't really ready to talk about it because she didn't know how she felt, how she wanted to proceed. She appreciated Emma's advice, but Emma was too honest. As much as she clung to logic and realism, in this case, she wasn't ready to process it.

"Are you sleeping with him?"

"Yes. We were sleeping. Somnambulists." Gina nodded emphatically.

"Don't get cute." Emma's brow had crawled so high

up into her hairline, Gina was sure it was going to get stuck. "You know what I mean."

"Can't talk about this now." Gina nodded toward the closet door.

"You're in deeper trouble than I thought." She shook her head.

"Yeah, so. You knew I was half in love with him in high school." Gina shrugged. That was no secret and maybe it would go a long way in getting Emma to be quiet about it.

"And you're all in love with him now, aren't you?"

Gina's shoulders sagged. "Yeah, so?"

Emma pursed her lips and sighed softly. "Are you in love with the man he is or the man you want him to be?"

"That's why we fought." Well, she obviously wasn't getting out of talking about it. So she might as well tell her the highlights. "I think I expected too much of him. And he expected too much of me."

"And now?" Emma prompted.

"Now he thinks Amanda Jane and I will be better off."

"Maybe you would be. Have you thought about that? I've never seen you like this in all the years that I've known you. He upsets you, unbalances you."

"No," Gina growled. "No, we wouldn't. Amanda Jane idolizes him. She's wanted a father for so long and I remember what that was like. Hoping that some-day he'd remember me. Someday he'd want me. Some-day he'd love me. And I wouldn't have to do this on my own and I'd be someone."

"You *are* someone."

"I know that." Gina shook her head. "But that ache? It never goes away. It never eases. I know who I am. I know what I can do. That doesn't change the fact that I still want a father."

"The thing is, would you have wanted Reed? I mean, if you're doing this for Amanda Jane. One man is not just as good as any other."

Gina thought about it, really considered what that meant. Even with his failings, even considering his stumble and the fact he could fall again. That he might screw up, even after all of his promises, he was a good man.

Would she choose him, if she had that choice?

Then she realized that she did have that choice. Right now, he'd offered her a way out. He'd given her the power to choose Amanda Jane's father. The man who would raise her. The man who would love her. The man she could always look to for comfort, for safety...

Would she choose him if she didn't have to?

The answer was yes.

"I can see it on your face." Emma sighed. "It'll be okay. It's screwed up, but I'm sure he loves you, too. Sometimes men do stupid things when they're trying to be manly." She rolled her eyes.

She laughed. "He said he loved me and I know that's why he's doing this, but that doesn't make it hurt any less. The problem is that we don't have trust, not like we need to."

"So how can you say you're in love without trust? Love is nothing without trust." Emma shook her head.

"I think the trust issue isn't with each other. It's trusting yourselves."

"How do we fix that?"

"I don't think anything is going to be an easy fix. Life isn't like that. It's messy and ugly, even when it's beautiful."

Amanda Jane popped out of the closet, shoes on and ready to go.

Gina took her hand and led her down to Emma's car.

Once inside Sweet Thing, Betsy knew exactly what to do for Amanda Jane. There was a kind sorrow in her eyes as she looked at Gina.

"How are you holding up?" she asked, when Amanda Jane had been settled with her "frosted frog legs."

"I'm okay." She nodded, and for now, that wasn't a lie. She was okay. "Being married is…different."

"My mom is currently making you more fried chicken than you could possibly eat in this lifetime or the next. You should expect the Ladies Auxiliary at your house very soon with their casseroles," Betsy warned her in a conspiratorial whisper.

"That would've been nice had they sent those over when my mother was dying of cancer." Gina bit her lip. "I'm sorry, I shouldn't have said that."

"You say whatever you want." Betsy patted her hand. "Yes, they should have. I agree. If I'd known you then, I would've stolen you to come eat at my house all the time. My brother did that with India."

Gina found a smile. "And you're both the kindest people I've ever known."

"If you look around, I think you'll see more of that here. Glory is a good place, Gina."

"Once you're on the right side of the proverbial tracks." Gina wasn't exactly bitter; she'd just seen the system in action.

"I don't think anyone knew how bad it was out there until your mom died. The way that you and Crys were trying to pay the bills, take care of yourselves and having to choose between paying the water bill and buying food."

"You always want to think the best of everyone."

Betsy nodded with a smile. "You're right, I do. And it's been a long journey for me to get to that place."

"You?" Gina cocked her head to the side. "But you're made of unicorn breath and rainbows, right?"

Betsy laughed. "Yeah, I'll tell you about it sometime if you want. Come after lunch rush someday and we'll chat. It was Jack that gave me hope."

"Are you telling fairy tales about me again, woman?" Jack, her husband, asked and wrapped his arms around her waist.

She slapped at him lightly. "Stop that. We're in public."

"This is Glory. It's not public." He planted a kiss on her neck and made his way over to the table where Amanda Jane was eating.

Gina sighed. She'd thought that Betsy had the fairy tale, and maybe she did. But in all fairy tales, the darkest times had to be weathered before the best. Sometimes, she lost sight of that. No, actually, a lot of times she lost sight of that.

"What for you this morning?" Betsy asked.

"I don't know. I had a hard night. Do you have any 'fix it' donuts?"

Betsy laughed. "You know, I just might." She reached into the case. "Try this one. It's Nutella cheesecake. If you can't fix everything with Nutella, well, it's beyond broke."

Gina paid for the treat and sat down next to Emma, who was eating something that looked a lot like a frosted frog leg.

"You're not really eating all of that?"

"Yes, yes I am." Emma nodded and took another bite. "I'm now a firm believer in dessert first and it doesn't get much firster than breakfast."

"Firster? Is that what your fancy law degree taught you?"

Emma grinned. "Yep."

They laughed and Gina tried the donut that was supposed to be the miracle cure.

After she took the first bite, she realized that maybe it was a cure-all—or there was just enough sugar to make her brain explode in euphoria, but either way, she felt a little better.

Amanda Jane finished her frosted frog leg and asked to go look at the case. As soon as she peered around behind the counter, Betsy said, "I'm putting your little one to work." She winked at Gina and handed Amanda Jane a tube of frosting. "Want to make your own frosted frog leg?"

Amanda Jane looked back to Gina. "Can I?"

Gina nodded, grateful to have her distracted not

only from her conversation with Emma, but from all the darkness that had come into her life lately. "Mind Miss Betsy."

"So." Emma began around a mouthful of pastry. "Tell me everything."

"I don't know, it just happened." She shrugged it off. "There's not much else to tell, really."

Emma rolled her eyes again. "Come on, details. I need to live vicariously. That night that Amanda Jane spent the night with Missy."

She nodded. "Yeah."

"Surely it didn't just happen that night. There had to have been signs, flirting…something."

"Some kissing." She shrugged. "But we agreed it was best to forget it happened. Dating with a child is exceptionally hard. Especially when you're both responsible for the same child. If it doesn't work out, you're left with a mess on your hands."

"That you have, anyway," Emma cheerfully supplied.

"Yes, that we have, anyway," she agreed. "I don't know what I'm supposed to do now."

"I'm going to tell you what I tell most of my clients going through relationship troubles. Although usually, they're ending relationships rather than beginning them. I tell them that a child knows when her caregivers are happy and content. She also knows when they are not. To be a good parent, to wear that hat, you have to be a good you."

"That doesn't make sense to me."

"Okay, just listen. You have to be happy yourself. In your own skin. If you're happy, no matter what the situation, she will feel safe and secure to blossom. At least that's what I've gathered from practicing family law."

"I know I need to fix this. I just don't know how."

"Talk to him." She ate another bite and sighed with pleasure.

"I tried talking to him last night."

"Last night when emotions were running high for both of you? I'm sure that Gray has been able to talk some sense into him and he might be in a more receptive place."

"Why are you suddenly in the Gray camp? Are you two—"

"No. Definitely no. We're just…sort of friends."

"Sort of friends? That was a pretty friendly kiss he laid on you at Frogfest."

"We will not discuss Frogfest. It did not happen." Emma sat up straighter, as if the more proper she was, the less likely it would be that Frogfest had occurred.

Gina raised a brow. "Oh, really? And you were doing what with him this morning? I mean, it's pretty early."

"One doesn't go bass fishing in the late morning or early afternoon. Dawn or dusk is the best. I mean, if you want to catch anything worth keeping."

"Uh-huh." She nodded to her. "So, if you can't stand him, why are you fishing?"

"A dare. Look, this isn't about me at the moment. Let's get you straightened out and then you can worry about me going fishing with Grayson James."

"I'd rather worry about you and Grayson James. That means I don't have to worry about me and Reed Hollingsworth." Gina took another bite of the donut. "Or worry about Grams."

"When was the last time you weren't worrying about something? Have you thought about all this pressure that you're both under?"

She sipped her coffee. "Lake of the Ozarks," she said more to herself than to Emma.

Gina remembered that was the last time they'd been happy. Her mother had scrimped and saved so they could go on that trip to the houseboat with Reed, his mother, and her one and only decent boyfriend. It was their first and only vacation, but it had been one of the happiest times she could remember. They'd eaten apples stolen off nearby trees, fish they'd caught themselves, and they'd told stories to each other out under the stars.

"Maybe you should go back there. Take Reed and Amanda Jane and just get away from everything. Start your family. Figure out who you three are together. Does that make sense?"

"It makes perfect sense. And I wish I could."

"Here's what you're going to do. You're going to tell Reed that you're going. You're taking Amanda Jane and that he should come, too. And tell him why. He'll go."

She wanted, no, needed Reed. She needed to feel his arms around her and she needed Amanda Jane. She wanted to wrap them both so tightly in her arms and just stay there.

Emma squeezed her shoulder.

"What's wrong, Gina-bee?" Amanda Jane was suddenly there.

Gina gave in to impulse and wrapped her in a fierce

hug. Amanda Jane hugged her back. "It's okay," Amanda Jane comforted her.

She realized how wrong that was. She should be the one comforting her, not the other way around. Yet, when Gina was a child herself, she knew that would've been exactly the role she'd assume. It made her feel as if it was something she could do. Some way she could affect the world around her—not that she'd thought of it in those terms, but being the one offering solace had always made her feel better herself.

"Can we find Daddy now?"

"We can go home and wait for him to come home." *If* he came home, Gina corrected herself silently.

"Okay."

"Make sure you thank Miss Betsy."

Amanda Jane did as she was told and Emma sighed. "I'll take you back to the house."

When they got back to the house, the parade of casseroles had begun. There were flowers and notes on the front porch as well as covered dishes in hot bags.

"I told you," Emma said. "And I bet Maudine's stoop is loaded, as well. Unless Grouchy Gunderson took everything inside." She said this with no rancor.

"No one likes a know-it-all," Gina grumbled.

She was surprised to see them, especially on Knob Hill. She didn't think the residents who breathed more rarified air were into that kind of thing.

Maybe Betsy was right. This was Glory and in this town, this was how things were done.

"You should put an announcement in the paper. Tell

people you're going to be gone or your stoop is going to be covered in spoiled food when you get back."

"I don't think that it's legal to refer to it as a 'stoop' on Knob Hill."

"Oh, you mean like the crick that runs to the Missour-ah back there? I suppose next you're going tell me that those snapdragons aren't yella."

"Smart aleck."

"Proudly." Emma grinned and then put an arm around her shoulder. "Hey, don't worry. Gray will bring him back, but can I suggest instead of beating this to death today you just tell him about your plan."

"Maybe." Gina wasn't so sure. "It could be good for Amanda Jane to go somewhere new, see some different things and have fun. Show her where we stayed, maybe let her see why it was one of Crystal's favorite places."

"Can I suggest something else?"

"As if I could stop you." Gina laughed.

"Don't talk about Crystal. I'm not saying you should forget her, but I'm saying this needs to be about you and Reed and Amanda Jane. You need to begin things as you intend to carry on. You need to build some foundations before you can do anything." Emma held up her hand. "I'm not saying that Crys isn't part of that, but you need to figure out what you mean to each other without her."

Gina sighed. "What about Grams?"

"She will be the first to tell you to take yourself on down to the lake." Emma adopted a bit of a holler twang. "And I'll be here to help her. So will Gunderson and the rest of them. If we need you, I can call you."

"I'm terrified something is going to happen while we're gone."

"If something is going to happen, it's going to happen whether you're here or there. Fix this. Fix your life."

"Sorry I ruined your fishing date."

"It wasn't a date," she reiterated.

"Sorry I ruined your undate."

"Now who's being a smart aleck?" Emma scowled.

"Me." Gina grinned.

Emma hugged her and planted a fat kiss on her cheek. "I'll see you later. Call me if you need me."

Gina waved her out and closed the door behind her, then sat down to wait for Reed. She was sure it wouldn't be long. Emma was most likely texting Gray and telling him to haul Reed back to the house.

At first, she'd thought it was silly, but she could see the wisdom in it now. It'd helped Gina, at least.

It wasn't long before the door opened and Reed stood there, blond, golden and still beautiful—even after the mess the night before.

"If I promise not to bite your head off, can we talk again?" She pursed her lips. "Please?"

"I'm sorry about this morning. I'm sorry about last night, too," he said.

"Me, too." She took a deep breath. "I think we've been under a lot of pressure to be a certain thing."

"Of course we have. We're parents now, we're living together, hell, we're married. It's like instant family, just add water."

She rewarded him with a small smile. "Reed, I think

we've always been family. It just took me a little while to see past my own mess."

"Maybe so." He looked so haunted that she regretted saying it.

"I'm making more coffee. Do you want some?" She changed the subject.

"No, thanks. I'm going in to the office for a while. I'll be home for dinner. We can make our plans then."

A wave of relief washed over her. He'd be home. For dinner. The same thing they did every night. He would be there. He wasn't leaving.

"Okay. Steaks on the grill?"

"Or one of those casseroles I saw in the kitchen. Might as well." He shrugged.

"Maybe there'll be some of Betsy's mom's fried chicken in one of those containers."

"I'm going upstairs to shower, then I'm heading out."

"Check in on Amanda Jane before you go?"

He nodded and climbed the stairs.

She watched him go, taking in his every movement and wondering what the future held for them.

CHAPTER TWENTY-THREE

MOST OF WHAT Gray had said made a lot of sense.

Except for the part about proposing to her. First, they were already married. Second, she didn't want this with him. Did she? All of this had spun out of control so quickly.

He stopped in Amanda Jane's room. "Hey there, princess."

She ran up to him and flung her arms around his neck. "You're not leaving?"

"No, I'm not leaving."

"Don't leave me."

He didn't want to make her any more promises he couldn't keep, but he kept thinking about his conversation with Gray, and his own self-doubt. It wasn't fair to put this on her. He wished she'd never heard any of their conversation.

"If you have to go for work, you have to take me with you."

He wanted her to feel secure, safe and loved. He realized that his own bullshit was getting in the way of that. "How about if we all go away together so we can take a bit of a vacation?"

"That would be okay."

"Good. I love you, Amanda Jane. Did you know that?"

"I love you, too, Daddy." She squeezed him tight.

In that moment, he begged the universe to let her be okay. He'd do anything as long as Amanda Jane was okay. He wouldn't run from his responsibilities, he wouldn't stumble again. He wouldn't hide.

If only it would keep this little girl safe and happy.

The logical part of him knew that such bargains were the tricks people played on themselves, but that didn't matter to him. This time his promise was to more than just her, it was to himself.

He'd fix this. He'd fix it all and he could. Not by letting them go, but by being the man they needed. Not because he felt he had to change for them; he had to change for himself. He wanted to be that man they could depend on.

The incident the night before showed him that maybe he wasn't going to fall, but he still needed some support. He needed to remember what it was like and why he'd chosen never to be numb again.

And if Gina hurt him, she hurt him. That was just life.

He laughed out loud remembering how she'd said he had a tender heart. That's what made her love him.

How could she love him? He was such a bastard.

He couldn't start that train of thought because then he'd start thinking they were better off without him.

Still, Amanda Jane needed him. If he bailed on her, he was a coward.

Reed was a lot of things, but he wasn't a coward.

Or at least, he didn't want to be. He supposed the rest remained to be seen.

He could've worked from home, but he needed the distance. Needed to put some space between himself and Gina.

Be happy.

As if it were that easy.

Be happy.

Yes, I will.

And like magic, they all lived happily ever after.

The hungry fire inside of him rebelled. It said, why not? Why not just decide to be happy and do it? He'd decided to teach himself the stock market. He'd decided he wasn't going to be poor. He'd decided he wasn't going to get high. He'd decided life would be better. Why stop there? Why not decide to be happy, too?

When he got to the office and took his messages from his secretary, he asked her to cancel all calls for the day. Instead, he tried to research some of the investment opportunities he'd been considering, but nothing appealed to him.

Or maybe it was because the words and the numbers on the page all reformed to point his thoughts back to Gina. Back to the decision to be happy.

And what came with that was asking Gina to marry him for real. Not today, not tomorrow, but someday. Maybe someday soon.

That was what would make him happy.

Would it make her happy?

He was some kind of wreck. Reed shook his head at the directions of his thoughts. He'd been ready to leave her and now he wanted to spend the rest of his life with her.

No, he'd always wanted to marry her. Back when they were kids, he knew she was exactly the marrying kind. He'd just never thought he was good enough.

For some reason she did.

Or she had.

He pushed thoughts of what she'd said about not trusting him out of his head. She'd been afraid, and he could admit he'd lashed out, said things that he hadn't meant to use to wound. Reed knew that she really did love him, even though he wasn't perfect.

Even though he couldn't *be* perfect.

His brain kept tumbling everything over and over on itself until he couldn't see the words in front of him at all. It was only Gina and Amanda Jane.

He called his secretary to come to his office.

"Yes, Mr. Hollingsworth?" Rae said as she stepped into the room.

"I need you to make reservations for a getaway. Lake of the Ozarks. Houseboat. Sleeps three."

"First-class, I take it?"

"Nicest they have."

"For this weekend?"

"No, tomorrow. Make it for three days," he instructed.

"I was just going to pay myself overtime, then." Rae slipped him a sheaf of papers. "These need your signature. I'll get those reservations taken care of."

She was out the door.

She was a little eccentric, but the woman got things done. He appreciated that in an employee.

Reed felt as if he'd hit some kind of turning point. As if maybe all the things he'd said about being better than where he came from to that reporter from *La Rue*, he hadn't believed them. Not until now. He'd been so ashamed of his past, but yet he'd worn it like a badge on his sleeve, daring anyone to take the daggers they'd offered and drive them home.

He turned off his computer and went outside. "Rae, just send the info to my phone. I'm leaving for the day."

"You got it." She smiled and went back to typing.

"Oh, and, Rae?"

She looked up at him.

"Give yourself the overtime on your time sheet. You deserve it."

"I have the best job in the world." She grinned.

Reed was on a mission. Work could wait. He had enough money that after a while, it would start to make itself. Why have the money if he wasn't going to enjoy the life he'd worked so hard to have?

Only this mission wasn't about pleasure.

It was about forgiveness. Reconciliation. Mostly with himself.

He drove the hour back to Glory but he didn't go to his house on Knob Hill. He drove to Whispering Woods. Back to the old trailer court that had seen the bulk of his youth—the place he'd tried so hard to forget.

The place where the Townsends' trailer had sat was empty. It was just a narrow lot with a naked water meter. Weeds had grown up over the spot, and it seemed wrong somehow. Reed wasn't sure what he expected to find, but this wasn't it.

The trailer next door was a brand-new double-wide, nothing like the single that had belonged to his mother. There were potted plants on the steps, a small metal shed and even some landscaping. It wasn't the dump that had squatted there those years ago.

He was tempted to knock on the door, but he knew his mother didn't live there. Her trailer had gone to the city dump when she died. There was nothing here for him but faded memories and ghosts.

Yet, it was important that he come here all the same. These ghosts waited for him; they needed him before they could rest. They needed to tell him goodbye just as much as he needed to say the same to them. They'd haunted each other for much too long.

He sat in his car for a long time, watching kids play. Some of the residents were the hopeless sort that he and his mother had been. But others were just people and he realized he'd demonized Whispering Woods as much as he had his mother.

Her sins and faults were her own, but it did little good to hold on to those things. He was more than this. More than the choices he'd made when he lived here.

He wished Crystal was here so she could make those same realizations. So she could let go of everything that hurt and—and he supposed she'd already done that. She'd tried to make provisions for them as best she could and she'd let go. Wherever she was, he knew that she wasn't suffering anymore.

Reed supposed that was all he could wish for her now.

He exhaled and started the engine. When he gave the

place a last once-over, he saw two kids on the roof of one of the trailers. They were pointing up at the clouds.

Nostalgia hit him with a fist and he remembered doing that with Crys and Gina. Part of him wanted to tell them to keep dreaming, keep hoping, but if they could still make things out of the clouds, they had no problem dreaming.

He still didn't go home. Instead, he drove through downtown Glory, thinking about all the things he'd resented about the place as a kid—all of the things that represented a life he didn't think he was allowed to have.

No one had kept him from it but himself.

He passed the old theater turned playhouse, several antiques stores, the Corner Pharmacy and the elderly couple walking down Main who waved at him. He parked the car and walked to the river park and sat on the bench for a long while, watching the muddy Missouri churn its way downstream.

This had been one of his favorite places. He'd imagined all the ways to leave, to have an adventure where he could make more of himself than what he was.

Reed had done that. He'd done all of that.

It was something to be proud of. He couldn't change his past, but he'd proved he could change his future.

His phone beeped and he saw that he had a text from Rae with the information for the houseboat. She'd even thought to include some pictures.

Then he thought about what home meant to him now.

Gina and Amanda Jane. Dinner together.

He'd almost thrown all of that away because he

couldn't see all the good things that had been entrusted to him.

He hoped it wasn't too late.

He turned his car toward home.

When he walked inside, it smelled of fried chicken.

He found Gina and Amanda Jane in the kitchen. Gina was pulling reheated chicken out of the oven and Amanda Jane was standing on a chair, using a mixer like a jackhammer to mash potatoes. She wasn't having very good luck keeping them all in the pot, but he didn't care.

There was something so right about coming home to them—to this.

Gina tucked a strand of hair behind her ear. "It'll be ready in a few."

"I can help. I'll pour the tea."

"I might have screwed up the tea." Gina blushed.

"How do you screw up tea?" He wrinkled his nose.

"That was my fault," Amanda Jane said, still hammering at the potatoes.

Gina reached over and stilled her little hands and turned the mixer off. "I think they're dead, honey."

"No. More butter." She was like a little general, commanding the potatoes.

"If we have any more butter, we're going have heart attacks at the table. It's fine. Let's sit down and eat."

Amanda Jane climbed down and went to the dining room.

Reed saw the pitcher for the tea sitting by the sink. It was half tea, half sugar. Literally. He raised a brow.

"I was pouring the sugar when she came in the kitchen and scared the life out of me."

"And the sugar out of the bag, apparently."

"Yes, she did at that."

He pulled out his phone and showed her the picture of the houseboat. "Hey, what do you think?"

Gina took the phone and stared at it for a long moment. "That's really nice, Reed."

"Do you want to leave tonight after dinner?" he asked her.

She looked at him, some expression written on her face that he couldn't decipher. "Yeah, I'd like that."

"I'm so sorry." He'd said himself that sorry didn't fix anything, but he was at a loss for what else to say to her.

"For what? Earlier?" She studied him.

"Everything."

"Me, too." She exhaled slowly, heavily, as if the contents of herself were under so much pressure any sudden change and she'd explode. "Let's stop apologizing. It seems that's all we're doing lately. I think I forgot how to be happy. So I want to try that."

"Okay." He nodded. It was something that they both needed. A break from the pain, a break from the sorrow and regret, and maybe they'd be able to find some hope together.

"I'm so *hungry*," Amanda Jane called from the dining room.

Gina laughed. "It's coming."

He found himself staring at her, just enjoying the way she moved.

"What are you doing?" She blushed and fumbled with a spoon.

"Just thinking that I'm hungry, too." It had been a long time since he'd looked forward to a meal the way he looked forward to this one.

This was what his dreams had been made of as a kid. It wasn't fancy, it wasn't extravagant. It was just a family meal. Simple, home cooking with the people he loved. No strangers that he wasn't supposed to anger or they wouldn't pay the bills, or wouldn't give his mother her "medicine." There was enough to eat, as much as they wanted with no strings attached.

There was conversation about plain, simple things, too. About going to Sweet Thing, eating frosted frog legs, about the butter in the potatoes, about Amanda Jane asking a question about something she'd read on the cover of a newspaper.

The only thing that could be purchased out of all of it was the food.

Not the warmth, not the sense of home and hearth, and not the absolute and utter devotion he felt for the other two people at his table.

CHAPTER TWENTY-FOUR

"Grams?" Gina said tentatively into the phone.

"Don't you go fussing on me like I'm going to break. Tell me whatever you have to tell me."

She laughed. "I was just checking on you. Reed and I were thinking of going out of town for a few days and I wanted to make sure you didn't need anything."

"What's the right answer here? Am I supposed to tell you everything is fine and to go or that I want you to stay and my old heart will break in my chest if you don't?"

Gina laughed. "I want to know how you feel. Honestly."

"Honestly? Like a bucket of Old Man Zorn's cow crap. But, honey, you go on ahead and go. I've got Helga and the Grandmothers if I need anything. Emma told me you might be taking a few days. I think it's a great idea."

"Really?"

"Really. I think you should go. I've already been through the hard part. I think you need this. Amanda Jane needs it."

There was so much she wanted to say to her, but it was all regret. It was all should have, so instead, she said, "I love you, Grams."

"I know you do. And I love you, too. To the moon and stars and back again. All I want is for you to be happy. That's the only reason I've done any of the things I've done."

"I know, Grams."

"Tell me all about it. Where are you going?"

"A pretty place at the Lake of the Ozarks. Just for a few days."

"That was your sister's favorite place."

"I know."

"I'm wondering if you'd like to take her ashes and scatter them. I think she'd rather be there than sitting on my mantel. Say goodbye to your past, put your ghosts to rest."

Emotion welled up and choked her. She didn't know what she was feeling. Grief, sorrow, joy, hope…it was all balled up into a sticky mess.

The drive to the Ozarks took about six hours. She'd never had Amanda Jane in a car for that long, but she seemed content to sleep. Probably the bellyful of fried chicken, and for that, Gina was thankful.

It was dawn when they finally arrived and an attendant came to meet them. The perks, she supposed, of having money to tip for the inconvenience.

Reed carried Amanda Jane aboard and they discovered that "sleeps three" meant a king-size bed in one bedroom and a single in the other.

"I'll put her in the big bed and you can sleep with her."

"Can I stay with you tonight?" she asked quietly.

"It's just…" Gina held up the box containing the ashes that Emma had brought over from her grandmother.

"Of course, Gina."

She breathed out a sigh of relief and he put Amanda Jane in the bedroom with the single.

Reed put his arm around her, and his presence was warm and strong, comforting her. "I know you don't want to leave her here by herself."

He understood without her saying a word.

"You have the money. Buy some property here, if you want it. Buy it for you, for Amanda Jane."

"That seems like a luxury."

"We can afford it," he answered.

"Taxes, upkeep, when I'm going to come here, what, once a year?" Yet the idea appealed to her. She'd be able to come see her whenever she wanted, bring Amanda Jane.

"If that's what you want." Reed rested his chin on her head. "Does it matter? It'll be a tribute to Crys. A pilgrimage so Amanda Jane doesn't forget."

She teared up again. "God, I can't stop crying. Every time I think I've finished, my face leaks again." Gina shook her head. "I really thought that I took care of her. I thought that she needed me more than I needed her, but I was wrong. I needed her. Needed to take care of her—or try to feel like I knew my place in the world."

"You have your place in the world. It's wherever you want it to be."

"You make it sound so easy."

He tightened his arms around her. "It is that easy."

"That's a different song than the one you were singing."

"I know. It kind of hit me. With a brick. The way those things tend to do."

It would be easy to surrender to his arms, and she wanted nothing more than to let him hide her from all the ugly things that she didn't want to face, but that hadn't worked in the past. She didn't see how that would change.

"Come to bed with me, Gina."

She wanted to ask if it was because she'd begged him, or if he needed comfort, too, but that would open up all the things she'd sworn not to talk about. Not yet, anyway. Her heart hurt, as though someone had been using it for a soccer ball. She couldn't take any more hits, so instead, she nodded and followed him to the master bedroom.

She stripped down to her tank top and panties and climbed between the sheets. He gathered her into his arms, and she exhaled so heavily, he asked her, "What is it?"

"This is the only place I feel safe," she confessed and then sighed again. "I'm sorry, I know you don't want to hear that."

"I thought we decided that we weren't apologizing anymore?"

She swallowed the lump in her throat. "I guess that's over."

He laughed. "No, I say we try it again. You're grieving. You have nothing to be sorry for."

"I have plenty to be sorry for. I am grieving and you were right about so many things. I think you are my drug of choice. I just want to get lost in you. I want to feel what you give me. I need to be close to you."

"After everything, you want me to touch you?" He sounded incredulous.

"I know, I shouldn't need you like this. I'll try to stop."

"I don't want you to stop."

Hope flared. "You don't?"

"But it still stands that I don't want to be a regret."

"What do you want?" Gina realized they'd spent a lot of time talking about what she wanted, what she needed, and even when he was angry and hurting, it was still about her.

"Now isn't the time to talk about that."

"Then let's not talk." She tilted her mouth up to his, desperate for that ambrosia of his lips and for a moment, she was sure he was going to deny her.

How many times had she laid herself bare for him and how many times had he pushed her away? When would she learn?

Then his mouth descended and crushed all thoughts from her mind. Time and space had been reduced to sensation. Only his hands, only his mouth, only his breath as he breathed new life into her.

He made her not care about the past or future, just the immediate present where he was all things. He made her want, made her need, but then gave her everything, fulfilled her, only to make her yearn again. It was like the tide crashing on the shore, bringing up the bounty of the deep, only to pull it away again.

It was a cycle she was more than happy to surrender to.

He trailed kisses down her neck, his lips grazing her collarbone as he drifted ever lower, as if he were seducing her even though he knew the deed was already won. Reed traced his hands over her skin, seemingly wanting to touch her everywhere. Not just her breasts, or her cleft, but found pleasure in the arch of her neck, the curve of her shoulder, the plane of her belly.

Reed kissed her everywhere. They were passionate, they were gentle, sometimes he nipped lightly at tender skin and other times it was more of a brushing of lips than an actual kiss. She felt as though he sanctified her somehow, made her more than she was.

When he finally had her bare, she was shy again. More so than their first time together. She felt more naked somehow, more exposed, but it wasn't frightening. It was good. Gina reveled in it, enjoyed the sensations, letting each one wash over her.

She cupped her fingers around the nape of his neck when he would've dived lower to bring her bliss.

"My turn," she said.

He moved to his back and allowed her the access she wanted to him. She returned the caresses, kissing, nipping, exploring his body with her mouth. Gina wanted to do to him what he'd done to her, she wanted him to feel all the ecstasy he'd given her.

Gina loved the taste of his skin, the way he felt like velvet-covered steel everywhere. His arms, his pecs, his abs and his cock. His thick, hard cock that was some kind of alchemy.

She dipped her head and took him deep.

He murmured her name.

Gina began to move over him, her hand cupping his shaft and stroking in the wake of her mouth. He didn't speak, but his hands fisted the sheets, curling tight. She increased the pressure and the speed until his hips arched up off the bed of their own accord and his face wore a mask of strained need. Then she slowed again, denying him the culmination he desired so that when she did let him have it, it would take him higher, be more intense.

She worked him, tasted him, choreographing each action to bring him the most pleasure.

His back arched, his hips thrust and he cried out her name this time, almost a desperate sound. Gina knew he was near completion, but she didn't stop. She wanted to bring him off this way and then drive him crazy again.

Gina liked watching the expressions on his face, the way he fought his culmination and the sense of power it gave her to be able to do this for him. It made her that much hotter. As she teased and taunted him, she was in a sense teasing herself. Every flick of her tongue against him, every jerk of his cock in response, it all made her cleft clench and ache to be filled with him.

His whole body stiffened and she knew he was on the edge, so she moved her hands and lips faster with more pressure until he reached his peak.

She lay on the bed beside him, satisfied with herself, but still wanting his touch. He didn't give her a second of reprieve before he was between her thighs, returning the gift. Gina found herself biting her lips to keep from crying out, to keep from howling his name. This was so much better than she'd ever imagined it could be.

Gina loved the way he touched her. The way he seemed to know just what she needed.

"Please, Reed."

He didn't stop to answer her, just kept teasing her as she'd done to him. Then that moment came where she was sure she was going to explode into a thousand stars, and then she did.

But that wasn't the end.

When she was still quivering from the bliss, he rose up above her and wrapped her legs around his hips. He pushed into her, driving home, driving deep and just like the first time, he looked deep into her eyes.

They were anchored together in that moment, in that pleasure and sensation, like one organism instead of two. Their bodies were joined, but so were their hearts. They moved in tandem together, striving to take the other to a new place, another rung farther up the ladder of ecstasy.

When she peaked, her lips fell open, but no sound issued forth, and if it had, it would've been swallowed by his kiss. She tasted herself on his lips, the evidence of her pleasure, and it wasn't long before his body spasmed and they were in heaven together.

When they drifted back to the real, she was content to lie in his arms and he seemed content to hold her.

She wanted this forever and it was hard to keep that inside, but she'd promised herself she wasn't going to put any pressure on him and asking for forever, well, that was definitely pressure. She could be content with what they had for now.

They slept in each other's arms for but a few hours, both knowing the chore that awaited them.

"Hey, sunshine," Reed whispered lazily when she woke up. "You ready to do this?"

"Not really, but that's not going to change anything, is it?"

"Afraid not. Do you want to get Amanda Jane?"

"Yes." Gina got dressed and found her in the galley of the houseboat, making toaster pastries.

"Good morning, Gina-bee."

"What are you doing?"

"Making breakfast."

"I can see that, but how many people are you feeding?"

"You. Me. Mama. Daddy."

Gina pursed her lips. "Mama?"

"I just want to," Amanda Jane said without further prompting.

"Okay. Whatever you want. Do you know what we're going to do today?" Gina asked her.

The solemn little girl nodded. "We're going to leave Mama here. This is where she wants to be. I don't want her to be hungry."

"Honey," she began, unsure of what to say.

"I know." Amanda Jane answered whatever it was that Gina had been going to say. "I just want to," she repeated.

Gina nodded. "But I think you have enough. None of us can eat that much."

"The rest is for the fish. They can have our breakfast and they can be lunch." She started arranging them on four plates.

Gina tugged her into a hug. "Oh, kiddo."

They took their toaster pastries onto the deck of the houseboat where a table and chairs had been set up for outside dining.

Amanda Jane placed everything just so, even the box at its own place.

They ate their pastries in silence, even Reed, watching his daughter with a wary eye. After they were finished, he said, "Are you ready?"

Gina picked up the plain brown box. "Do you want to help, Amanda Jane?"

She shook her head.

Gina thought she knew what she wanted to say, but when faced with the moment at hand, it didn't matter to Crys. She'd never hear it, never know how much she'd be missed, never know all the good things she could've had, if only she'd tried.

Gina couldn't help but be angry, especially when she looked at her niece's face. But she was heartbroken, too. Heartbroken that Crys had always been in so much pain, both emotional and sometimes physical.

"Tell Mama I love her," Gina said. "And I love you. I promise I'll take good care of Amanda Jane and we'll try to be happy. Just like you wanted." She looked to Reed.

"I'm sorry, Crystal." He seemed to be enumerating

his sins in his head, but that was okay. This was for him, not for her. "Thank you for her." He nodded to Amanda Jane.

"Do you want to say anything, honey?" Gina asked Amanda Jane.

She shook her head.

Gina opened the box and let the wind take the ashes, carrying what was left of Crystal out onto the dark waves where the ashes disappeared.

Amanda Jane took the toaster pastry and let it drop into the water below.

Gina realized what she was doing then. They'd watched a documentary not too long ago about the Day of the Dead and how they honored their dead with offerings of flowers and food. It was a strange little something to have stuck in the girl's mind, but stuck it had. It was her way of grieving and keeping Crys with her even though she was gone. If it comforted her, Gina didn't mind it.

"She wanted us to be happy. So we have to try and be happy."

Amanda Jane turned her face into Gina and hugged her tight. "I'll try," she sniffed.

"That's why we came here. She was the happiest here. So we're going to do the things that made her happy. That's how we'll keep her in our hearts."

"Being happy hurts," she said.

She stroked her hair. "Sometimes, little one."

Reed embraced them both. "You're going to look back on this when you're all grown up and you will always miss her, but you're going to remember the good parts about today, too."

They held each other, sharing their grief, their good-byes, until Gina pulled away. "She said to be happy. We're not being happy. Let's take this thing for a ride."

They spent the day out on the water, splashing and playing, Amanda Jane in her floaties and her inner tube. Fish swam around their feet and legs, and Amanda Jane was delighted with the experience.

Hearing her laugh, it somehow made everything better, and Gina held the tender spark of hope in her heart for both her future and the love she longed for.

Gina looked out over the water, watching as the sky turned from purple velvet to the pink and gold of dawn and bloomed like a cosmic flower. The water lapped gently at the sides of the boat and she sighed.

"It really is beautiful here, Crys. I can see why you'd want to stay." Tears pricked her eyes again. "That was the best of times coming here with Mom, being out on the water and daydreaming about moving here. We'd all get jobs at one of the shows in Branson and we'd live on a little houseboat…eat fish every night that we'd caught. It was our dream."

She'd spoken as if Crys could hear her.

Gina leaned against the rail and sighed again.

CHAPTER TWENTY-FIVE

REED THOUGHT ABOUT everything he'd heard about Jack McConnell. He'd been the hero who'd done good, even though he'd come home a mess. Reed was nothing like a former navy SEAL. He'd never done anything so noble, but maybe there was a place for him in Glory, after all.

Maybe he didn't need to be the rich bastard on the hill, maybe he could just be a guy who was good with numbers who had a family in some small, charming midwestern town. He could have everything he wanted.

He was enough.

Reed had wanted that, to know he was enough, to really feel it. But he'd been afraid of it, too, because it meant that if he failed, if he didn't live up to his word, it wasn't anyone's fault but his own. It gave him control over his life, over his destiny.

There was a part of him that was content to hide behind his faults, to chalk up any failures to his bad blood, bad childhood, his past mistakes.

But none of that had dominion over him, he realized. He had dominion over himself.

That was a terrifying prospect.

Going forward, he'd rise or fall on his own—though he supposed it had always been that way, rising or falling on his own merits. But he'd used his stumbling blocks like a security blanket and the time for that was done.

His first instinct was to share this discovery with Gina, but he knew it wasn't the right time.

She was still reeling.

He was still reeling for that matter.

But now he had hope.

Maybe that was what he'd been lacking before. That was the secret alchemy that really would make everything okay.

GINA HAD BEEN having nightmares since they'd gotten back. She woke up screaming if she wasn't in Reed's bed.

The first night back, Amanda Jane had come running into her room, terrified that something bad was happening to her. She never remembered what her nightmares were about when she woke up, but Gina could hazard a guess. Fear of abandonment, helplessness—both things that were the innermost ring of hell to her.

After a week back, she couldn't take it anymore.

She found herself padding barefooted, after everyone had gone to bed, to Reed's room.

She knocked lightly and he opened the door wearing nothing but those soft lounge pants she liked so much. Gina tried not to lick her lips, or think about the passion between them.

It seemed as if it had been a onetime thing. Since they'd been back, it was almost as if it had never happened. She was tired of chasing him and had determined not to, but she was tired of being afraid to go to sleep.

"Another nightmare?" he asked.

"Yeah." She nodded. It had to be the anxiety of her new situation. All the fears she'd choked down, giving him all of this control. It was strange that he was the one she'd turned to when he was part of the problem.

"Come here." He tugged her toward the bed. "Just stay with me. You don't have to sleep alone."

She crawled into the bed, grateful for his invitation.

He pulled her close and suddenly, everything that could be right with the world was.

"Do you remember what they're about?"

"No." She was still shaking.

"It's not really a surprise that you're having nightmares with all the upheaval in your life in these last months. All the stress you were under before? What surprises me is that you haven't popped like a tick."

She laughed at the description. "So this is really okay? You don't mind?"

"Having you in my bed every night, Gina? No. How could I mind?"

His words warmed her, even though she didn't want them to. She wanted to be an island, a rock; she didn't want to need him or need his touch. Especially when he could take it away so easily. "I don't want to be here if you don't want me here."

"I want you here."

She curled against him. "I love how you smell."

He stroked her back gently. "You keep nuzzling like that, you're going to get more than a nap," he teased.

She looked up at him. "I always want you, Reed."

His hand stilled. "I don't want to push you."

She wet her lips. "I don't know what we're doing here, but I'm okay with it. I'm more than okay with it. This is where I want to be whether I'm sleeping or… other things."

"Other things, huh?" he teased and pulled her closer.

She slipped her hand up over his back. "Be quiet. Since you're teasing me, I'm going to sleep."

"Good. You probably need it. There's time for 'other things' later."

"How is it so easy for you?"

"Easy? Sweetheart, it's hard. Very. Very. *Hard.*"

"Is it, really?" She let her hand trail down to his hip and when he didn't stop her, she cupped him. "I see that you are telling the truth."

"You don't have to do that if you just want to be close."

"I want both. After all this time, I don't know how you could doubt that."

"I guess I still have a problem believing that you really want me."

Even though his confession stabbed at her heart, it warmed it, too. He was confiding in her, trusting her.

"I just never want you to feel like you owe me anything. And I want you to trust me. I want to trust you."

She wanted to reassure him. "I'm here for you. Because I have feelings for you. Because I need you, but because you're you. Not because of anything you have. I'll remind you as many times as you need to hear it."

"How about you make this an every-night thing?" he asked quietly.

Warmth bloomed. "Yes."

She turned over, nestled herself against him. "How do you think Amanda Jane is doing?"

"I think she's doing as well as anyone could expect. She's had a lot of upheaval, as well. I was going to ask if you wanted to take her to Glory Days this weekend."

"Ugh. Anyone I knew in high school that matters to me I still talk to." Glory Days was an alumni festival that consisted of a carnival, fund-raising efforts for the high school, and a class reunion for all the different class years.

"She might like it, though. The carnival part. The funnel cake."

"The seeing people judging us…"

"Hey, I didn't even finish high school here. I'm not really concerned about what they think about me. I just want Amanda Jane to have some fun."

"Frogfest didn't kill me, so I don't guess Glory Days will, either."

"That's my girl."

She was tempted to ask if she really was his girl. She wanted to be, but him inviting her to spend all of her nights with him was victory enough.

"Did you ever go to Glory Days when we were kids?"

"Once or twice," he said.

"I did. I'd go and watch from the sidelines. I'd pretend like someday, I'd come back to Glory and I'd go to Glory Days in a white coat that had *Dr. Gina Townsend* stitched on the pocket and somehow, that would make everything shiny. It would whitewash my life so it was just like that coat."

"And now?"

"And now, I don't think it needs to be whitewashed. It is what it is."

That felt good to say, but even better because she believed it to be true.

"I went back to Whispering Woods before we left for the Ozarks." His fingers made lazy whorls on her skin.

"Really? And what did you find there? Skeletons and closets?" She never wanted to see that place again. She couldn't fathom why he'd go back.

"I found my future."

"I think you need to explain that one to me."

"I was so worried about not looking back that I forgot to look forward."

That resonated with her. "I think I understand what you mean. We wouldn't be who we are now without who we were."

"Neither of us has anything to be ashamed of." He lay silently, but she could feel that he had more to say. "I saw a couple of kids hanging out on top of a double-wide, pointing out shapes in the clouds. You remember we used to do that?"

"I remember we used to spend a lot of time on the roofs of yours and mine." Some of those times were the memories she wanted to keep.

"It reminded me to keep hoping, keep dreaming."

"Did you forget?" she teased.

"Yeah, I think I might have. I'd been so buttoned-down trying to secure that good life that I forgot to live it. I don't want to do that anymore. I don't want to teach Amanda Jane to do that. I think I was afraid that if I let myself go, if I gave myself permission for anything, that part of me would take it as permission for everything and I'd fall."

"You're not going to fall," she reassured him, and when she said it, she believed it. There was no doubt in her voice, or her mind.

"See, that's just it. I know that now."

"I'm glad."

"What about you, Gina?"

"What do you mean?"

"What's your happy?"

This, right here. That was what she wanted to say. "Medical school. Knowing that Amanda Jane is safe. This is going to sound horrible, but knowing that Crys can't be hurt anymore."

"I don't think that's horrible."

She exhaled and it was as if the weight on her shoulders that had been holding her down left her body with it.

"So we're going to Glory Days?"

"Why not?"

"Oh, I can think of plenty of reasons why not." She snorted.

"You already agreed. Stop trying to get out of it."

"Fine." She shifted around, trying to get comfortable again. "Let it be noted I'm only going for Amanda Jane."

"Not for me?"

"Nope." She grinned, liking how easy this play was

coming between them. It was as though they'd always been together.

But then that bothered her. It was as if it was too easy.

For a moment, she considered slapping herself. Nothing about this had been easy and just because they had a few things that happened to go smoothly, Gina was suddenly daring the universe to throw some rough road in her path. It was almost as though if it wasn't rough, she didn't know how to process it.

Her stupid brain wondered if maybe that was why he wanted her. She fit so easily into the world he was forced to inhabit. Amanda Jane already loved her and Gina had confessed she loved him.

No, no. He'd told her that he loved her.

But did he really?

There was a lot to be said for the ease of things. When they'd started this journey he'd talked about all the ways he'd protected himself from gold diggers. That he didn't date, didn't have one-night stands, didn't do anything that could endanger himself financially. Maybe there was a reason he was so caught up on only being wanted for his money—because that was what occupied the most real estate in his mind. His cash.

She'd already signed an agreement and he knew what he had to pay up front.

But that would make her little better than a whore.

He'd never treat her that way.

That little voice in her head, the one that said she wasn't good enough, that she had to try harder, be more, it kept repeating all of these things back to her and for some reason, no matter how thin the argument, it seemed to sound better than all of her logic and reason.

Because she'd known from the beginning that she could be a doctor or she could have Reed Hollingsworth. She didn't get both. That's not how it played out for girls like her.

"Hey, did you fall asleep on me?"

She didn't respond. She couldn't. Just let him think she was asleep and then she wouldn't be tempted to ask him stupid questions—but she'd spend the night wondering about stupid answers.

He shifted behind her and settled, holding her close.

"You're just so easy to love, Gina."

Rather than take from that that he loved her, all she heard was the easy part and it played into her fears about being ready-made—like a ramen-noodle family unit that fit all the things he wanted.

It was cheap and it was easy.

She tried to reassure herself that it was nothing of the sort—but what they had? Maybe it wasn't the traditional definition of easy, but with what they were used to? Yeah.

Gina replayed every interaction over and over again, looking for all of the times when she was sure she'd just been easy.

She thought about every time he'd tried to turn her down for sex and she'd been convinced that he was just trying to look out for her, but maybe he didn't want her at all, that stupid, ugly little voice said.

Why she gave it any time in her headspace she'd never know. No, she did know. She let it stay because it pushed her harder, made her keep trying, made her do more and mostly kept its promises.

If you work harder, you'll get better grades.

If you get better grades, you'll get scholarships.

If you get scholarships, you can go to med school.

If you're quiet enough, it won't wake Mama.

If you're good enough, she won't get sicker...

That was where it had lied. But it had come through on all the others.

So when it told her she wasn't pretty enough, wasn't smart enough, just wasn't enough, she tended to listen because it was right nine out of ten times and Gina didn't think she was special enough to be that one percent, to be that exception on more than one thing.

It was the thing that told her med school or Reed Hollingsworth.

Too bad he was so easy to love, too.

CHAPTER TWENTY-SIX

GLORY DAYS WAS LOUD, bright and completely obnoxious. At least to Gina's way of thinking. That was probably because she hadn't wanted to come. But Amanda Jane was immediately intrigued by all of the lights—especially the lights on the Octopus, the spinning ride that had, contrary to its name, more than eight arms that swung the cars around.

The day dawned cloudy and soft, with the promise of rain. But that didn't stop the revelers.

Gina was relieved to see a friendly face when she spotted Emma in the crowd. Amanda Jane saw her at the same time and pointed her out.

Emma waved and made her way over.

With Grayson.

Gina couldn't help but be the tiniest bit ornery. "So, no kissing booth this time?"

Emma narrowed her eyes. "You shut up."

Grayson laughed.

"You, too," Emma added.

"If I want to kiss a woman, I don't need a kissing booth," Gray offered.

"Who asked you?" Emma grumbled and blushed.

He arched a brow. "Me. I asked me because I'm thinking about kissing *you*."

Amanda Jane giggled and faux-whispered, "You should."

Gina decided she liked watching their banter. It was like watching a tennis match with razor blades, but she was sure if either of them were to actually be cut, the other would feel…somewhat bad.

Gray had a fire that Emma had been missing in her life. So she was glad to see some spark.

Amanda Jane turned to Gina. "Octopus. Octopus."

"I'll take her, if you want to talk to Emma," Gray offered.

Amanda Jane looked up at him. "I think they're going to talk about you."

"I think so, too." Gray winked at Emma and Emma rolled her eyes.

"Is it okay to go?" Amanda Jane asked.

"Sure." When they were out of earshot, Gina turned on Emma. "You can't tell me there's nothing there."

"There's not. He's just a flirt. I don't take him seriously." But the stain on her cheeks said otherwise.

"That kiss at Frogfest—"

"Let the Frogfest kiss die a good death. Really. It's over, done with. Neither of us was that impressed." She shook her head. "Maybe we should even give it a Viking funeral. Light it on fire and send it out to sea. And never mention it again."

"Why are we here again?" Gina sighed.

"Glory Days, of course," Emma teased.

"Reed thought this would be good for Amanda Jane, to focus on something else besides all the craziness."

"How did the trip go?" Emma asked.

"Oh, you know. It went." The shoe was most definitely on the other foot now. She didn't want to talk about her feelings. The last weeks had already been so crazy, she didn't want to analyze it to death.

"And?"

"And what?" Gina fidgeted with her hands.

"Sexy times?"

She blushed. "Maybe. But I still don't know what we're doing. I wonder if he wants me just because it's easy."

Emma shot her a look.

"I know, I know, nothing with us has really been easy. But as far as things go on our road? What we have now is easy."

"Why would he shortchange himself like that? That doesn't make any sense. I think you should talk to him."

"I don't want to. Things are…good. They've finally settled. I don't want to rock the apple cart." Gina bit her lip.

"It's already rocking if you don't know where you stand."

"You're probably right." Gina sighed.

"I'm always right, but it's nice to hear. And settling is just that. Settled. Like mud at the bottom of the Missouri. You don't want to be settled. You want to be happy."

"Enough of me. I want to know more about this friendship of yours with Grayson. And you better indulge me, or I'm going to sic Grams on you with her matchmaking friends."

"Never say that! They'll have me married and spitting out babies before I know what's hit me. With Grayson, it really is just a friendship."

"Uh-huh. Keep telling yourself that. He looks pretty comfortable with kids. Doesn't that just hit you in your ovaries?"

"Stop matchmaking. I'm happy in my single status." Emma looked around. "Where's Reed?"

Emma dropped that bomb on her as if it was nothing. Which meant it was everything. "Emma—" She reached out for her.

"Can't do it now. Thought I could. Reed. We were talking about Reed." Her face had gone white.

Gina looked at her friend and squeezed her hand and let her change the subject. Emma would talk again when she was ready. "He was supposed to be getting cotton candy." Gina looked around for him.

"There's Missy." Emma pointed at her and she was walking with Judd Wilson. "Why don't you practice your matchmaking skills on her and the good sheriff?"

"Because it looks like she's already figured out where she wants to be."

Judd Wilson, the sheriff, tipped his hat at them and he guided Missy toward them.

Missy hugged her tight.

Gina allowed the hug and let herself lean on the other woman for just moment. What surprised her was that the burly sheriff was next. "So sorry, Gina." He swooped her up in a giant hug. "You need anything, you call me, okay?"

She found herself overcome with emotion at the display and nodded, throat tight.

Grayson and Amanda Jane made their way back to the group and Emma said, "I do believe this is what they call a clique. We're standing around in the middle of all the fun whispering about people we know."

Amanda Jane put her hand in Gina's and indicated she wanted to tell her something. Gina leaned down and Amanda Jane whispered in her ear, "The sheriff likes Missy."

"Yes, I think so." Gina nodded.

She smiled.

As they chatted, it occurred again to Gina that this was a good place to raise Amanda Jane. She'd been worried about people holding her past and her roots against her, but that was what made the town strong—roots, a sense of tradition and self. These people, what had happened to her, to Crys, to any of them, it hadn't been their fault.

She couldn't blame a whole town for what a few residents had done, or not done.

Another woman she didn't know came up and hugged her. Gina was frozen, and stiff, but the woman smelled of fresh basil and lemon. Something about it was so homey and comforting, that she allowed the embrace.

"Bambina." Her Italian accent was heavy. "If you and your family would like, come stay at Cora's Cottage for a weekend to have a getaway at home. I'll cook for you."

"Thank you, that's very kind." She realized that was Marie Hart. Crystal had talked about Johnny quite a bit when they were in middle school.

Marie patted her cheek. "It will all be well. You'll see."

It was as if she was some kind of old-world fortune-teller, happening into her life at just that time to deliver just that message.

A hand on her elbow caused her to turn around and see Reed. "Walk with me?"

"Amanda Jane—"

"Is staying with Emma and Gray for the moment."

"It sounds like you want to talk?"

"I do. Let's go this way." He took her hand and led her to a quiet corner under the trees that was secluded.

"What did you want to talk about?"

"Us."

"Haven't we talked that to death?" Her hands were shaking; she didn't know why.

If she were being truthful, maybe because she was afraid everything was about to crash and burn all over again.

"No, I don't think so. Will you listen to what I have to say?"

"Of course." Even though she was afraid. Whenever they talked about their relationship, it was always something bad. The whole rocking of the apple cart she'd been trying to avoid? She had this sneaking suspicion that this was going to flip the apple cart over and all her apples were going to roll down the street and get smushed into applesauce.

But that was unreasonable. It didn't have to be bad.

"I think we need to define our relationship for Amanda Jane."

Yeah, it was definitely a crash and there were flames everywhere. She could see the apples rotting and turning into hard cider.

"I know things have been unsettled, but she's seen us sleeping in the same bed. She's trying to label our roles and I think if we do that for her, it will give her more of a sense of security."

"What does that mean?" She tried not to freak out, to be angry. She tried to trust. At every stage in this relationship when things fell apart, or things burned, it was because they didn't trust each other. It was time for that to stop. But she was having a really hard time with this one.

"It means I think we should really *be* married. I know it's done on paper, but let's just call it what it is."

Just like the whole of their relationship, this was everything she wanted and nothing at all.

"That's not a good enough reason."

"Her happiness and well-being isn't good enough?" He seemed surprised.

"To actually have a marriage? No, Reed. It's not." She took a solid gulp of air. "That's committing to forever."

He just wanted her because it was easy—because she fit. It was no effort to confide his past—she'd been there. It was no effort to make her fit into this future—she'd be there.

The part that hurt the worst, was that he didn't understand. He was sitting there under a tree offering her almost everything she'd ever wanted.

But she wasn't going to settle for almost. Emma was right. Settling was for mud. She didn't want mud.

"Gina—"

She stood up and put her hands out in front of her. "I'm not angry with you, but I can't be around you right now."

"I don't understand."

"That's the problem. We'll talk later, but right now, I just—" She had to flee him, this feeling. She suddenly understood what it was like to be willing to do anything to get away from a stimulus. Anything to numb it and make it stop.

She didn't think it could get any worse, but it did because he let her go. He didn't chase her, he didn't try to reassure her, he didn't—he did exactly as she'd asked.

Gina knew that was no cause to be upset. If she wanted something from him, she should tell him. She couldn't expect him to just know.

Except she did—because he should.

If he wanted her to commit to spending the rest of her life with him? How horrible it was to love someone more than they loved you.

Emma saw her and grabbed her arm. "What happened? What wrong?"

"Just watch Amanda Jane."

"No, the boys can do that. I'm watching you." Emma followed her.

Gina didn't know where she was going, only that she had to go. She had to get somewhere she could breathe.

"What did he do?" Emma said when she finally slowed down.

"He asked me to make this marriage real."

"Oh, the horror," Emma drawled, making it clear that she didn't find it to be as objectionable as Gina did.

"It is a horror. He asked me to define our relationship for Amanda Jane."

"That's the dumbest thing I've ever heard." Emma's expression turned gentle. "Honey, he's already told you that he loves you. What more do you want?"

"To know that I'm not the easy choice."

"This again? So what if you're the easy choice? All these things that you've been saying are things that you're supposed to look for in the person you want to spend your life with. Why don't you want to be the one who fits with him?"

Emma pursed her lips. "Do you want it to be hard? Do you want him to run some gauntlet to prove how he feels? I think he already has. Look at the last few months. What else could he possibly do?"

"Love me."

"He told you he loves you. He's shown you he loves you." Emma shook her head. "He just didn't do the things that you've earmarked as proof. Would you rather have some workhorse checking things off a list or do you want a flesh-and-blood man who thinks you're the moon and his daughter is the stars?"

"I guess I thought that if someone ever asked me they'd at least have a ring, or it would be special."

"How was it not special?"

"I guess I'm still more of a little girl than I realized." She shook her head. "I made a conscious choice to put my trust in him and I'm not... I want it all. I want fireworks. I want a ring. I want everything. I thought less would be okay, that it didn't matter. But it does. "

Emma put an arm around her. "Oh, honey. I think we're all little girls when it comes to things like this. When Amanda Jane is older and she wants you to re-tell the story of how he proposed to you, you're going to say you got married for a custody arrangement? Or Glory Days under a walnut tree? Maybe if that was where you had your first kiss. Or that was where you knew it was love—I understand where you're coming from, I do. He screwed the pooch on this for sure. But do you really think that he's only asking for Amanda Jane or is he asking for himself?"

"I guess that's the problem. I don't know."

"Don't you think that you should find out?" Emma urged.

"I think I've already made up my mind that he's only asking for her. I'm afraid to believe that it's because he loves me." That was the guts of it. Again, it came down to the lack of trust. But Emma was right, too. She didn't trust herself enough to believe that she was worth it.

"Do you remember what Crystal said to you there before the end? Be happy. Stop being afraid. If you don't want to be with Reed Hollingsworth, then don't. But if you do? I suggest you go ahead and grab life by the balls. None of us know how much time we have or what blessings we'll be given. I thought I had all the time in the world to have children. Now, I can't. Even though that makes me want to bawl and rail at fate, I won't. Because I'm still here. There are worse things that can happen to you than loving too much."

"I'm sorry, Emma. All my silly crap when you've got big things, serious things happening in your life." In being a good caregiver, she didn't want to forget to be a good friend, too.

Emma waved her off. "Serious things? Love is pretty serious. No, I withdraw that from the jury. It doesn't have to be serious, but it is important."

"I'm scared, Emma. I've been scared. I keep thinking I'm this warrior woman, but I'm really not. Everything I do is motivated from fear."

"So stop it. And who says that warriors are never afraid?"

"Just…" She shook her head. "Stop it?"

"I know it's easier said than done, but if you want Reed, go back and get him."

"After I just ran out of there like an idiot?"

"He'll understand. If you're going to be married to the man he's going to see you being stupid plenty more times than this." Emma grinned. "Well, not to say that you were being stupid. Maybe *wary* is a better word. Nothing you feel is stupid. There's a reason you felt that way."

"Would you say that's true in all cases?"

"Probably."

"Then I feel like I hope you and Gray end up together." She couldn't resist dropping that in there.

"I should've seen that one coming."

"Yes, you should have." Gina laughed.

"You know what? We're going shopping."

"Why in the world would I do that?"

"Because there's a certain way you want this done? You tell him. In no uncertain terms."

"I am not going lingerie shopping and I'm not proposing to him."

"You *are* going lingerie shopping and you're going to tell him how to propose to you." Emma's fingers moved quickly over the keys of her phone.

"What are you doing?"

"Telling Gray that he and Reed have Amanda Jane. Reed was the one who was so hot for Glory Days, anyway. I wanted to go to Lynnie's and get a pedicure."

"No."

"Yes. It's time you asked for what you want, Gina. You're never going to get it otherwise. You have to believe you deserve it and reach for it. Be happy."

"How is making an ass out of myself going to make me happy?"

"I guess you'll just have to see."

Her phone rang and initially, she wasn't going to answer it. She wasn't even going to look at it, but just like when her grandmother had fallen, she had a sense in her gut. It was a call she needed to take.

It was Dr. Ness.

Instinctively, she knew he'd have their test results for the DNA marker for hereditary breast cancer.

It seemed as though her whole life, Amanda Jane's life, was hung like a star on this very moment. But it wasn't. Whatever was meant to be would be. Finding out about it, quantifying it, that wouldn't change anything.

Or maybe it would. Maybe it would give them a fighting chance.

"I have to take this, Emma. It's Rob."

Emma nodded.

Except when she answered, she wasn't sure what to say. "Hi."

"How are you, Gina?"

"Kind of dying waiting to know."

"The lab was going to mail you the results, but I thought you'd like to hear it from me. Amanda Jane is negative."

"Thank God." It felt as if a weight had slipped from her shoulders. The rest of what he had to say didn't matter, as long as she was okay.

Fear knotted. No, it did matter. But whatever Rob had to say next, she'd deal with it because her niece was fine. She was safe. At least from this.

"And so are you," he continued.

Her knees went weak and Emma barely caught her as she crumpled with relief. "Thank you. Thank you so much."

"Take care of yourself, Gina. Call me when you're ready to do your ER rotation and I'll get you set up with us. That is, if you want to do your practicals here."

"I would love that. Thank you. I mean, I already said it, but that's so generous."

"We got our test results," Gina told Emma as she put away the phone and blinked back tears. "We're negative for BRCA-1."

Emma squeezed her. "I'm so happy for you. This is the best thing we could've hoped for."

"I have to call Grams."

Three hours and some credit card swipes later found Gina home and gussied up in ribbons, lace and something that she couldn't sit down in or she wouldn't be able to stand back up.

"I don't think I've ever seen a movie where the heroine seduces the hero over a macaroni-and-cheese-with-bacon casserole."

"You don't watch the right channels. You can seduce anyone with bacon." Emma nodded.

"That wasn't the image I wanted."

"It's the one you've got." Emma winked at her.

"This is dumb. I should just talk to him."

"I promise you that this is not dumb. When you see the way he looks at you, it will give you the confidence you need to tell him what you want. I'm going to take Amanda Jane to a movie and keep her overnight. We'll have a great slumber party and I'll send her home late tomorrow stuffed full of sugar and maybe with a puppy," Emma teased.

"As long as it's not a pony."

"I can promise, no ponies." Emma sniffed. "I never had a pony. But back to the subject at hand. After tonight, you will know for sure whether he wants you for you, or wants you because you're easy." She snickered.

"I look easy." She flicked a pink ribbon that hung from the general direction of her cleavage.

"No, you don't. You look beautiful." Emma smiled at her. "This is your chance. You're not good girl Gina, you're not the poor kid made good, you're a woman who knows what she wants and she's going to reach out and take it, okay?"

Gina nodded. As always, Emma knew just what to say.

"What if..." She trailed off.

"What if all that stuff that keeps rattling through your head is the truth? Then, honey, this was just a dress rehearsal, anyway."

CHAPTER TWENTY-SEVEN

AFTER THE WAY she'd run out of the park, Reed wasn't sure what to expect when he came home. The look on her face when he'd suggested a real marriage was like he'd suggested pudding was made out of something vile.

Gray assured him all would be well, but he wasn't so sure. They'd come so far, through so much, and he'd screwed it up, just like he knew he would. Just like he told her he would.

But that self-hate voice that liked to berate him, it wasn't as loud as the other one that said maybe he'd just gone about this all wrong. Maybe his timing was bad.

Maybe he should've bought a ring.

He didn't know what the hell he was thinking except he just wanted her to say yes. He wanted her to define their relationship for him and he'd used Amanda Jane as an excuse.

Reed was sure there was a lesson in that. Maybe if he'd been more honest about his needs, his wants, maybe they'd be met.

That was a novel idea to him and he was sure that it was for her, too. Not all was lost. Or that's what he kept telling himself on the way home.

Something smelled delicious in the kitchen. He held

up his hands in mock surrender. "I surrender. Just let me have some of tha—" He stopped midsentence. The sight in the kitchen was definitely not what he expected.

Yes, he definitely wanted some of that, but it wasn't the roasted lamb that had just come out of the oven. It was Gina herself.

She was laced up, beribboned and wrapped in pink silk. Her long hair hung soft and wild around her shoulders and she was definitely a sight.

"It's stupid, isn't it?" She blushed, the stain on her cheeks matching the color of the negligee.

"It is the furthest thing from stupid. Do you really not know how beautiful you are?"

"Emma said I should tell you exactly what I want."

"I'm a fan of that." He nodded. "When you left…" Reed closed his eyes. "Woman, if you want to have a serious discussion, I can't do it when you look like that."

"Emma said that was a good thing."

"Emma is saying a lot of things but I'm not trying to spend my life with Emma."

"Am I easier than Emma?"

His eyes widened. "I really don't know what you want me to say here. Or do. I want you. I love you. And you shut me down. Explain it to me."

She pursed her lips. "The way you asked me… I don't need you to skywrite it, or shower me with diamonds, but I'd like to know that you're asking me because you love me. Because you want me. Not because you want to tell Amanda Jane some label we put on ourselves." She took a deep breath. "And not because being with me is easy."

"Being with you is the furthest thing from easy, Gina."

"It's easier than with anyone else. We're already legal. How would you explain what we have to someone you were trying to date? And even more so, what kind of person would tolerate that kind of treatment? Or being second place all the time?"

"Don't you think that could be because we belong together? Not because you think I'm shortchanging us both."

"Emma said that, too."

"I guess Emma can keep talking. But again, none of this is about Emma," he said softly.

She strode over to him, the kitten heels causing her hips to sway in a pronounced manner.

"Then what is it about?"

"I think it's about finding glory."

"What does that even mean?" She braced her palms on his shoulders and didn't shy away when his hands encircled her waist.

"I think it's both literal and figurative. I think it started when I came back. When I could see this place as something more than a prison, more than something trying to keep me down. That wasn't Glory, that was me. I think we're both seeing the town for what it is and the future we can have here."

He dragged his cheek against hers and inhaled the sweet, feminine scent of her.

"And I think the figurative is finding the glory in ourselves. In the lives we've been given and not being afraid to embrace it. I was. I'm sorry for that. If I'd been honest, if I'd done it the right way—" Reed found that once he'd plunged forward, it got easier. The words kept coming and the feelings he'd been afraid of weren't so giant and terrible, after all. She'd felt the same things about herself.

"There is no right way. If I'd already found my glory, I wouldn't have needed you to do it a certain way. I could've just said yes because I knew you loved me. Because I loved myself enough to let you love me."

"We're quite the pair, aren't we?" Reed asked.

"We are, but I don't think we should punish ourselves for it. I think we've done that enough."

"No more sorries?" He leaned down to bury his face in her neck. "Should we keep with that theme?"

"I think I like that, so I don't have to apologize for earlier."

"Our slates are pretty even, Gina. But if you just let me untie this ribbon—" he fingered the pink scrap that kept the filmy material in place "—I'd say we'll both be in the clear."

She pulled the ribbon for him and the material slid to the floor.

"Wow, that happened just like I wanted it to." She flashed him a smile.

"How else do you want things to happen?"

"I want you to take me upstairs, or right here is fine, make love to me and then I want to live happily ever after."

"We can try that." At one time her words would've caused him to feel a noose tightening around his neck, pressure of expectations that he could never live up to.

But he felt none of that, only the thrill of taking his woman to bed and knowing that she was there for him.

Because she wanted him.

Because she loved him.

Her needs weren't so different from his own. She wanted to know he wanted her for herself, he could understand that. He wasn't going to berate himself for his clumsy attempt earlier because what they'd gotten out of it was so much better.

She told him what she wanted from him and he found he could give it to her. There was a lot to be said for living to be happy, letting go of the fear.

Gina looped her arm around his neck. "Yeah, we'll just try it. If the happy-ever-after doesn't work out we could always go to Vegas instead for happy right now."

He swept her up. "We can do both."

"I like how your brain works, Mr. Hollingsworth."

In that moment, it was as if they'd been together forever. It was easy, because it was right. He carried her up the stairs and to his bedroom.

"I think you should consider moving."

"Me, too." She leaned in, her breath warm on his neck. Gina pressed her lips to his skin, her mouth hot.

"Better watch that or I might drop you."

"Then you'll just have to take me on the stairs."

"And then we'll be on some documentary about how sex sent us to the emergency room," he teased.

She pressed her palm to his cheek. "I love you."

It resonated inside of him, the ringing of some long-silent bell that he never knew he had. It was that sound that finally silenced the dark things, and healed the things that hurt.

He put her down on the bed and stared at her for a long moment before returning the sentiment. His eyes drank her in, his fingers and hands devoured the texture of the cream of her skin; he wanted to experience her in all ways.

This time between them was different. For Reed, it had always been about more than lust, more than physicality, but the barriers were finally down and they were both raw, bare in a way that they hadn't been with each other before.

Every touch, every caress, it all had another meaning, another layer.

It felt damn good, that was for sure, but it wasn't only about the physical stimulation. There was so much more between them—and he could show her with his mouth, his fingers and even his cock.

He pulled her on top of him, allowed her to take the reins. Trusted her to push them both toward that spiraling pleasure.

She moved them together, their bodies finding that synchronicity, that harmonic where their every motion was as one.

He surrendered to it, to her, and the waves of pleasure took them and washed away all the old hurts, all the old angst. It was like being reborn.

They were lying in each other's arms, sated and content, when she asked, "So are you going to ask me again?"

"No," he answered and kissed the crown of her head.

"What?" She sat up and looked at him.

"No. I'll ask you again when we're both ready."

"I don't like you," she said, but the insult didn't have any teeth. Not when she lay down again, replete and happy against him.

"Yes, you do. You love me."

"Doesn't mean I like you."

He grabbed her again. "Great. How about some hate sex?"

She slapped at his arm. "How about…no?"

"How about you wrap those long legs around my shoulders?"

Gina blushed. "How about yes?"

"Yeah, how about that." Reed winked and rose above her only to enjoy the trip down.

THE FOURTH OF JULY was a couple weeks later and the biggest of spring and summer events, what with the proximity to Fort Glory. It was a whole-week affair from parades to a community barbecue until finally, the night of the Fourth, everyone chose a venue from which to watch the display.

Many of the residents of Glory would go to the lake on Fort Glory and spread out blankets early in the morning and stay all day feeding ducks, eating slow-smoked hot dogs, hamburgers and sometimes a whole pig.

Kids ran around playing, setting off fireworks way too early and eating ice cream.

Gina and Reed brought Amanda Jane and they chose

a spot down by the river with their own little grill. They invited Gray and Emma to join them as well as Betsy and Jack.

Betsy's brother, Caleb, crashed the party. He was technically on duty with his partner, India, but in Glory, even crime stopped for fireworks.

Patriotic music blared over the speakers that were normally used for the tornado sirens and for once, Gina Townsend was happy in the moment.

She wasn't worrying about what came next, or tomorrow, or what had come before. She was living in the breath and she was, most important, happy.

Caleb reached over a hand and tried to steal another cupcake from Betsy's picnic basket, but Jack blocked him without even looking.

"Come on, I need another one."

Jack eyed him. "No, you don't. You're going to get fat and then India will have to take care of all your light work and your heavy work."

"I work out every day. Give me the cupcake," Caleb demanded, serious.

Betsy slapped his hand. "No. There aren't going to be any left for Amanda Jane."

"Hmm. Just for that, I'm going to follow her on her first date in the police cruiser."

Amanda Jane looked up from where she was throwing down snappers on the concrete walk so they popped. She shook her head. "Nope. You can't follow me."

"And why not?" Caleb grinned, waiting to hear what she would say.

"Because you're going to be driving. We're getting married, you know." She threw another popper down and laughed.

"Oh, really?" Caleb answered.

"That is if India will let you have him." Betsy cast a side eye at the statuesque blonde who was midbite on a double cheeseburger.

"She can have him. All yours, kiddo." She chomped another bite. "But by the time you're dating, he'll be old."

"Old?" Amanda Jane turned up her nose. "Like my daddy?"

"He's older than your daddy." India kept chewing.

"Gina-bee, I think I need to rethink my strategy." She looked at Caleb. "I'm sorry. I've changed my mind." But once she'd snagged the last cupcake, she went back to throwing snappers.

India laughed. "That's cold. So cold."

Gray and Emma were strangely subdued, quiet. But as the darkness started to fall and the sky faded from blue to inky velvet, she noticed that they'd linked hands.

"Can I ask her yet?" Amanda Jane whispered to Reed.

"No. Not yet."

"What are you two up to? No more sugar tonight or she'll never go to bed." Reed was bad about indulging her, but sometimes, a little indulgence was a good thing.

Reed pulled her against him. "You'll see."

"Oh, this sounds like trouble."

"Daddy, now?" Amanda Jane asked.

Reed laughed. "No. Not yet."

"Yes, yet." She nodded emphatically. All attention was on Amanda Jane and Gina really wondered what kind of trouble they'd gotten into.

"No, wait for the purple one."

As the first fireworks of the night began, the sky exploded with starbursts and in the center of all the commotion two words had been written in the sparks.

Marry me.

She shot a quick glance to Reed, who smiled at her. "Now, Amanda Jane."

Amanda Jane gave her a small velvet-covered box.

Gina accepted it with shaking hands. Inside was a solitaire diamond ring.

"Will you marry my daddy?" Amanda Jane clapped, knowing what the answer would be.

She turned to Reed. "Much better."

"Do I get an answer this time?"

"Yes. I was just…living in the moment. Feeling it happen around me. Missing Crys, but loving this life. Loving you." She flung her arms around him. "Of course I'll marry you."

It didn't matter that they'd already signed the paperwork, that according to the state of Kansas, they were already married. Or that they were married in their hearts. This was the moment that she'd always remember.

And he knew it.

He whispered into her ear, "See, this is that happy-ever-after thing you were talking about. I think it starts now."

Amanda Jane was pulled into the embrace and their friends clapped for their joy, because together, they'd found glory.

EPILOGUE

"ANY OTHER DARK secrets you plan on keeping from us?" Helga asked Maudine as they sipped their sweet tea from the rocking folding chairs and watched the light show.

"It wasn't really a dark secret."

"Oh, it most certainly was," Ethel Weinburg said from her place on the checkered blanket, her feet tucked neatly beneath her red-and-white-striped crinoline. "You managed to keep it a secret from me, and I know everything." Ethel wasn't shy about adding that.

Maudine shrugged. "I didn't want it to be a big deal. There were more important things to focus on."

"And those things are now accomplished?" Regan Marsh asked, her fingers drawing little circles in the air as she conducted the music along with the big band that played patriotic tunes from the makeshift gazebo stage.

Maudine exhaled heavily, the scent of sulfur still in the air and the cheers and claps still coming from where her granddaughter had set up base. "I suppose, but this matchmaking gives me purpose. Speaking of matchmaking, where exactly is Marie?"

"She had a guest who checked in to Cora's Cottage," Rose Cresswell whispered as she took a bite of cheese.

"It's the Fourth. What does that matter? She should've made him wait," Ethel said.

"Nuh-uh." Rose shook her head. "He was her husband's commanding officer."

"And what does that matter?" Regan asked.

"I just smell a romance." Rose sipped her tea.

"Who do you think we should help next, then?"

"Helga's grandson."

Helga narrowed her eyes. "He doesn't need any help. He's doing just fine."

"Or he's told you not to meddle." Rose grinned.

Helga arched a brow. "I think there are more dire candidates."

"Such as?" Ethel stirred her tea with her straw.

"Caleb Lewis and India George. They're a perfect match, don't you think?" Helga smiled.

"I think if they were going to get together, they already would've done it." Ethel wrinkled her nose.

"Pish." Maudine perked. "I love this idea. If anyone needs our help, they do."

"Relatives are easier," Regan said.

"Who said this was about easy? It's about doing good things in our community," Maudine said.

"It's about entertaining ourselves and living vicariously is what you mean," Ethel corrected her.

"To-may-to, to-mah-to." Maudine shrugged.

Rose grinned. "Actually, I think I have a plan."

Another meeting of the Grandmothers was in session and new hearts and happily-ever-afters were on the line and another round of fireworks exploded in the sky.

* * * * *

Return to Mustang Creek, Wyoming, with #1 *New York Times* bestselling author

LINDA LAEL MILLER

for her new *Brides of Bliss County* series!

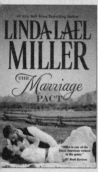
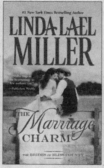
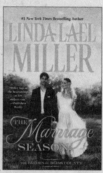

Will their marriage pact be fulfilled?
Pick up your copies today!

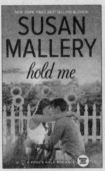

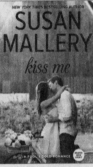

Come to a small town in Oregon with
USA TODAY bestselling author

MAISEY YATES

for her sexy, heartfelt new
Copper Ridge series!

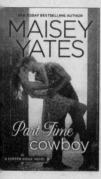 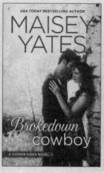 

Available now! Available now! Coming July 28, 2015!

Can these cowboys find the love they
didn't know they needed?

Pick up your copies today!

HQN™

www.HQNBooks.com

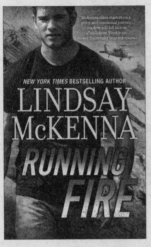

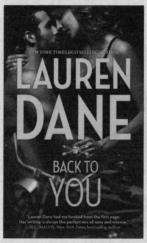

From the creator of *The Originals*, the hit spin-off television show of *The Vampire Diaries*, come three never-before-released prequel stories featuring the Original vampire family, set in 18th century New Orleans.

Family is power. The Original vampire family swore it to each other a thousand years ago. They pledged to remain together always and forever. But even when you're immortal, promises are hard to keep.

Pick up your copies today and visit
www.TheOriginalsBooks.com
to discover more!

HQN™

www.HQNBooks.com

From #1 *New York Times* bestselling author

NORA ROBERTS

come two remarkable tales of the O'Hurleys' dynasty
of dazzling talent and sizzling passion.

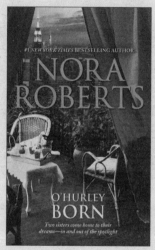

Two sisters come home to their
dreams—in and out of the spotlight.

Pick up your copy today!

Be sure to connect with us at:

Harlequin.com/Newsletters
Facebook.com/HarlequinBooks
Twitter.com/HarlequinBooks

Get 2 Free Books,
<u>Plus</u> 2 Free Gifts –

just for trying the Reader Service!

YES! Please send me 2 FREE novels from the Essential Romance or Essential Suspense Collection and my 2 FREE gifts (gifts are worth about $10). After receiving them, if I don't wish to receive any more books, I can return the shipping statement marked "cancel." If I don't cancel, I will receive 4 brand-new novels every month and be billed just $6.49 per book. That's a savings of at least 19% off the cover price. It's quite a bargain! Shipping and handling is just 50¢. I understand that accepting the 2 free books and gifts places me under no obligation to buy anything. I can always return a shipment and cancel at any time. Even if I never buy another book, the two free books and gifts are mine to keep forever.

Please check one: ☐ Essential Romance ☐ Essential Suspense
194 MDN GJAX 191 MDN GJAX

Name _____ (PLEASE PRINT)

Address _____ Apt. #

City _____ State _____ Zip

Signature (if under 18, a parent or guardian must sign)

Mail to the **Reader Service:**
P.O. Box 1867, Buffalo, NY 14240-1867

Want to try two free books from another line?
Call 1-800-873-8635 or visit www.ReaderService.com.

* Terms and prices subject to change without notice. Prices do not include applicable taxes. Sales tax applicable in N.Y. This offer is limited to one order per household. Not valid for current subscribers to the Essential Romance or Essential Suspense Collection. All orders subject to credit approval. Credit or debit balances in a customer's account(s) may be offset by any other outstanding balance owed by or to the customer. Please allow 4 to 6 weeks for delivery. Offer available while quantities last. Offer only available in the U.S.A.